THE BRIDGE IN THE CLOUDS

William, Mary and Alice Constant have spent the last three school holidays staying with their Uncle Jack and his girlfriend Phoebe at Golden House. During this time they have met and befriended an Elizabethan alchemist, called Stephen Tyler, who has discovered the secret of time travelling and has called upon them to help him in the great task of saving Golden Valley from the hands of his wicked assistant, Matthew Morden, and his descendants.

Under the Magician's guidance the children have entered the bodies and minds of animals and birds. They have assisted in the birth of Jack and Phoebe's baby, Stephanie; they have fought off the evil badger baiters and thwarted the terrible plans to turn the Golden Valley into an adventure park.

Now it is deep autumn and they have returned for the half term holidays. At once they are thrown into the most crucial and desperate adventure of all. Matthew Morden is on the point of discovering for himself the art of time travelling and his evil influence is permeating the whole valley. The time has come for a final confrontation; the last great battle is about to be fought . . .

The Magician's House Quartet
The Steps up the Chimney
The Door in the Tree
The Tunnel Behind the Waterfall
The Bridge in the Clouds

THE BRIDGE IN THE CLOUDS

Being
the Fourth and Last Book
of
The Magician's House

William Corlett

RED FOX

For Mary

* * *

The Magician's House
is for
Mum and Dad
who were here when I started the quartet
but had both gone before it was finished.

A Red Fox Book

Published by Random House Children's Books
20 Vauxhall Bridge Road, London SW1V 2SA

A division of Random House UK Ltd
London Melbourne Sydney Auckland Johannesburg
and agencies throughout the world

First published by The Bodley Head Children's Books
1992

Red Fox edition 1993

7 9 10 8 6

© William Corlett 1992

Phototypeset by Intype, London
Printed and bound in Great Britain by
Cox & Wyman Ltd, Reading, Berkshire

RANDOM HOUSE UK Limited Reg. No. 954009

Papers used by Random House UK Limited
are natural, recyclable products made from wood grown in
sustainable forests. The manufacturing processes conform to
the environmental regulations of the country of origin.

ISBN 0 09 918391 9

Contents

1	Return to Golden House	1
2	Beef Stew	8
3	A Midnight Meeting	18
4	The Dawn Conference	29
5	Rattus Rattus	41
6	A Conversation with Meg	49
7	An Experiment	59
8	Jack's News	72
9	A Ghost Hunt	82
10	The First Journey	92
11	The Autumn Garden	105
12	Doubts and Divisions	119
13	A Potential Buyer	129
14	Rattus Returns	138
15	Into the Enemy Camp	145
16	A Voice in the Dark	156
17	The Second Journey	165
18	As It Was	176
19	The Magician's Glass	185
20	The Beginning of the End	192
21	The Enemy Gather	203
22	Battle Stations	215
23	The Battle Royal	233
24	The Circle of Energy	252
25	A Walk Through the Woods	261
26	Departures and Arrivals	273
27	The Bridge in the Clouds	282

THE BRIDGE IN THE CLOUDS

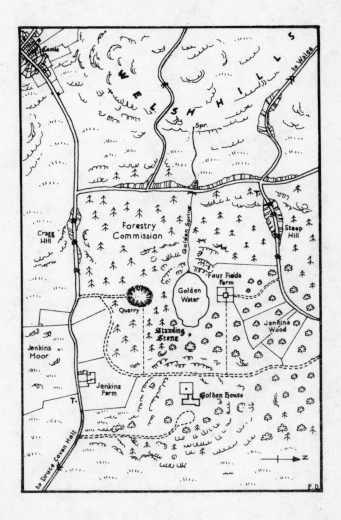

1
Return to Golden House

Mary sensed there was something wrong as soon as they reached the house. There'd been more renovation work done while they'd been away and there were lights shining from one or two windows in the Elizabethan wing, which before would have been dark, but these minor changes excepted, everything seemed much as usual. Nevertheless, she felt uneasy as soon as she saw the place.

It was already dusk when Mr Jenkins' car came to a halt on the drive. The trees were dark against a cloudy sky and a thin breeze was blowing down from the heights beyond Goldenwater.

'Wind from the west,' Mr Jenkins remarked, as he lifted their cases out of the boot. 'Winter's on its way. Now, you'll be all right? Regards to your uncle and aunt. I'll not stop. There's a Farmers' Union meeting tonight. I'll be late, if I don't get a move on. I sometimes think life is one long blooming meeting these days. Glad to have been of help. Call in and see us, if you get the time. Cheerio, then . . .' and he drove away into the dark, the rear lights of his car glowing red, until they disappeared from view round a twist in the drive.

Mary felt a wave of sadness envelope her as she went through the door and yet there was a fire burning in the hall grate and the welcoming smell of cooking issued from the kitchen.

'Where is everybody?' Alice said, running ahead and calling out, 'Hello? We're here!'

Even Spot seemed strangely subdued as he came to meet them, and Meg, who appeared after him from the kitchen door with her arms outspread, was obviously nervous beneath her cheerful greeting.

'Here you are at last!' she said, fussing round them and drying her hands on her apron. 'Your uncle should be back any minute. I'm afraid Phoebe's taken to her bed. Best not go until she calls. She's not feeling quite herself . . .' and, still chattering, she hurried them towards the fire and shut the door against the chill air.

Mary thought it was like watching a play, where everything is meant to be believed but at the same time you know that none of it is real. She confided these feelings to William and Alice as soon as they went up to their rooms to unpack and settle in, having refused a cup of tea because supper was, according to Meg, almost ready.

'I thought it was a bit funny that Mr Jenkins came and met us at the station,' William said, agreeing with her.

'No, it wasn't!' Alice protested, 'if Phoebe isn't feeling well and Uncle Jack had to go into town. Honestly, you two! You're always looking for problems. I'm just glad to be back. I've hated this term, so far. I wanted to be here all the time.'

She was sitting on the floor, with an arm round Spot, who sighed and gazed at her with sad eyes.

'I'm sure something bad's happened,' Mary said,

looking at her reflection in the mirror on the chest of drawers and rearranging her fringe with her fingers. 'Has it, Spot?' she asked, and as she spoke, she turned and crossed to crouch on the floor in front of the dog, who continued to stare silently, using his 'haughty' expression.

'It's always quite difficult to get him talking when we've just arrived, isn't it?' William said, sitting on the side of Mary's bed. 'D'you remember last time? We thought the magic had stopped altogether.'

'That wasn't last time, that was the Spring holidays,' Alice said, 'and it hadn't, of course. It was just you. I knew everything would be all right. It always is, isn't it, Spot?' and she kissed the dog lovingly on the top of his head.

'All the same,' William insisted, 'it does take time. It's as though we have to get used to the magic all over again. As though we have to get back into the right frame of mind.'

'But I am!' Alice complained. 'I haven't thought about anything but being back here all term. That's why I've been getting such hopeless marks. I haven't been able to concentrate on anything else. Everything's so boring compared to the magic here.'

'Yes, I know,' William agreed. 'But even so we have to sort of get back on to the Magician's wavelength. Something like that.'

'Well, don't take too long about it,' Spot growled, making them all jump with surprise.

'Oh, Spot!' Alice exclaimed, 'It's working!' Then she hugged the dog again. 'I've missed you so much. The Simpsons have a puppy called Tess, but I couldn't make her talk to me at all. She just yapped and scratched all the time and got quite impatient with me. I really did try. I stopped myself

3

thinking . . . and everything. . . . But it was useless. She probably thought I was quite mad.'

'Not all animals are like us, you know,' Spot said, disdainfully. 'You can't go expecting every puppy you meet to have a conversation with you. It's we who are different. It's we who do the talking.'

'And us,' Alice insisted. 'We talk to you as well.'

'Animals have been able to understand humans for years,' he told her. 'But humans never bothered to listen to us until now, that's the difference.' Then, getting up, he went quickly out of the room, saying, 'I won't be a moment,' and he disappeared on to the landing and down the staircase.

'No! Hang on a minute, Spot!' William called, following him. 'Don't go! There's masses we have to talk about . . .'

'Who are you yelling at?' Jack asked, appearing on the landing in front of him. 'Sorry,' he said, following William back into the girls' room and speaking breathlessly, as if he'd run up the stairs. 'I had to go into town. I thought Phoebe was going to fetch you – but this bug thing must have got the better of her,' and, as he spoke, he hugged Mary and swung Alice right up off the floor as he planted a kiss on her cheek. 'Oh, it's lovely to have you back! Thank goodness Mr Jenkins was in! If Meg hadn't been able to reach him, you'd all still be sitting at Druce Coven!'

'How did she?' William asked suddenly.

'Who? What?' Jack asked, turning and giving him a hug as well.

'How did Meg ask Mr Jenkins to come and collect us? If you'd already gone in to town?'

'Ah! The great event! Of course, you haven't heard! What if I was to say 314 to you?'

4

'I don't know what you're talking about, Uncle Jack,' Alice said and, as she spoke, she stifled a yawn. It had been a long journey. She and Mary had come from London and changed trains at Bristol. Then, when they'd reached Druce Coven Halt, they'd discovered that William's connection at Manchester had been delayed and they'd had to sit in Mr Jenkins' car for almost half an hour, waiting for him to arrive. Alice was tired and hungry. She wanted her supper and bed.

'Come on. Think!' Jack was saying. '314. What is it?'

'A number of some sort,' Mary said, trying not to let her voice sound bored. She'd forgotten that Jack had an unfortunate habit of sometimes treating them as if they were children.

'And what does a number suggest?'

'You've had a telephone put in,' William said.

'Brilliant, William! You obviously inherited the brains for the entire family!'

'Uncle Jack! Please!' Mary said, sounding as though she was talking to a silly child. Then she added, 'It's an awfully short number. Are you sure there aren't more figures than that?'

'Masses,' Jack said. 'There's the whole dialling code – but I haven't learned them yet! Anyway, we're on the phone, at last! It was put in last week. Since when no one has called us – not one solitary person! We sit there staring at the thing, willing it to ring . . . and nothing happens!'

'Maybe that's because no one knows you've got it,' William said.

'Yes,' Jack said, laughing, 'that could have something to do with it! Oh, I am glad you're all back! We've really missed you.'

5

'We're not here for long, though,' Alice sighed. 'Half term holidays are really far too short.'

'Never mind, a week's better than nothing!'

'It's ten days, actually,' Mary said.

'Even better! So – supper in five minutes! Meg's done the cooking tonight . . .'

'Is Phoebe very ill?' Mary asked.

'No,' he said, cheerfully, then he frowned. 'It's just a bug, I expect. She'll be over it in no time, now you're here. Come on down as soon as you're ready.'

Jack went out on to the landing and they heard him speak to Spot as they squeezed past each other on the narrow spiral staircase. A moment later the dog bounded into the room. He was carrying something dangling from his mouth that glittered in the electric light.

'That was close!' he exclaimed, dropping the object on the floor in front of Mary. 'If Jack had seen this he'd have wanted to know where I got it.'

'The pendulum!' Mary exclaimed, picking up the solid gold lump on its thin chain that the Magician had left with them during the summer holidays and which they had entrusted to Spot's safekeeping when they had returned to school. 'Look! It's the Magician's pendulum. Where did you hide it, Spot?'

'I never reveal my hiding places,' Spot replied. 'Once you do they cease to be of any use.'

'How is Mr Tyler?' William asked, feeling a tingle of excitement as he looked at the pendulum hanging from Mary's hand.

'Don't know,' Spot shrugged. 'We've not seen him since you were last here.'

'I expect you will, now we're back,' Alice said.

6

'I hope so,' the dog growled, quietly. 'We really need him at the moment. Jasper will come and see you later. He said to tell you to expect him.'

'What about Cinnabar?' William asked eagerly. 'Does he know we're back?'

'Probably. Jasper will have spread the word through the forest,' Spot replied. 'But it's not a good time for the fox just at present. The Hunt will be meeting soon. He'll have to go carefully!'

'What's been happening while we've been away, Spot?' Mary asked. 'I've got this awful feeling that something is wrong.'

'It's the humans,' Spot explained.

'Which humans?' William asked, feeling immediately apprehensive.

'Jack and Phoebe.'

'What about them?' Mary said.

'They don't like each other any more,' Spot growled and, before they could question him further, he turned and slunk out of the room with his tail between his legs.

2
Beef Stew

When the children went down to the kitchen, Meg was standing at the range, stirring a pan, and Jack was spreading a cloth on the table.

'Where's Steph?' Mary asked, noticing that the baby's playpen, in its place by the fire, was empty.

'She's upstairs with her mother,' Meg replied without looking round.

'She hasn't gone to bed already, surely?' Jack asked.

'I took her up about half an hour ago,' Meg answered.

Jack frowned.

'No, I meant Phoebe. Isn't she coming down for supper?'

'I don't know, dear. I went up to see her and she asked me to bring the baby up, which I did. That's all I know.'

'But if Steph's been put down already, she'll be awake half the night, bawling the house down. You know what she's been like recently.'

'Apparently she's teething, dear,' Meg said. 'Babies are all a bit of a mystery to me – but I'm learning fast!'

'Yes, I know she's teething – but all the same!' Jack snapped. 'If we want her to sleep through at least some of the night, it's stupid putting her to bed so early.'

'You tell her then, dearie,' Meg said, catching Jack's irritability. 'It isn't for me to say. I'm not the child's mother.'

Jack sighed and crossed to the door, saying:

'Can you kids finish laying the table? I won't be a minute,' and he went out, slamming the door behind him.

Meg glanced over her shoulder at the sound then went into the larder. As soon as they were alone, William looked at his sisters and pulled a face, as if to say that they'd better keep out of whatever was going on. But this warning had no effect on Alice.

'Why's everybody so cross, Meg?' she asked, setting knives and forks in front of each of the chairs at the table.

'Nothing for you to worry about, pet,' Meg said, returning to the table with a loaf of bread on a board.

'But what's wrong with Phoebe?' Mary asked.

Meg looked at her and raised her eyebrows, but she remained silent.

'Uncle Jack told us she's got some bug or other,' William reminded her.

'I hope it isn't catching,' Alice said, putting salt and pepper on the table. 'I don't want a bug – not when we've got hardly any time here.'

'What's for supper, Meg?' William asked, kneeling in front of the cupboard again. 'I need to know which plates you'll want.'

'Stew, dear. Beef stew,' Meg replied.

Alice looked round, with her mouth open.

'Beef?' she said. 'But we never eat meat when we're here!'

'Well, you will tonight. That's what Phoebe arranged.'

'But she's a vegetable!' Alice said indignantly. 'Vegetables don't eat meat.'

'I just do what I'm told, dear. She said to get the stewing beef out of the larder and make a stew, and that's what I've done.'

'But – where did the meat come from?' William asked, sounding equally amazed.

'The butcher, dear. Where else would it come from?'

'You mean Phoebe went and bought it?'

'I doubt it came as a gift!'

'But I don't understand,' William said. 'She never buys meat.'

'No, well, now she has. Of course, she won't be eating it herself. Nor could she bring herself to cook it. Come to think of it, maybe that's why she's taken to her bed. Just the thought of the flesh in the house was too much for her.'

'But if it makes her feel so ill – why go and buy it?' William said. 'I mean, we're used to her vegetarian cooking now. We actually like it.'

'You'll have to tell her that yourselves, dear. It's got nothing to go with me. I just get on with things.'

There was an awkward silence. Meg had turned her back on them again and was testing jacket potatoes with a knife to see if they were cooked.

'Oh dear, Meg,' Mary sighed, after a moment. 'I'm sorry to be a nuisance . . . but I can't eat meat any more.'

'Why can't you?' Meg asked, looking round.

Mary shrugged. 'It makes me feel sick,' she replied. 'I don't know why, exactly. Even just think-ing about it now is making me feel a bit funny.'

'Since when did this happen?' Meg asked, sounding cross again.

'Well, really since we started coming here,' Mary said nervously. Meg seemed so irritable, which was unlike her.

'In that case, you'll have to make do with eggs. Vegetables and eggs. Faddy eaters!' and, grumbling, she limped back to the larder.

'Can I have eggs as well, Meg?' Alice called, glancing at Mary and pulling a glum face.

'You can eat what you like!' Meg snapped, then, turning to William, she said, 'and I suppose you'll be wanting the same?'

William looked surprised and shook his head. 'No, I don't mind having stew,' he said, sounding as uneasy as the girls.

'Oh, how very kind of you! Very accommodating, I must say!' Meg muttered and then, to their amazement, she threw down the oven cloth she was carrying and limped over to the hall door. 'I'm going to my room,' she said. 'All this upset! I'm not used to it!' and, still grumbling to herself, she went out of the kitchen.

'Crumpets!' Alice exclaimed, as soon as they were alone.

'What was all that about?' William asked.

Mary frowned. 'It must be what Spot was saying – about Phoebe and Jack not liking each other any more.'

'I don't know why he ever liked her in the first place,' Alice said, then she also frowned.

'That's not fair, Al!' said Mary, 'she's all right. Even you got to like her in the end.'

Alice shrugged, remembering. 'Suppose so,' she said. 'But . . . what is going on then? Why's everybody being so bad-tempered? Where's Spot? He'll tell us.'

The dog hadn't followed them into the kitchen and when they looked for him in the hall, there was no sign of him.

'D'you suppose I should go and apologize to her?' Mary asked as they returned to the kitchen and she crossed to the range to warm herself.

'For what?' Alice said.

'For not wanting to eat the stew.'

'I'm not going to apologize.'

'I don't see why you won't eat it anyway, Alice,' William said. 'You're not a vegetarian.'

'I am when I'm here.'

'I hope they're not going to divorce,' Mary said, rubbing her hands over the heat. Then she shivered. 'Oh, I'm suddenly cold!'

For a moment they were silent as they each thought about what she'd just said.

'How can they divorce?' Alice asked. 'They didn't even get married yet.'

'You know what I mean . . .' Mary replied, her mind deep in thought.

'But why all this fuss about buying meat for us?' William wondered.

'Oh, what does that matter now, Will?' Mary complained. 'You always bother about the unimportant things.'

'It's just . . . so out of character for her. I mean, even if she and Jack aren't getting on well, that doesn't explain why she's suddenly gone off and bought meat. It's against her principles.'

'If they split up,' Alice asked, out of the blue, 'what would happen to Golden House?'

'I don't know,' William said, with a shrug. Then

he frowned as the full enormity of what Alice had just asked sank in.

'They'd sell up, wouldn't they?' Mary said quietly, and, as she spoke, she turned to look at the other two.

'Not necessarily,' Alice said quickly. 'Maybe one of them would stay here.'

'Who?' Mary asked. 'Jack wouldn't want to live here all on his own. And Phoebe certainly wouldn't. She hates the place.'

'No, she doesn't,' Alice protested. 'She loves it. She told me.'

'Well, she wouldn't stay here on her own anyway, would she?' Mary said. 'And, if she went, she'd take Stephanie with her. She'd be more likely to get custody of the child – besides Jack couldn't look after her.'

'He'd have a job to feed her, that's for sure!' Alice said solemnly, then she almost giggled.

'Oh, shut up Al!' William snapped. 'This is serious. If she took Stephanie away – what would that do to the Magician's plan?'

'How can we know?' Mary said. 'He's never really explained to us what his plan is, has he?'

'But our first task was helping Stephanie to be born and we do know that the Magician wanted an heir in our time and that Phoebe is really a Tyler, though her family is now called Taylor. We do know that much,' William said, then he continued, 'but where does that get us? What does any of it mean? I hope one of you understands it, because it's a total mystery to me.'

'We'll just have to ask the Magician,' Alice suggested eagerly. 'He'll explain anything, if we only ask.'

'Spot said he hasn't been here for ages,' William said glumly. 'And after we rescued the contract that Lewis and Crawden drew up . . . he never came to see us. Even though we needed him desperately then. In fact, when you think about it, the last time we saw him was in the tunnel behind the waterfall and even then he didn't exactly tell us what to do.'

'I think he would have, if only we'd asked the right questions,' Mary said thoughtfully. 'The trouble is the really important questions only come into your mind later. Like now, there's lots we want to ask him, because now more has happened that we need to make sense of.'

'Maybe that's why he time travelled in the first place,' William said. 'We know you mustn't change the past, but maybe, if you know the future it helps you to influence the present.'

'But surely, if you change the present, you alter the future,' Mary said. 'And wouldn't altering the future, be as dangerous as altering the past?'

'I don't know,' William admitted. 'I haven't a clue. I told you, I don't know any of the answers.'

'There's only one person who does,' Mary said, 'and that's the Magician.' Then she added bitterly, 'but he's never here when we need him!'

'So?' Alice demanded. 'Like you said, Mary – at the end of last holiday – we'll have to go to him.'

'We've tried all that,' William groaned. 'We don't know how to.'

'Maybe this will help us,' Mary said and, as she spoke, she produced the golden nugget, the Magician's pendulum, from the pocket of her jeans.

They stared thoughtfully at the piece of gold dangling from Mary's hand.

'You know,' William said, sounding depressed

again, 'after all we've been through and after all that we've done, I don't feel we're any further forward than we were when we first discovered the steps up the chimney. We still don't really know why we've had to do all the things we've done. We still don't know the reason or the purpose . . . for anything.'

'Except saving the badgers,' Alice said. 'We knew why we had to do that. But then that was our idea anyway . . . the badgers didn't really seem to be part of Mr Tyler's plan, did they?'

'He came to their help, though,' Mary said.

'But saving Goldenwater from the developers – what was all that about?' William said. 'I've thought about it so often since, but I haven't a clue why it really mattered to him. I mean, we didn't want the place spoiled . . . but why should it matter to him? He's been dead four hundred years! I'm sure all this country will be completely different in another four hundred years from now – but that doesn't mean I'm going to try and do something about it – so why does he?'

'Because he's a Magician – and you're not, are you?' Mary said. Then she continued more thoughtfully, 'You couldn't do anything about it, even if you wanted to. But he can. And there has to be a reason why he wants to – there has to be.'

'Well, I wish he'd tell us what it is then,' Alice sighed. 'I mean I don't mind risking my life – but I would like to know why I'm doing it.' Then she giggled again. 'It's frightfully tiring, being a heroine all the time!'

'If Jack decided to sell Golden House,' William said, ignoring her and still deep in thought, 'what would happen to the land, I wonder?'

'It isn't Jack's land anyway,' Mary pointed out. 'It belongs to Meg.'

'All right then, suppose Meg drops dead or something, what'll happen to the land then?'

'It would depend on who she's left it to,' Mary said.

'I thought she was going to leave it to Jack,' Alice said. 'She was going to leave Four Fields to us, if it hadn't burnt down . . .'

'But if Jack sells the house,' William insisted, 'what will Meg do with the land then? She won't have anywhere to live. She's only living here because she's a friend of Jack and Phoebe. If they sold up . . . she'd have to find somewhere else. In order to do that she'd need money and the only way she can get money would be by selling the land . . .'

'And guess who'd buy it,' Mary said, grimly.

'Who?' Alice squealed.

'Who d'you think, Al?' Mary asked wearily. 'It's obvious.'

'Crawly Crawden?' Alice said. 'But then, in that case, we wouldn't have won at all. We'd be right back where we started when those vile men first came and wanted to turn Goldenwater into an amusement park – or whatever it was they wanted. All we've done would be useless.'

'And Morden would win after all,' William said.

The name Morden hung on the air like a dark shadow but, before any more could be said, Jack came briskly into the kitchen from the hall.

'Right!' he said. 'Supper! Phoebe isn't feeling too good, so you'll have to wait till tomorrow to see her. Now, let's have a look at what there is to eat. This stew is a mistake, I'm afraid. A bit of a misunderstanding . . .' and, as he spoke, he removed the saucepan from the top of the kitchen range. 'Jacket potatoes, vegetables and fried eggs. How does that sound?'

Mary stuffed the pendulum back into her pocket and William started to lay the table once more.

'Alice,' Jack called from the larder, 'can you go and tell Meg we'll be eating in five minutes time, please?'

Jack continued to bustle about, preparing supper, as though he hadn't a care in the world and when Meg returned with Alice she also seemed to have completely forgotten her bad temper and the irritation she had shown to the children only a few minutes before. As for the beef stew, it was never mentioned again. It was as though it had never been made. Meg immediately offered to fry the eggs for Jack and he accepted with enthusiasm.

'Phoebe just wants some bread and butter and a pot of tea,' he said, brightly. 'I'll take the tray up as soon as the kettle's boiled . . .'

Mary watched all this activity and listened to the cheerful chatter with increasing disbelief. It made her strangely depressed again and she thought once more how like a play it all was; a play being specially staged by Meg and Jack for the benefit of William, Alice and herself. 'But they aren't fooling any of us,' she thought, 'and, what is more, they know they aren't.' Then, not for the first time since she arrived back at Golden House, she felt a cold shiver down her back. 'It's bad, this time,' a voice whispered in her head. 'This time is going to be the hardest of all.'

3
A Midnight Meeting

When Mary woke, the first sound she heard was the rain. It was torrenting down outside the window. She could hear it drumming on the roof above her head and rushing and swirling down the tiles. At first she supposed it was this that had dragged her out of the deep, comfortable sleep she had fallen into as soon as her head touched the pillow. But another sound, low and urgent, now penetrated the darkness of the room. It was a strange reedy whistle, one of those half-familiar sounds that, coming unexpectedly, have to be worked out; the sort of sound you know well without at first being able to put a name to it. . . .

'Jasper!' Mary whispered, recognizing at last the owl's call, and she sprang out of bed and ran to the window, turning the latch and pushing it open. Gusts of cold air blew into the room, carrying the drenching rain so that it soaked her face and hair and trickled down her neck, wetting her pyjamas.

'Where are you?' she called. 'Jasper!' Her voice was swallowed up by the night wind that moaned and whined round the house.

'What's happening?' a sleepy voice behind her asked. 'Shut the window, Mary! It's freezing!'

Mary pulled back into the room and closed the

small dormer window. Then, shaking water out of her hair, she hurried towards the landing to get a towel from the bathroom.

'It was Jasper,' she said as she went. 'Come on, Al! I think he wants us.'

'Not now!' Alice grumbled. 'I'm asleep!' But, of course, she wasn't any more and by the time Mary came back from the bathroom, wiping her face with a towel and having woken William as she was passing, Alice was already pulling on her jeans.

'What time is it?' she whispered.

'Nearly midnight,' Mary replied, starting to dress.

'Why can't we do whatever we have to do in the morning?' Alice sighed. 'Why does it always have to be in the middle of the night? Well, I shan't clean my teeth again, I've only just done them. Honestly! I was in the middle of a fantastic dream and . . . Oh, it's freezing in this room..!'

'Shut up, Alice!' Mary whispered, pulling on a thick sweater. 'You don't have to come. No one's making you. Go back to bed, if that's what you want!'

But Alice had no intention of letting Mary go off on an adventure without her and so she followed her out on to the landing, where William joined them, moments later, carrying a torch.

'You're sure it was Jasper you heard?' he asked, yawning.

'Pretty sure,' Mary answered. 'But anyway, now we're all awake we may as well go up to the secret room. It's going to be even more difficult to go there during daylight now Meg is living in the house.'

'Yes,' William agreed, then, as he was making for the head of the stairs, he stopped and added,

19

'Although, actually I've been thinking about that. We ought to talk to Meg. I mean she knows much more about what's going on than either Jack or Phoebe – and she already knows about the secret room, because her grandfather, Jonas Lewis, was always drawing plans of the house – and he knew all about it . . .'

'And she said she'd help us all she could – last summer, when we were fighting the Crawdens. She did, didn't she?' Alice added eagerly. 'She knows about the Magician and everything. I think Will's right, she won't give us away. She's our friend . . .'

'Well, she wasn't very friendly tonight,' Mary said ruefully. 'She was really bad-tempered.'

'We ought to ask her about that, as well,' William said. 'We've got to find out what's been going on while we've been away.'

'Oh, please, can we move and have this talk somewhere else?' Alice pleaded. 'It's freezing on these stairs and if it was Jasper who Mary heard, he'll be waiting for us and he hates being kept waiting.'

A light was shining under Jack and Phoebe's bedroom door as they tiptoed along the gallery and they could hear Stephanie crying. Realizing that at any moment the door could open and Jack or Phoebe could come out, they hurried down the stairs and made for the great inglenook fireplace, in which the embers of the fire still glowed and smoked.

'Just a minute,' Alice whispered, as they were passing the kitchen door. 'I must get Spot. He'd never forgive us if we went without him.'

As soon as she opened the door, the dog bounded out, his tail wagging. He raced across the hall to join William and Mary in the fireplace, without hesitation, as if he'd been waiting for them.

'Come on!' he whispered urgently, looking back over his shoulder at Alice. 'Meg is quite likely to appear suddenly. She spends most of the night wandering about.'

The inside of the chimney was smoky and sweet with the smell of pine and apple. Jack had used trimmings from the fruit trees in the walled garden and pine cones from the forest to kindle the log fire and the scent lingered long after the fire had gone out.

William led the way up the stone slabs to the ledge, carrying the torch so that it shone on the steps for each of them. Then he edged his way to the back corner of the fireplace and disappeared round the protruding wall to where the steps up the chimney started. Followed by Mary and with Spot and Alice close behind, he began to climb up towards the wooden smoke door and then on to the very top of the old medieval tower where the secret room was situated under the eaves of the house.

The room was in darkness. As William held the torch for Alice to see her way up the final steps, Mary passed him and, feeling her way carefully, she went and opened the shutters of the circular window that looked out over the back of the house towards the walled garden and the heights beyond, now completely hidden from view by the night. Releasing the catch on the window, she pushed it open. At once rain entered the room. The wind was much stronger on this side of the house than it had been through the bedroom window. It filled the room with swirling, damp air, and slammed shut the door at the top of the stairs with a shattering bang that echoed and reverberated like an explosion.

'Mary!' William whispered. 'You'll wake people.'

'What people?' Mary asked, turning to look at him. 'No-one can hear us up here, and anyway, I didn't do it on purpose. Why must you be so bossy, William?' Then, as her eyes gradually grew accustomed to the dark, she gasped. 'What's happened here?' she exclaimed.

William turned the torch and ran the bright beam slowly round the room. The floor was littered with crumbled plaster and the beams of the steeply-raked ceiling were thick with dirt and cobwebs.

'What a mess!' Alice said. 'It's usually quite clean up here.'

'What's happened?' Mary said again.

William's torch glinted on the mirror, hanging in the corner of the room. He crossed over to it.

'Look at this,' he said, holding the torch so that the mirror was fully illuminated. 'It looks as though it's been dusted while the rest of the room has been completely ignored.'

'It's not just ignored, Will. Look at all the mess!' Mary insisted. 'It's as if someone has deliberately scattered dirt everywhere.'

It was true. The floor was covered with the sort of filth that gets trapped under floorboards and round the sides of drains after years and years of habitation. Black, evil sludge; some dry as dust but other bits dank and slimy.

'And what a horrible stink!' Alice added and, as she spoke, the other two also noticed that the room had a most peculiar smell: a pungent, rotten, odour. Alice crinkled her nose. 'It's disgusting!' she said.

'What has happened?' William said, turning and addressing Spot.

The dog had remained perfectly still and silent since entering the room. He stood with his tail down between his legs and his head hanging low. Now, as William spoke to him, he didn't react. He seemed scarcely to have even heard. He was a picture of such forlorn misery than Alice ran and knelt beside him on the dirty floor, putting an arm round him.

'Oh, Spot,' she whispered. 'Don't be sad. We're here. We'll look after you.'

The dog sat down, staring at her with mournful eyes.

'It's the Magician, isn't it?' Mary said, from the darkness behind them. 'Something's happened to him. He isn't . . . ?' she couldn't bring herself to say the next word. She dreaded so much that what she feared might be true that she just shook her head and left the sentence unfinished.

'Isn't what?' Alice's voice was small and tearful. 'What are you saying, Mary?'

Mary shook her head again, still unable to speak without her voice trembling uncontrollably.

'You think he's dead, don't you?' Alice whispered. 'That's what you mean.'

'I don't know,' Mary replied quietly. 'But something very bad has happened. I knew it as soon as we got here. And now, seeing the room like this. . . . Oh, where's Jasper?' she said, sounding almost irritable. 'We need him.'

'I'm here,' a mournful voice hooted and, looking towards the open window, they saw the great owl sitting on the candle sconce, staring out at the driving rain.

'We didn't hear you arrive,' William said, shining the torch at the bird.

'No,' Jasper said. 'Well, I am here and you are here . . .' and the last word ended in a sad, lingering sigh.

'Is he dead, Jasper?' William asked, his voice shaking as he spoke. 'Mr Tyler? I mean, I know he really is, but – in his own time – has he died now?'

'Not yet, I think,' the bird answered.

'How would we know?' Spot whined pitifully.

'I'd know,' the owl replied. 'I'd . . . feel it. When the Master . . . goes . . . then surely . . . I'll feel it. The woods will know. Merula and Falco, Lutra, Cinnabar, Bawson . . . the great company of his friends, his companions . . . You, little boy and your sisters . . . we will all know . . . somehow. But, nevertheless, I think it is very close . . . his death, I think, will be soon. I feel it . . . I know it . . .'

They were silent as the owl's words slowly sank in. The reality of what he was saying was more terrible than anything they could possibly have contemplated. Each of them was locked into their own grief. They didn't want to share it with anyone else. It was a private pain. Alice clung to Spot, who leaned against her. The owl remained staring with unblinking eyes out into the night. William switched off his torch, not so much to save the battery as to draw some comfort from the obscurity of the dark. Only Mary, overwhelmed as she was by grief, couldn't allow herself to believe what they were all contemplating.

'We must go to him,' she said firmly. 'We *must*!' As she spoke she felt a sense of urgency, of determination, quickening in her body.

'We don't know how to,' William said wearily.

24

'We don't have to *know* how, William,' she said crossly. 'We just have to want to . . . want to enough. We can't let him die, all alone in that house, without us there. We have to tell him that everything is all right. We have to tell him that we'll always remember him. We have to tell him that, no matter what happens, he has a descendant who will grow up to know about him and about the wonderful things he was able to do. We have to let him know that we'll teach Stephanie how to understand the animals and how to love all the things that he loves and that he has taught us to love. I don't know *how*, William. . . . But we will go to him, because we must and because we want to. . . . Or, at least, I . . . I want to . . .' and a great sob broke from her and tears ran down her cheeks and she was shaking so much that she had to lean against the sloping roof for fear of falling.

William walked slowly across the room and, feeling in the dark, he found her hand and held it.

'Well, that's it then, isn't it?' he said, trying to make his voice sound cheerful. 'If we're to go to him, Jasper, can you help us?' and he switched on the torch again, shining it in the direction of the bird.

'Help you?' the owl trilled, and as he spoke he turned his staring eyes and blinked at them. 'Perhaps. Perhaps, together, we can achieve what you hope for. I . . . don't know very much. But I can . . . sometimes . . . understand. With my understanding and your knowledge, we together may be able to . . . do the impossible. It's worth a try. We must have a meeting of the company. This will take all our concerted effort. You are in command, now. You

25

three. That is how the Master wanted it to be. He told us, when he met us at the secret place . . .'

'You mean the meeting we had at . . .' William started to speak, but Spot sprang at him, nipping his hand with his teeth. 'Ow! Spot!' he exclaimed. 'That hurt!'

'Don't speak secrets, little boy,' the owl hooted. 'Never speak secrets. This place is no longer safe. Can't you smell it?'

'What is that smell?' Mary asked.

'The smell of decay,' the owl answered.

'The smell of poison,' Spot growled. 'It's the smell of food that's gone bad.'

'But where does it come from?' Alice asked him.

'Rats,' Jasper replied.

'They're everywhere now,' Spot said. 'Jack puts traps down, but there are more than he can catch. They're probably listening to us now. Can't you sense them? They're in the walls and under the rafters.'

'Oh, stop! Please!' Alice said, in a small voice. 'I don't like it here. I hate rats. They make me feel all crawly.'

'What's happened?' Mary whispered. 'Why have the rats come back?'

'They're up to something, but we don't know what,' Spot said. 'I should have killed that first one, at Christmastime. The one that was sniffing about while the baby was being born. I knew I should, but I didn't.'

'I stopped you, didn't I?' Alice said. 'I was in you . . . I remember the smell . . . I knew you wanted to pounce . . . but I was so afraid.'

'Well,' Spot said, nuzzling her, 'you humans aren't used to dealing with rats like we are. A nice sharp pounce while they're not expecting it. That usually does the trick.'

'Don't talk about it any more, please, Spot!' Mary pleaded. She was remembering the first time she flew in Jasper and the mouse they had for supper. 'It's no wonder I've gone vegetarian,' she said to herself and she shuddered.

'Has Morden been here?' William interrupted her, an idea suddenly occurring to him.

'Not yet, I think,' Jasper replied.

'Well we've got to get to his time before he gets here to ours,' William said.

'Why?' Mary asked. 'What are you thinking, Will?'

'I'm not sure, but I suspect that once he manages to time travel he'll be all-powerful and the Magician, if he really is ill, won't be able to control him . . .'

'So, you mean, we must?' Mary said.

'Something like that,' William replied. Then, looking round, he raised his voice. 'If any of his spies are listening, they can tell Morden that we'll see him in his time before he ever manages to reach us here!'

The owl blinked. 'Very well,' he said, 'I'll gather the company soon after dawn,' and, without waiting for a reply, he spread his wings and launched himself out of the room into the dark, rain-drenched, night.

'Come on,' Mary said, 'we'd better get some sleep. We'll have to be up early. I've brought my alarm clock this time.'

'But we can't just go off, without saying anything,' Alice said. 'Phoebe and Jack will go bananas if we're missing at breakfast time!'

'That can't be helped,' Mary said. 'This is too important to worry about little things like that.' And, with a determined nod, she hurried towards the door and started down the stairs without even waiting for William with the torch.

'Come on, Al!' William said, closing the window once more and securing the shutter across it. 'She's right. We may as well go back to bed, there's nothing more we can do up here. It feels as though Mr Tyler hasn't been here for ages.' Then he added sadly, 'Almost as though he's never been.'

'But he has,' Alice said firmly. 'We know he has – and that's what's important. We've seen him. We know he exists. We know the magic that he can do. And . . . and I agree with Mary! If he can't come to us, we'll just have to go to him, that's all.' And she followed William out of the room, glad of the torchlight on the dark, twisting stairs.

4
The Dawn Conference

They reached the tunnel behind the waterfall just as the first streaks of dawn were touching the tops of the distant hills and the trees of the forest were gradually emerging from the dark mass of night.

It had still been dark when they let themselves out of the kitchen door but, with Spot leading the way and the light from William's torch, they had managed to find the narrow path from the forest track that led up the steep escarpment towards Goldenwater.

Near the yew tree, where the secret house was completely hidden from view by the thick branches, they met Bawson, the badger, hurrying to the meeting. He greeted them with a low bark but was too shy and too nervous to engage them in conversation.

'It's his bedtime,' Spot explained. 'Many of the creatures are a bit scared as daylight approaches.'

'Scared of what?' Alice asked breathlessly as she ran beside him.

'Humans, mostly,' Spot growled. Then, seeing how hard it was for her to keep up, he stopped and stared at her, his tail slowly wagging and his tongue hanging out.

Alice's heart raced faster. Spot's big, brown eyes seemed to see right into her. She reached towards him, wanting to stroke his soft, smooth head and, as she did so, she saw not a hand, but a paw stretching in front of her. Then, as this paw touched the ground, she and the dog, together as one, sprang forward up the last steep ground to the plateau at the top of the heights with the silent reaches of Goldenwater glimmering at a distance, black and still beneath the night sky.

'Oh, Spot!' she whispered in her head. 'This is better. We humans find it difficult to keep up with you . . .'

'Quite!' the dog agreed, and she knew he was laughing at her.

Mary had already reached the side of the lake when she heard the harsh, chattering voice of Pica, the magpie.

'Where are you?' she called, scanning the sky for a glimpse of him.

'Here!' a voice rasped in her head and she felt herself rising up off the ground into the cold breeze.

'Oh!' she gasped, taken completely by surprise.

'Listen! the bird voice said.

'I'm flying!' she whispered.

'Just listen!' the voice repeated.

At first she could hear nothing more than the sound of the breeze in the trees below them. But then a sudden, exuberant cascade of singing broke the silence. If sound could be likened to running water, she thought, then she was listening to the clear music of a mountain stream.

'What is it?' she whispered.

'Alauda, the skylark. During the summer months she's always the first to greet the dawn. But it's late in the year for her to be singing. We are living in strange times!'

'It's beautiful!' Mary whispered, listening to the cheerful, enchanted and enchanting sound.

'Tasty too,' Pica said.

'What?' Mary cried, not believing that she'd heard the bird correctly.

'You can make a nice little snack of a young skylark,' the Magpie remarked, then, dipping his wing, he turned in a slow arc and headed up the centre of the lake as the first light began to soften the eastern horizon behind them and more and more birds joined in the chorus to the dawn.

William saw Cinnabar first. The fox's red-brown tail glimmered momentarily in the shadows as the animal streaked through the trees near the bridle-path to Four Fields, heading for the end of the lake.

'Cinnabar!' he whispered, excitedly, making the fox stop in his tracks.

'Too much haste, not enough care!' William heard the familiar voice exclaim.

'I'm here!' William called.

'I know where you are,' the fox said, sounding almost cross. 'This isn't the best of times to call a conference, you know.'

'Sorry!' William said, not hiding his disappointment that their meeting seemed to be starting with an argument.

'I don't like the dawn,' Cinnabar said. 'Not this dawn, not at this time of year,' and, as he spoke, he looked over his shoulder nervously. 'The hunting starts soon. We foxes have to learn new ways. The winter may be hard, but the hounds and the men in red are a greater danger.' As he spoke he padded along beside William, his breath smoking on the cold air.

All around them now, birds were singing and the

31

light was growing, glittering on the surface of the lake and touching the clouds with hues of apricot and violet.

'What a hard life you have,' William said sadly. 'The dawn looks so beautiful.'

'Beauty?' Cinnabar barked. 'You can't eat beauty! What's the point of beauty? Come on!' he said, springing forward. 'We'll be last there at this rate!' and, gathering William to him, they raced together towards the distant waterfall.

The cave at the end of the tunnel was crowded when Cinnabar and William entered it. They could see Alice standing beside Spot and Mary was sitting on a protruding rock, with Pica on her shoulder. There were birds of every description clinging to the walls and perched in crannies. Some of them were familiar to the children; there was Merula, the blackbird and Falco, the kestrel . . . but the swallows and the swifts had already left for warmer climates. Lutra, the otter was there, together with several ducks. There were rabbits and stoats, Bawson, the badger, some squirrels, a vole . . . even a spider on a gossamer web. They all had their backs to the entrance and were facing Jasper, the owl, who had perched on a ledge with a clear space on the ground in front of him.

'You're here at last!' he hooted as soon as William entered. 'Well, come on! Come on! Don't loiter about! Here we all are. You too, Mary! And you, Alice! We are here at your behest, after all.' And, trilling impatiently, he ruffled his feathers and blinked.

'You'd better go and stand with him,' Cinnabar whispered to William. 'He gets put out if he's kept waiting.'

'But . . . but . . . we didn't ask for the meeting!' William protested.

'You are in charge now!' the owl hooted. 'With the Master not here, it's up to you three!'

'Us?' Mary said. 'But we don't know anything.'

A mallard duck, who was standing near her, quacked irascibly. 'I haven't had my breakfast yet,' he said and he eyed a frog, and would probably have pounced if the frog hadn't had the good sense to sidle away out of his reach.

Then Bawson, the badger, raised himself up on his hind legs.

'Tell us what to do,' he said. 'The Master hasn't been here for so long that we don't know whether to expect him back or not. The woods are full of strange rumours. My people fear the lampers and baiters will come back . . .'

'The Hunt starts soon,' Cinnabar said.

'I's been told the waters of Goldenspring will run with poison. That's what I's heard,' Lutra, the otter said staring with bright eyes at William, as if he wanted him to say whether the rumours could possibly be true or not. 'I's been told that if we have another hot summer, the springs will start to dries up and there won't be pure water no mores. Then what'll happens? What about the fishes? What about us? All of us? There isn't nothings that lives that doesn't depend on pure waters. Waters is life.'

Now more and more complaints started to be voiced. The birds were saying that their food was in shorter supply than they'd known for years. A stoat had heard a rumour that the farmers were putting down poison . . . 'along all the hedgerows. What will we eat, if they poison the land?' he asked, in a plaintive voice.

'Silence!' Jasper commanded, trying to restore order to the meeting.

'We won't be silenced!' Bawson growled. 'We're desperate. Someone has to take charge. The Master is an old man. He's done a lot for us, I know that. Without him, and these human children here, I would be dead and my family scattered. And the old woman, of course – old Meg. She's been our guardian, but now she doesn't come so often . . . and these children go away . . . and the Master. . . . He promised us . . . he promised that there would be others who would follow after him when his time came to be called away. He promised us that we wouldn't be abandoned.'

'Why won't he come?' Cinnabar barked. 'Where is he? Is he sick? Do we know this to be true? Or has the other one finally got the better of him? That's what I want to know. There are stoats and weasels that would have it so. More and more of our wild creatures are turning to Morden. I've heard there are new creatures moving in along the banks of the river – creatures from across the water, bred by men in captivity and now escaped. Vicious and strong and cunning. Trying to take over our land. They won't even have heard of the Master. Morden could soon win them over. He'll have more on his side than us a hundred times over. We'll have war on our hands.'

'Shut up, Cinnabar!' Spot growled. 'That sort of talk is only making things worse. It's all rumour.'

'I heard that the Master's house is over-run with rats,' a rabbit said. 'Or is that also a rumour?'

'There are a lot of rats,' Spot agreed, sounding uncomfortable, 'but haven't there always been?

There used to be a lot of your sort – until the great death.'

'Oh!' sobbed the rabbit. 'And who brought the great death?'

'Humans,' Jasper said and all the eyes of the company turned on the three children.

'But not humans like us!' Mary exclaimed. 'I know what you mean by the great death. We've been told about it . . . Myxomatosis . . .'

'A long word for a cruel fate,' the rabbit sighed. 'Why did humans punish my race? Why? What had we ever done to you?'

'It was a long time ago,' Mary mumbled.

'It isn't over even now,' the rabbit added. 'The great death will never go away completely.'

'Why do they hunt my people?' Cinnabar asked.

'Why do they torture mine?' the badger asked.

Once again the children could feel all the eyes staring at them through the gloomy light in the cave.

'Maybe,' William said, when he could bear the silence no longer, 'maybe some questions can't be answered . . .'

A growl and a hiss and a squeak and a chatter of disapproval ran through the company.

'That's no answer!' Jasper said, in a lofty voice.

'I know it isn't!' William said crossly. 'I just said . . . some things can't have simple answers. Like . . . the rabbit asked about the great death. But what about the rats at Golden House? Are they to be allowed to live?'

'That's quite different,' a stoat said, sounding impatient.

'Why?' William asked. 'Why is it?'

'Because the rats at Golden House are Morden's creatures . . .'

'And were all the rabbits that died in the great death the Master's rabbits?' William demanded. 'Is that what you're saying?' He got no reply. 'And anyway, why is it all right for Morden's creatures to be killed and not for the Master's? That doesn't seem right to me . . .'

'Little boy!' Jasper cut in, sounding like a schoolmaster. 'Don't talk about things you don't understand . . .'

'But I don't understand any of it!' William cried, his voice so loud with impatience that he silenced all the chattering around him. 'I don't even pretend to. It's you lot who keep asking us questions. If you must know – the myxomatosis was introduced because there were so many rabbits they were taking over . . . I know . . .' he said, capping the rabbit's shrill protest, 'I know it was horrible – I know it was wrong . . . but that's why it happened. Humans did it – but it wasn't entirely for bad reasons. And the rats at Golden House – if they're not stopped, they'll take over the place. They have to be killed. Even the hunting, Cinnabar . . . I know it's cruel. I don't like it . . . but you foxes kill the farmers' hens and chickens and ducks. That's why they hate you . . .'

'And humans?' Jasper asked, in a lofty voice. 'Are they not "taking over" as you put it? Do they not kill chickens and ducks? Is there one law for humans and another for the rest of us, William? Is that what you're saying?'

'Well,' William countered, 'haven't you just suggested that there's one law for the Master's

36

creatures and another for Morden's? You don't seem to mind Morden's rats being killed, do you?'

There was a terrible, long silence. William hung his head. He felt he had ruined everything. He knew that he had alienated the meeting. He could sense the disappointment and the antagonism that surrounded him. He wasn't even sure that it didn't come from Mary and Alice as well as from the animals and birds.

Alice, who had been silent throughout the entire meeting so far, reached out a hand towards Spot, who was sitting on the ground in front of her. He looked up at her with troubled eyes, but didn't come towards her. Mary, who was standing next to her, put an arm round her shoulder, as if trying to give her the comfort that had just been refused by the dog. With this show of kindness, Alice felt tears stinging in her eyes. Not wanting to been seen to cry in front of all the staring eyes, she turned towards Mary and buried her face on her sister's shoulder.

'Perhaps,' said Cinnabar. 'I will see you this weekend, little boy?'

'Yes!' William said eagerly, hoping to make amends.

'You'll no doubt be riding with the men in red?' the fox snarled and turning, with a swish of his tail, he ran lightly down the tunnel towards the distant torrent of the waterfall.

'Cinnabar!' William cried. 'That isn't fair, Cinnabar!' he shouted after him, and his voice shook.

'Bad times for foxes now,' Bawson said, in a sad voice. 'Bad time for all of us.' As though his words were a signal to the others they started to file out of the cave, hopping and sliding, scurrying and flying until, at last, only Jasper and Spot remained with the children.

'Jasper!' William pleaded. 'Help me, please!'

'Oooh!' the owl hooted mournfully. 'Help us all!' and, without waiting for a response, he spread his wings and flew away down the tunnel.

'Spot!' Mary said. 'Don't you leave us, please Spot.'

'They're just wild animals, you see,' the dog said quietly. Then he sighed. 'Just? I say just? We dogs have been tamed so long, we don't know what we are.'

'I love you, Spot,' Alice said in a small, tearful voice.

The dog looked at her with searching eyes. Then he seemed to nod and make some deep decision inside his head.

'Love,' he said. 'That's what humans gave us. Did you know that? Wild animals don't love. They protect, they defend, they feed and nurture their own kind. But until they come in contact with humans, they don't begin to love.'

'But surely that's a good thing?' Mary exclaimed.

'Good?' Spot asked. Then he continued gruffly, 'Yes, of course. But difficult. Because when you love, you can also hate. Wild animals do not know hate either. Oh, they hunt and kill and have certain enemies. But these are natural enemies. Until you know love – you do not know hate. Or hurt. Cinnabar now is hurting, because he has come into contact with a human and the human has not behaved how he expected him to do. You humans, with your love and your hate . . . you make life very complicated.'

Then, unexpectedly, he licked Alice's hand. She

immediately sank on her knees in front of him and put her arms round him. But, almost as she was embracing him, the dog pulled away from her and sprang round, all the hairs on his back sticking straight up and a low growl forming in his throat.

'Now what?' Alice exclaimed, tearfully believing that she had done something wrong again.

'I don't know,' Spot growled. 'Something. . . .' His nose twitched as he scented in the direction of a dark corner of the cave to their right. 'Something . . . something ratty.'

'A rat?' Alice gasped, standing up and backing away hastily.

'And yet . . .' Spot said, putting his head on one side, 'not Morden. . . . A rat and not . . .'

A sudden hiss stopped the dog in mid-sentence. Alice immediately put her hands over her eyes, which is what she always did when she was scared.

'What is it?' Mary gasped.

'Where is it?' William whispered.

'Up on the rocks, up there,' Spot barked and he bounded forward, reaching upwards, with his front paws leaning on the steep side of the cave.

'I can't see anything,' William said, straining his eyes in the half-light.

'It's there though. I can smell it,' the dog muttered. 'Rat smell, but different. Who are you?' he barked. 'Stand and declare yourself! You! Rat! Who are you? Where are you from?'

There was a moment of agonizing silence. Then a sleek black shape sprang down towards them from the dark, making Mary scream and William take a step back.

The creature landed at their feet, standing in a shaft of light that filtered down from the opening in

39

the cavern roof, high up above. They saw a sleek, black body and a long, worm-like tail. Spot faced it with all his hackles up, but he didn't pounce; he seemed, if anything, confused.

'Who are you?' he asked again.

'My name is Rattus Rattus,' the creature replied.

'I've never seen one like you,' Spot growled.

'I don't belong here,' the rat replied.

'Then where have you come from?' William asked.

'Oh, William!' Rattus Rattus exclaimed. 'Don't you know?'

'Mr Tyler?' Mary gasped, relief and hope flooding through her body.

'Well, not in person,' the rat replied. 'But, yes, I am the Magician's rat.'

'I don't believe you,' Alice said, still with her hands over her eyes. 'Mr Tyler wouldn't have a rat.'

'Alice!' the rat hissed. 'Shame on you! Why should the devil have all the best tunes? You will find that I'm going to be very useful to you. Very useful indeed.'

'Useful?' Mary asked, suddenly feeling nervous again. 'How – useful?'

'How else will you manage to infiltrate the enemy's camp without me?' Rattus Rattus said and he squeaked with laughter.

5
Rattus Rattus

A horrible silence greeted the rat's words. Alice still had her hands over her eyes but now, by opening her fingers, she was able to steal a quick look at him.

'Hello!' he said, his jet-bright eyes twinkling in the gloom. And he gave her a broad grin.

Alice reached out a hand and pulled Spot closer towards her.

'The Master told me that you were brave, Alice. What sort of bravery is this?'

'I don't like rats,' she whispered.

'That's not very nice, is it?' he said. 'And how many rats have you known, may I ask? Are you intimately acquainted with a rat? Have you had dealings with one? Have you ever, in the whole of your short life, tried to get to know a rat? Well? Have you?' and, as he spat out the final question, he leaped towards her, his tail swishing and his teeth flashing.

Alice screamed and ducked back behind Mary.

'Get away from me!' she gasped. 'Spot, do something!'

The dog growled and stood his ground. He was now between the rat and the children. The two animals sized each other up.

'You'd be no match for me, Sirius,' the rat said, his voice cold and menacing. 'Don't even think what you're thinking. One move and I'll be at your throat. I am a famous duellist. I learned the art on board a man-of-war sailing against the Spanish pirates and when I fight I always win. None of your gentlemanly sorties for me. If I engage in combat, I go for the kill.'

Spot growled, a long, low sound. But his tail was between his legs and he took a step backwards.

'How do we know you have anything to do with the Magician?' he asked. 'You could be a spy. You could be Morden's rat.'

'I could,' the rat agreed. 'That's why I'm going to be so useful to you.'

'Useful?' Spot growled. 'How could a rat be useful?'

'By making other rats believe that I am one of them, perhaps?'

'Which you most likely are anyway,' Spot said.

'He might be what he says,' William said, trying to sound braver than he really felt. 'He does know all our names.'

'That's not much of a proof,' the rat said disparagingly. 'Do you really think that Morden's creatures don't know your names? They know your names, they know your movements, they're watching you all the time.'

'They don't know we're here,' Spot said. 'They don't know about this place. They haven't found the Cave of Dreams.'

'Not yet, no,' the rat agreed. 'But they will soon. That's why we must attack them first. We have to be one jump ahead of them. That's our next job. That's why I'm here.'

42

'The Magician wouldn't use a rat,' Alice insisted.

'The Magician would use any creature, or thing, that was going to help him,' the rat said. 'He even uses little girls who are scared of animals hardly bigger than one of their feet.' And, as he spoke, he dodged quickly round Spot and jumped at Alice, landing with a thud on her foot, where he clung, tail flicking and teeth bared.

'Spot!' Alice screamed, and she kicked out, trying to rid herself of the dreadful creature. At once Spot swung round, his hackles up, barking savagely.

With a shriek of laughter the rat leaped away and streaked up the rough wall of the cave to a high ledge.

'Oh! Oh!' Alice sobbed hysterically. 'Get it off me! Get it off me!' And, still sobbing and shaking, she dissolved into noisy tears.

'It's all right! It's all right, Alice! He's gone!' William had to shout to be heard above the din. Spot was standing on the ground below the ledge, barking and growling. Alice was crying. The rat was squeaking gleefully.

'Shut up!' Mary yelled. 'Shut up, all of you!' Her voice was so loud and so unexpected that it did the trick. Alice stopped in mid-sob, Spot in mid-bark and the rat hissed into silence.

'That's better!' she said. 'Much more of that noise and we're bound to be found by Morden's spies.'

'So don't you think I am one of his spies any more?' the rat whispered sibilantly.

'We don't know,' William retorted. 'But if you are on our side, as you claim to be, then you have a very peculiar way of showing it.'

'It's a puzzle, isn't it, William?' the rat whispered.

43

'The Magician left us one present,' Mary said. 'If you are who you say you are, you must know what it is.'

'Easy,' the rat replied. 'His pendulum. His golden pendulum.'

'That's right!' Mary gasped.

'But that proves nothing, Mary,' the rat said. 'After all, Morden's crow tried to take it from you. Morden himself saw that you, William, had it. What does that prove?'

'But it was lost. It fell into Goldenwater.'

'Yes. And the crow saw it happen. He would of course have told his master.'

'But the crow didn't see what happened later,' Mary insisted.

'You found it again and now it's in your pocket,' the rat countered, in a singsong voice.

'Oh, this is hopeless!' Mary sobbed.

'Looks like you're going to have to trust me,' the rat squeaked. 'After all, deeds are more revealing than words.'

'What does that mean?' William asked.

The rat sat up on its haunches and shrugged.

'If I serve you well, I will be a friend. If I serve you ill, I'll be an enemy.'

'But by then it may be too late,' William said crossly. 'By then you may have led us into all sorts of danger . . . or worse. We could lose everything to Morden if we trust you.'

'You don't seem to have much faith in yourselves, William. Are you so useless that you'll let one little rat ruin the enterprise?'

'One little rat!' Alice exclaimed. 'You're a horrible big, slimy rat and of course we're scared of you. We don't go jumping at people out of the dark, trying to frighten them. We don't squeak and . . . and . . . Oh!' she exclaimed, fear and frustration making her lose her words, 'go away . . .' and, picking up a stone from the floor, she threw it with all her strength. It hit the wall of the cave just above the rat's head, then rattled down to the ground again. The rat hissed and arched his back.

'Don't, Alice!' Spot growled. 'Don't make him lose his temper!'

'Spot, you must know if the Magician has a rat,' William said.

'I've never heard of one,' Spot replied.

'But then you've never been to the Magician's time, have you, dog?' the rat hissed.

'You mean . . . you came from *then*?' William asked, surprised.

'Of course. Didn't I tell you?'

'You said you weren't from round here.'

'Neither I am . . .'

'How is he?' Mary asked, cutting in anxiously and quite forgetting her fear.

'The Master is far from well,' the rat replied.

'Is he . . . ?'

'Dying?' the rat finished Spot's sentence for him. 'I asked him that.'

'Well, what did he say?' Mary whispered, afraid again of the possible answer.

'He said that we are all dying from the moment of our birth,' the rat replied.

'Why did he send you?' William asked.

'Because he cannot come himself. Not this time. Perhaps never again. He sent me because he didn't want you to be alone.'

'He sent a *rat* to keep us company?' Alice said, her voice full of disbelief.

45

'Alice! Alice! Stop this now!' the rat said, trying to keep his patience. 'I am Rattus Rattus. I am honourable. I am renowned. I am very close to the Master and I am becoming exceedingly weary of your attitude. I am Rattus Rattus! I have fought battles the length and breadth of the known world. I have travelled the seven seas and seen the sun rise over distant lands. But when I met the Master I chose to stay with him. I know the reputation of my race. We have been stoned since our conception. The stone you threw was only one in a great line of stones, Alice. Though I didn't think to have one of the Master's friends treat me thus. I may be a rat, but the Master saw only the good in me and he brought out that good. He made me gold.' His voice sounded distant with wonder. 'The Master saw in me possibilities that ordinary people never know. I am Rattus Rattus. I will not cease to be the rat I was when I was born. I will always be a rat – just as you will always be a human and Sirius will always be a dog. We cannot escape our form. But the alchemy, if it is allowed to work, will free us of our baser self and allow us to shine. I may be a rat. I may fight like a rat and think like a rat and look like a rat. But I am, so far, the only gold in this cave.'

He said the words so simply that he didn't seem to be boasting.

Mary, who had listened and watched in silence, turned now and looked at the others. They were all staring solemnly up at the high ledge on which Rattus Rattus was perched. Each one of them, with their heads tilted upwards straining to see him, looked small and vulnerable, each one of them had a rapt, expectant expression. Alice had stopped crying and William wasn't frowning, as he usually did when he was trying to work something out. Spot's hackles were down and his tail was slowly wagging.

'We need your help,' Mary said, speaking for all of them. 'If you have come from the Magician's time . . . can you take us back there with you?'

'Ah!' Rattus Rattus said, sounding sad. 'The Master warned me that that is what you would want. But he says it would be far too dangerous, far too difficult. That's why he sent me instead; to help you here, in this time.'

'But we must go to him,' Mary said, pleading with the rat. 'We want to see him so much!'

'And he . . . he wants to see you. But he says that is an old man's whim. An old man's vanity . . .'

'Could we do it?' William asked. 'With your help?'

'Time travel? I don't know,' the rat replied. 'It isn't a skill to be borrowed or learned; it is an art . . . no, more than an art. It is in your being. If you want it enough . . . you will manage it. If you want something for the right reason, you can do anything. But remember . . . if you travel back to our time, you will also have to know how to return.'

'But Morden is trying to come here,' William said, 'and the Magician told us he was close to doing so. But he's selfish and greedy and he's doing it for all the wrong reasons . . .'

'Precisely,' hissed the rat.

'So how is it that he can manage it?'

'He wants it enough. He wants it so much, he thinks of little else. His mind is ever focused on your time. In this future he sees his destiny, his release, the fulfilment of all his dreams.'

'But he's horrible,' Mary said. 'He brings evil with him. I don't believe that he can travel and yet we can't. How can that be possible?'

'In the same way that greedy people manage to turn base metal into gold, Mary, if they work really hard and are diligent in their lust . . .'

'Then evil can win,' William said, shaking his head. 'There seems no point in going on.'

'They make fool's gold, William. Like Jonas Lewis made. But his was a small mistake in comparison to what Morden is dreaming. It is one thing to have a bit of gold revert . . . but imagine if you time travelled for the wrong reasons and then the magic stopped.' Rattus Rattus paused, letting his words sink in. 'Imagine travelling to another time and not being able to get back. Where would you be then? Lost. Lost in time. Nowhere. Oblivion. Believe me, listen to me, time travelling is not an undertaking to be embarked upon without a great deal of thought. Get it wrong and you could be lost for ever.'

'I don't understand,' William sighed.

'Never mind,' Rattus Rattus said kindly. 'I don't somehow think that such a fate will ever befall any of you. Now you must go back to the house before your absence is noted by our enemies. I will come to you in your rooms at the top of the tower. Not the secret room, your bedrooms. The adults – Jack, and Phoebe Tyler – they need help. They could ruin everything. There is much work to be done. Expect me . . .' and, in mid-sentence, he disappeared from their sight.

'Just like Stephen Tyler used to do,' Mary whispered.

6
A Conversation With Meg

Meg was in the kitchen when they arrived back at the house. She was sitting, huddled up close to the open range, drinking from a mug.

'There you are,' she grumbled, as they came in from the yard. 'You shouldn't have gone out without your breakfasts. You'll get me into trouble.' But she didn't make a move to get them any food. She seemed depressed and distant.

'What's gone wrong, Meg?' Mary asked, crossing over to the fire. She was cold, although she hadn't noticed it when she had been hurrying back from the cave.

'Wrong?' Meg asked, looking blankly at her.

'Yes,' Mary said, turning to her. 'Look, we're not stupid, you know! It's obvious that something's happened. . . . Something bad.'

'Phoebe's got a bit of a bug, that's all,' Meg said, trying to sound bright but not being able to meet Mary's eyes.

'Meg,' Mary said, crouching down beside her, 'please tell us. We only want to help.'

'You're just children,' Meg said.

'So what?' William asked impatiently. 'We may

49

be young, but we do have brains, you know! We have eyes in our heads! We can see that something's going on!'

'If you're so clever, there's no need to ask then, is there?' Meg snapped.

'Oh, Meg!' William exclaimed, frustrated and disappointed at the same time.

'You said you were going to help us,' Mary said, still crouching beside the old woman, and feeling the warmth of the fire burning her cheek. 'Last summer, when the Crawdens were trying to buy you out. We helped you then and you said that you'd help us in return.'

'Well, I did, didn't I?' Meg retorted. 'I did help you. I didn't sell up to them. That's what you wanted, wasn't it? Well, I did that for you! I didn't sell Henry and his son the land round Goldenwater when I could have done. I didn't even know it was mine to sell, if I'm honest. But it was, apparently. It belonged to my family all the time!' She scratched the back of her hand thoughtfully and shook her head. 'How did you know that, I wonder? Or do I wonder?' She turned and looked at each of them in turn. Alice was sitting at the table eating a thick slice of bread and butter that she'd cut and spread while the others were talking. William was leaning against the dresser, with his hands in his jeans pockets, staring at the ground. Mary had pulled away from the heat of the range and was sitting on the floor, with her knees drawn up under her chin. 'I shouldn't have listened to you,' Meg continued, her voice becoming bitter and complaining. 'I could have sold the land and gone away. Somewhere a long way away. If I'd sold Henry the land, this whole story would be over, once and for all.' Now it was more as though she was talking to herself. Her voice was distant and puzzled, as though she was speaking thoughts that haunted her mind. 'It was a mistake ever coming back here. A Lewis back in Golden House! I should have known it would bring nothing but misery.' She shivered, as if suddenly cold, although the heat from the fire was intense. Then she fell silent again and when Mary next looked at her there were tears running down the old woman's cheeks.

'Oh, Meg!' Mary said, sliding across the floor towards her and putting both her arms round her. 'Don't cry! Please don't cry! It's going to be all right, I promise you. Somehow! We're here now. We won't let everything be spoilt . . .' Then, running out of words to say, she looked desperately back over her shoulder at Alice and William, as if asking them for help.

William crossed to the other side of Meg, and Alice got up and ran to kneel in front of her.

'Don't cry!' she said, swallowing a mouthful of bread and butter before she spoke. 'Please, Meg!'

'Just tell us what's happened,' William said. 'We really need to know, Meg.'

The old woman looked at each of them in turn and then she nodded.

'Difficult to know where to begin, dears,' she said, quietly. Then, as she stared at the glowing embers in the grate and her voice gradually gained in confidence, she told them what they wanted to know. 'It started soon after you'd gone back to school – and not so long after I moved in here really, when I come to think of it. But, at first, everything seemed to be going well. I thought things were working out for the best. My leg was mending nicely. I was still having difficulty getting up to the sett, but Dan, that young builder who helps Jack, he was keeping an eye on my badgers for me. We've had no trouble since that to-do in the spring and Bob Parker, my policeman friend, keeps me up to date on any happenings – so I'd hear if the baiters were about again. To tell you the truth, I was beginning to quite enjoy myself here. I knew that I mustn't get in Jack and Phoebe's way. It isn't easy having someone else living in the house with you, not when you've a young family. So I stayed in my room when I wasn't doing a bit of housework – anything to help Phoebe; washing and ironing, she didn't like me doing the cooking, but I did a bit of painting for them and baby-sat once or twice while they went off to town for the evening. They went out to supper with that woman from the museum one time and another they went to a play somewhere. It seemed to be working out nicely. I was being useful to them and, as for myself, it was nice having a bit of human company after all the years alone. Only she wasn't happy. I could see that. There are some people who are never really very happy. I think Phoebe's one of them. She broods. Of course, they're neither of them getting much sleep. The baby cries all night and sometimes with me during the day as well, though I can usually get her off for a while. It must be difficult for them. I couldn't stand it! Not now! Time was I wanted children. . . . But now . . .' She shook her head, lost in some distant thought, then frowning, she forced her mind to concentrate once more. 'No,' she continued, 'Phoebe and Jack have been bad-tempered with each other . . . for a long while, I think. But it was the rats that finished everything. I felt they'd followed me here. It was a plague of rats that swarmed through my cottage at Four Fields,' she shuddered, remembering. 'I thought, then, I'd never see so many again! Little did I know! It was the rats that drove me out of my own house. But the first time I saw one out there,' as she spoke she jerked her head in the direction of the hall, 'I thought – what's the odd rat? You know – I mean, this is an old house, built over water, you're bound to get the odd rat. . . . So I didn't think too much of it. Gypsy – I mean your Spot, I still think of him by the name I gave him – he soon chased the nasty thing away. But the next time, there were two or three in the hall and then I did begin to worry. I told Jack, but he didn't seem to take much notice. Then, this particular morning – it seems like only yesterday, but it was a week or two back – I came along the corridor from my room . . .' she paused and shook her head as if trying to rid herself of some memory. Mary could feel her body trembling. When next she spoke, her voice was a whisper. 'There was a real swarm of the things. They were all crawling round the chimney-breast in the hall. I've never in my life seen so many rats. More by far than had come up at Four Fields. There were . . . hundreds of them. I screamed, I don't mind telling you. I screamed the house down! Jack came running down from their room. He must have wondered what on earth was happening. Well, he soon saw! He was pretty horrified, I could see. But no more than I was. They ran, of course, once he came . . .' She paused again, frowning. 'But before that . . . it was like as if I'd happened on them by chance – caught them by surprise . . .' The anxiety in her voice made it high and shrill. 'They didn't run away from me. In fact, now, I think,

53

looking back, that they were . . . confronting me. If I'd been here on my own . . .' her voice dropped to a whisper again, '. . . I don't know what might have happened. Even when Jack came they seemed a bit . . . cocky, a bit . . . sure of themselves. But, at least for him, they did run . . . they did go. It was then I told Jack about the steps up the chimney . . .'

'You told him?' William said. 'Why?'

'I had to, dear. There was no choice,' Meg said. 'That's where they went, you see. Straight up to the ledge and then out of sight in the back corner – like water out of a bath, they went. I have never in my days seen anything like it . . .'

'Did he go up there?'

'Oh, yes! He's got some courage, has that one! He went right to the top. Tickled pink he was with the idea! He knew about the room, but he'd no idea about the steps. A real secret staircase! But he wasn't too happy about what he found up there.'

'What did he find, Meg?' Mary asked, feeling her skin crawling with apprehension.

'So many rats, dear, he said the room was seeth-ing with them. It's a miracle to me how he got out alive. I waited down here. Gypsy had come in after I'd screamed and he'd followed Jack up. But not me. I was too scared. And I was right to be, I reckon. They only got out of that room by the skins of their teeth! They were pretty shaken, both of them. Jack said I wasn't to tell Phoebe; that it'd only frighten her; that he'd tell her in his own time. So I didn't. I didn't say a word. I gladly left that to him. It's not that we don't get on, she and I, but I don't find her easy, I have to admit. Well, anyway, he didn't wait long. It was the following day that I heard the two of them having an unholy row. They were shouting and raging. I'd never heard them like that. She's always been a bit moody as I say, but he's never raised his voice to her. He did that day – and she answered him straight back! They went at it full tilt! It was embarrassing really; I didn't know where to go. I was in here. They were out there in the hall. I couldn't help overhearing . . .'

'What was the row about?' William asked.

'The rats, dear. Jack was saying they'd get Mr Jenkins along. That they could put poison down in the secret room . . . out of reach of the baby and the dogs and cats. He said it'd be for the best, that that's what he was going to do. But she started screaming! It was like merry hell let loose! She wouldn't have them poisoned! Would not have it. She would not have killing in her house. That's what she said. Then the real battle started. He was saying it was as much his house as hers. She was saying she didn't recognize him as the man she thought she was living with. She told him how much she hated living in Golden House. She said it was haunted; said it was a bad place. He told her she was being childish; he said it was she who'd wanted to move here in the first place. On and on it went; all the things they'd both bottled up inside themselves coming out; bitter and cruel. I wanted to stop them, but I didn't know how to. I just stayed in here. I covered the baby's ears with my hands – silly of me, I know! But I didn't want her to hear her mother and father hating each other as they were then. In the end they both slammed off their separate ways. Next day Jack went into town and came back with a load of traps. Horrible things! It's a horrible thing, a rat trap. But he was worried that if he put poison down, they could crawl anywhere to die and then birds or other animals could be poisoned as well. He didn't like what he was doing, but he felt he had to. I understood! It was a difficult decision, but you couldn't just leave them running wild and do nothing. It was the numbers of them apart from anything else. Anyway, he didn't say anything to Phoebe and he told me not to mention it either. As if I would! I just wanted the rats out of here. I don't mind admitting I was scared by it all. He even wondered whether he should stop you lot coming for half term. . . . But he decided to wait and see if they went away. That can happen – they just move on sometimes, as if they have found somewhere better to live. Meanwhile Jack was setting the traps regularly. He caught quite a few and after a while there was no sign of them any more. . . . There are some about still, but it isn't so bad when you can't see them. Jack catches the odd one in a trap – but at least there aren't swarms like before. As for him and Phoebe, they've continued to be distant with each other. It's almost as though she knows what's going on, but in some way, without the evidence, she doesn't have to make a stand about it – and maybe she's really as glad as I am that the rats are being kept down. At least, that's what I thought but then, three days ago, she went over to the outhouse to get some kindling for the kitchen range here – which she said I'd let go out! Me? I said I didn't know fire-watching was one of my duties . . . as I say, we're chalk and cheese really. Though I do try. If I think I'm going to lose my temper, I just walk away. But she makes me so mad, sometimes. . . . Anyway, she'd found one of the traps, with a dead rat in it, in the outhouse. She came storming back in here. Did I know about

this? Ranting and raving at me. What was I supposed to say? I wasn't going to lie. I said if she'd
seen the numbers she'd probably have wanted to
leave the house – let alone put down a few traps.
Well, that did it! "Leave the house?" she yelled at
me. "Leave the house? I'd happily leave this house
once and for ever and not set foot in it again, not
as long as there is breath in my body!" Or words
like that. And out she stormed, banging the door
after her. She hasn't spoken a civil word to me since
and every conversation she has with Jack seems to
end in a row. She stays in her room and only comes
out to feed herself and the baby . . . until yesterday
morning, that is. She seemed, suddenly, in a better
mood. She arranged with Jack that she'd collect
you from the station. He was glad – because he said
he had something he wanted to do in town. I never
know what either of them are up to. Whatever it
was he had to do, it must have been a sudden
decision. He'd definitely said he'd go to the
station . . . but anyway, she was all sweetness and
light. She'd go for you. It would be good to be out
of the house for a bit . . . but first she'd get the
shopping. . . . Nothing was too much trouble. . . .
Well, by the time she returned, she seemed to have
lost the good mood! She arrived back after Jack had
already gone. He's got a motorbike now, did he
tell you? Nasty dangerous things! They must have
passed each other on the road but, if they did, she
didn't mention it to me. She came in from the back
yard, laden down with shopping. And amongst the
bags was one from the butcher's. I couldn't believe
it! I mean, to tell you the truth, I've missed not
having a bit of meat since I moved in here. But I've
put up with it and I must say, she's a good cook.

But why, suddenly, out of the blue is she dumping a bag of stewing beef in front of me? "Cook this!" she says. "As this is now a house of death, you may as well cook dead animals for them." That's you she meant. Then she rushes out, all tearful, and goes up to her room, leaving me still looking after Stephanie – who, I have to add, is sleeping as peaceful as an angel in her cot! Well, I thought I'd just let Phoebe be for a while, in the hope that she'd calm down. But it was getting nearer and nearer to the time when she should be leaving to collect you. I waited until the last minute but there was still no sign of her. . . . So I went up and knocked on her door. She just told me to go away. She would not listen to me. She seemed oblivious of the fact that you were even expected. I think she's gone off her head! I do! I think she's gone mental! In the end I telephoned Mr Jenkins. I didn't know what else to do and I have to say I hate those machines and am not used to them. Thank goodness he was in. . . . But what will become of it all? I don't know. This has always been an unhappy house. But I've kept away from it till now . . .' She was shaking her head and she'd started to cry again, silent tears coursing down her cheeks. 'I shouldn't have come back,' she whispered. 'Is it all my fault? Is it some sort of a curse? The curse of the Lewis family? I don't know. I don't know anything any more. I wish I'd stayed with my badgers. Badgers are less complicated.'

7
An Experiment

There was a long silence after Meg had finished speaking. She remained sitting as close to the kitchen fire as she could be without burning herself. 'I can't get warm,' she murmured. 'I'm always cold here.' Then, as if remembering that the children were in the room, she put down her mug and pulled herself up out of the chair. 'What am I thinking about?' she said, 'I should be getting you some breakfast . . .'

'No, Meg,' William interrupted her, putting a restraining hand on her shoulder. 'You sit still. We can do it.'

The morning, outside the window, looked dull and overcast, a perfect counterpart to the atmosphere in the house.

While they were sitting at the table Phoebe came in from the hall, carrying Stephanie. It was the first time the children had seen either of them since their arrival. But now, because of all they'd been told, they felt shy and nervous in Phoebe's company. She was quiet and strained with them also. She was wearing a dressing-gown and looked pale and sickly.

After an awkward greeting, the children gathered round Stephanie, relieved to have a focus for their attention. The baby at least seemed genuinely pleased to see them. Mary took her from Phoebe and, as she held her in her arms, the baby beamed up at her and blew bubbles, which Alice said was 'undoubtedly wind' in a knowledgeable voice. 'Babies,' she explained, 'never smile; they burp.'

Phoebe, meanwhile, had crossed back to the door, where she hesitated as if uncertain what to do next.

'Where's Jack?' she asked.

'Out, dear,' Meg said in a flat voice. She'd scarcely looked round from the fire when Phoebe had entered and there had been no acknowledgement or greeting exchanged between them.

'Where?' Phoebe asked.

'I don't know, dear,' Meg replied.

This short exchange was followed by another awkward silence.

William eventually felt that some effort should be made so he enquired after Phoebe's health.

'I'm all right,' she replied. 'I just feel so tired all the time. When Jack comes home, will you tell him I want to see him? Oh, and Meg, will you look after the baby for a while? I must try to get some sleep . . .'

'Yes, dear,' Meg said, rising and taking Stephanie out of Mary's arms. 'Don't I always look after her?' and she cooed and fussed over the child, who burbled happily back at her, raising a tiny hand and touching her cheek. Without another word, Phoebe turned and went out of the room.

Mary frowned as she watched her go.

'She looks so ill,' she said as the door closed.

'She'd look a sight better if she got dressed and came down and did some work,' Meg grumbled. 'Of course she looks ill, stuck up in her bedroom all the time. She needs a bit of fresh air on her cheeks.' Then, putting Stephanie into her pram, she sat beside her, gently rocking it backwards and forwards. In a very short time the baby was asleep.

'Poor little thing! She's as tired as they are. She'll sleep for a bit now. The teeth coming through hurt, you see. She can't help the crying.'

Eventually, after the children had washed up the few things they had used for breakfast, they escaped from the room with the excuse that they had home-work to do.

'They give you work to do in your holidays?' Meg asked. 'That doesn't seem very fair.' Maybe she knew that they were lying. If so she didn't say anything. Only, as they were going out of the room, she looked over her shoulder and said in a firm voice, 'Mind, don't you go up to that secret room. It's not safe now. You promise me?'

Alice was about to promise when William cut across her.

'We can't promise anything, Meg,' he said. 'You know we can't.'

'Oh well,' Meg grumbled. 'At least I've warned you.'

As soon as they were out of the kitchen they breathed a sigh of relief.

'It's all so gloomy,' Alice said. 'I've been looking forward to being here but now . . .' she shrugged and wandered over towards the fireplace, staring at it. 'I suppose it's because Mr Tyler isn't coming any more,' she said.

'But he's been dead for hundreds of years!' William exclaimed.

'No!' Alice protested. 'He isn't dead yet. Ratty Ratty, or whatever his stupid name was, told us.'

'Alice,' William insisted. 'He's been dead for four hundred years.'

'Then why are we worrying about him dying?' she asked.

William frowned.

'Well, because, once he's dead – in his own time – we won't be able to see him again.'

'Why not?' Alice insisted. 'We could just go back to an earlier date, before he died.'

'I think, maybe, our time and his are running parallel. Like two straight lines.' Then he shook his head. 'I don't know really . . .' he sighed.

Mary, who had been silent, seemed suddenly to make up her mind about something and crossed towards the fireplace with a determined expression on her face.

'I'm going up there,' she said.

'To the room?' Alice asked. 'Oh, we can't! Please, please, Mary, don't make us go up there! You heard what Meg said, the rats have taken it over!'

'I'm going all the same,' her sister said, disappearing into the fireplace.

'Why?' William asked. He also seemed reluctant to follow her.

'Because it's the nearest we can get to Stephen Tyler and because now we need him desperately,' Mary replied.

'Aren't you scared?' Alice whispered.

'Of course I am!' she snapped impatiently and, without any more discussion, she went up into the gloom and hurried up the spiral staircase to the top without stopping to think any more about the possible consequences of such an impetuous decision.

In daylight the room looked more of a mess than

ever. Mary opened both the circular windows, letting the fresh morning air blow in. Then, turning, she waited for the other two to join her.

'I hate the smell most,' Alice said, following William into the room and remaining close to the door, in case she had to make a sudden getaway.

William walked over to stand in front of the mirror, the only piece of furniture in the room.

'The Magician's Glass,' Mary said, crossing slowly to join him. 'Didn't he call it that? Or have I just made it up?'

'No, you're right,' William said. 'And he said something about it being the other way round in his time. Concave instead of convex.'

'Is concave when the glass goes in?' Mary asked.

'Concave is like the inside of a bowl, convex is like it is now, the outside of a bowl. Mr Tyler said that, in his room, the glass reflects backwards and forwards across itself . . . I suppose from one mirrored edge to the other. The mirror, reflecting the mirror, would reflect the mirror . . . and so on.'

'Like the ones in the Simpsons' bathroom,' Alice said, eagerly. 'You remember, Mary!' Then turning, she explained to William. 'The Simpsons have two big mirrors opposite each other in their bathroom and, when you stand between them, it's like looking down a long corridor. The mirrors just go on reflecting each other, backwards and forwards . . . for ever.'

'Really – for ever?' William asked.

'Well, the image gets smaller and smaller,' Mary said, trying hard to remember, 'and the corridor sort of . . . bends.'

'Bends?' William said quietly. 'Why would it do that?'

'I don't know,' Mary said. 'I always wonder what's round the corner . . .'

'That's it,' William said, suddenly. 'That's it!'

'What is?'

'It bends! Light . . . bends. I'm sure that's what we were told in physics. Light . . . bends. And a reflection is only an image sort of carried on light . . .' He frowned. 'That's why it would seem to veer away, I think. . . . Because nothing is exactly straight.' More half-remembered facts were now flooding into his mind, making his voice excited. 'Like . . . if a rocket is shot out into space. . . . It doesn't actually go straight. . . . It goes off in an arc . . . following the edge of a huge circle . . .'

'In that case wouldn't it, in the end, come back to where it started from?' Mary asked.

'Yes. But millions and millions and trillions of years later . . .'

'Like a science-fiction boomerang,' Alice said.

'That's it!' William said again, his excitement making him want to jump up and down.

'What is?' Mary exclaimed, almost irritably.

'In Mr Tyler's study . . . in other words in this room, but in his time, as opposed to now. . . . That mirror is like the inside of a glass bowl. Right? That's what he told us. . . . That it reflects backwards and forwards across itself . . .'

' "To infinite nothing", that's what he said,' Mary said, remembering.

'Just like your friends' bathroom mirrors.'

'So where does that get us?' Alice asked.

'Time,' William said. 'I'm sure it must have something to do with time. You know how they say that if you went for millions of miles out into space

64

and then came back . . . you wouldn't have aged, like the people on earth had aged?'

'But that's just a story, William,' Alice protested.

'Is it? Then where did the idea come from?'

'I don't know. From someone's imagination,' Mary said.

'Well, Mr Tyler did say we should use our imaginations, didn't he? So, all right then – let's! We need another mirror,' William continued, his mind leaping ahead.

'What for?' Alice asked.

'If we put another mirror opposite this one, and positioned it just right . . .'

'It wouldn't work, Will,' Mary said.

'Oh, Mary!' William cut in, irritably. 'Don't block everything! We can at least try . . .'

'No! Wait a minute! Let me finish! It wouldn't work because this mirror is . . . the outside of a bowl . . . whatever that word is?'

'Convex,' William said, thoughtfully, realizing what she was getting at.

'I'm sure the corridor effect would only come about with two flat, reflecting surfaces opposite each other.'

'And yet there must be a point,' William said, staring at the curved glass, 'right in the middle of that glass, where it is flat and, if we angled the other one properly, those two flat surfaces would be pointing straight at each other.' He frowned, deep in thought again. 'What we need is another mirror,' he said. 'Where is there a mirror? A big mirror?'

'There's one in our bathroom,' Alice said.

'It's fixed to the wall.'

'There's a dressing table mirror on the chest of

drawers in our bedroom,' Mary said. 'It's not very big.'

'What we really want is something huge . . .' William shrugged and shook his head. 'We'll try with the one from your room. I won't be a second!' He hurried out of the room and they heard his footsteps clattering down the stone steps into the distance.

The silence that followed his departure was dull and oppressive. Mary walked over to the window, looking out from the back of the house towards the walled garden and the steep cliff of the forest beyond. Although the sill was high, she could just see over it. The autumn colours of the leaves were muted by the dull light and a damp breeze was blowing after all the rain in the night. Only a few birds were singing in the trees and, above, clouds were piled across the sky, like hanks of grey wool.

Behind her, in the room, Alice had sunk down into a squatting position on the floor, near the door.

They both remained silent, lost in thought. Mary was remembering how certain she had been at the end of the summer holidays that when they were next here they would travel back to Stephen Tyler's time. She'd believed that, in order to do so, all that was required was for them to want it enough. But now, faced with a real need to get there, it seemed an impossible task.

Alice, meanwhile, was wishing that some magic would happen, she didn't care how. She saw no point in trying to work things out, as William was always doing. She just wanted an adventure. She sighed, dolefully. We're only here for a few days, she thought, and it's not going at all how it's supposed to.

* * *

William hurried up the stairs to the landing. The excitement of actually getting on with something made him feel elated.

The mirror in the girls' room was in an oblong frame of carved wood that stood, propped up on the top of the chest of drawers like a large photograph, supported by a strut attached to the back. He knew, as he was picking it up, that it was not going to be easy to use it for the experiment he had in mind. Someone would have to hold it in position for one thing, which meant that all three of them couldn't be between the two reflections at the same time. But it would be better than nothing. At least it would help him to work out his theory.

Picking the mirror up, he hurried out of the room and ran quickly back down the spiral staircase to the gallery. Just as he was starting down the main staircase, a door along the gallery suddenly opened and Phoebe came out.

'Where are you going?' she asked, seeing William on the stairs.

William froze. The mirror was too big to hide, though he tried to position his body between it and Phoebe, who was now leaning over the banister rail, looking at him.

'What are you doing with that mirror, William?'

'Nothing . . . I was just . . . I wanted to borrow it for a minute.'

'Borrow it?' Phoebe asked, puzzled. 'What on earth for?'

'Just for . . . an experiment I'm doing,' he said, brightly.

'I never know what you children are up to,' Phoebe said, frowning and sounding distracted.

'We're not up to anything,' William said, shaking his head feebly. 'It's just . . . a little experiment.'

'Well, don't break it,' she said, going back into her room.

William waited for a moment and then, when she didn't return, he continued quickly down the stairs and across the hall. As he stepped inside the shelter of the hearth, he sighed with relief. But if he had glanced up at the gallery again before he started to climb up the slabs to the stone ledge, he would have glimpsed Phoebe, standing in the shadows up on the gallery, watching him, with growing suspicion.

* * *

When William reached the secret room the two girls were still waiting for him in silence.

'That was close!' he said, coming in. 'I bumped into Phoebe. She wanted to know what I was doing with this,' as he spoke he lifted the mirror up in front of him, holding it with both his hands.

'What did you say?' Alice asked.

'I told her the truth,' William replied. 'I said I wanted it for an experiment. Now . . .'

Crossing and standing in front of the mirror on the wall, William held up the one from the girls' bedroom and began to angle it so that the two reflections were perfectly positioned opposite each other. Mary and Alice moved slowly towards him, watching with fascination.

'It's not very good,' he said, speaking to himself. 'It's difficult to see properly. If one of you went and stood between . . .' Alice hurried forward and placed herself in front of the mirror on the wall, with William behind her.

'What can you see?' William asked.

68

'Me!' she replied. 'I can't see the other mirror at all, because I'm in the way!'

'Oh! It's no use,' William said, disappointed.

'Let me try,' Mary said, taking the mirror from William. She bent and peered at the side of the frame, trying to see the reflection in the wall glass. 'Move, Alice! I can't see anything with you standing in the way!' As soon as Alice had stepped aside Mary could see herself, with the mirror, reflected in the one on the wall. Concentrating on the reflection she said; 'There is a sort of corridor, if you look right in the centre. But both glasses are too small for it to work very well.'

Alice turned round to look at Mary. Then she screamed!

The noise took both Mary and William so by surprise that Mary almost dropped the mirror she was holding and William spun round, thinking immediately that Alice had seen a rat.

'Oh!' he gasped, staring, like Alice, in the direction of Mary.

'What? What is it? What's happening?' Mary asked, panic in her voice.

'Morden!' William whispered.

'Where?' Mary asked desperately.

'In the mirror,' William said.

'Can he see us?' Alice whispered, not taking her eyes off the man's face that was staring at her out of the mirror that Mary was holding.

'I don't know,' William replied, his lips hardly moving as he mouthed the words.

The face in the mirror was as clear as one of their own reflections would have been. The man they were looking at had shoulder-length black hair that was receding on the temples so that the hairline formed a curious peak in the centre of his forehead. His face was very pale and his eyes very dark. His neck and shoulders were also in the image. He was wearing a white, open-necked shirt with a broad collar, edged with lace. He stared intently out at them, his eyes not moving, nor even blinking. It was as if he were concentrating so deeply that, though his eyes were open, he saw nothing.

'Is that him?' Alice whispered.

William nodded his head, never for an instant taking his eyes off the face in the mirror.

'That's the man I saw up at the lake, during the summer. When the crow first took the pendulum from me.'

'William, I can't hold this much longer,' Mary pleaded. She was beginning to shake, and her fingers, gripping the sides of the frame, were clenched so tightly that the bones showed white through the skin.

'Just wait . . .' William hissed, urgently. 'Just wait . . .'

As he spoke, the man, Morden, raised a hand. From his thumb and forefinger dangled a golden nugget on a thin chain.

'The pendulum!' William whispered. 'He's got the pendulum!'

'No!' Mary said, her voice shaking, but firmer than before. 'He can't have! It's in my pocket.'

'Then he must have one of his own,' William answered.

'He can't see us,' Alice said. 'I'm sure he can't.'

As they continued to watch, the pendulum started to swing slowly, backwards and forwards. Morden's eyes followed the motion, from left to right, from right to left. But then, suddenly and without any apparent prompting on his part, the slow, rhythmical motion began to speed up. Morden watched with obviously growing amazement as the piece of gold started to turn faster and faster, going in a circle, like a propeller, and, as it did so, it began to swing forward on its chain from his thumb and forefinger until it was spinning so fast in front of him that the golden lump disappeared into a single circle of light, framing his startled face.

'William!' Alice cried out, her voice terrified. 'He can see me now! I'm sure he can! He's staring at me!'

'What's happening?' Mary screamed, her arms beginning to shake so violently that the mirror she was holding tilted and turned.

The expression of the face in the mirror, Morden's face, looking through time across four hundred years, turned from one of intense concentration to utter surprise, followed by shock and finally horror. He opened his mouth and, a moment later, a shriek of such terror broke the silence in the room that both William and Alice involuntarily put their hands to their ears.

Then two things happened in such quick succession that it was difficult to know which came first. The glass in the mirror that Mary was still holding, splintered, with a deafening cracking sound, into a thousand glittering particles and, at the same instant, Phoebe appeared through the door behind Mary, her hands outstretched in a gesture of defence, her eyes wild with fear.

"For God's sake!" she cried, "What the hell is going on here?"

8
Jack's News

The children spent the morning up in their rooms, until Jack returned from town just before lunch. They had been sent there by Phoebe.

'It's like as if we're naughty babies,' Mary complained as she stumped off into the bathroom to comb her hair, because the mirror had been utterly destroyed. 'Like being sent to bed without our suppers. It's ridiculous! Who does she think she is?'

'D'you suppose she'd been up to the secret room before?' William asked. He was sitting on the side of Alice's bed, with his hands in his pockets, staring out of the window.

'How should I know?' Alice snapped. She was still in a state of shock and whatever the other two said to her only made her more irritable and bad-tempered.

William glanced at her, but didn't retaliate. Sometimes it was wisest to leave her well alone when she got into one of these moods, otherwise there was a danger of provoking her and the mood could last for hours and get increasingly worse until life wasn't worth living anywhere near her.

'Maybe she was too cross to notice much,' Mary said, coming back into the room.

'Who?' William asked, surprised that she seemed to be reading his thoughts.

'Phoebe, of course!' Mary snapped, flopping down on the bed.

'Oh, Phoebe! I thought you meant Alice!'

'Do you mind, William? I am not cross,' Alice said, 'I'm furious! How dare she treat us like this? How dare she? I've a good mind to go down and really tell her what I think of her . . .'

'Alice!' Mary said, in a bored voice. 'Just leave it.'

'Well,' William observed, continuing the earlier conversation, 'she certainly noticed the broken glass! I thought she was going to have a fit.'

'She practically did have one,' Mary said and she started to laugh.

'Oh, both of you – shut up!' Alice yelled. 'What does it matter about Phoebe? I never did like her. She's always been bad-tempered. What happened before she arrived up there is far more important.'

'I agree, Al,' William said.

'We actually saw that horrible Morden person. He was looking at us out of the mirror that Mary was holding. But how?'

'I don't know,' William said, his mind obviously elsewhere.

'The reflection,' Mary said. 'I'd positioned the mirror so that it was reflecting the glass on the wall. So, what you saw in the mirror I was holding must have been contained in the mirror behind you.'

'But we didn't see anything in the mirror on the wall,' Alice protested.

Mary shrugged. 'It's the only explanation, all the same. Morden must have been looking into the glass in the Magician's study and somehow our mirror picked up the reflection.'

'And then he saw us. That's the bit that frightened me,' Alice said quietly. 'Suddenly he was looking straight at me!'

'So it was you, Alice, that made him scream like that!' Mary said and, still lying on her back, she giggled.

'I wish we knew how much Phoebe was aware of,' William said, quietly. His concern was understandable. Phoebe's reaction, when she had broken in on their experiment, had been one of absolute fury. She had hurried them out of the room and back down the secret staircase so quickly that there hadn't even been time to close the two windows. Once they were back in the hall, she had told them to go up to their bedrooms and wait until they were called. She had been so angry with them that none of them had thought it wise to argue.

'Well, she couldn't have seen the face in the mirror,' Mary said. 'I mean, I wasn't able to see it myself because I was facing the wrong way and she came in behind me.'

'Then what was she so afraid of?' William said, in a puzzled voice, staring out of the window again. 'Because she was. You couldn't see her face, Mare, because of having your back to her, but she looked absolutely terrified when she came into the room. It was like as if she'd seen a ghost or something.'

As William said this, Mary frowned. His words had nudged a fragment of memory in her mind; something so vague that ordinarily she might hardly have remembered it.

'That's odd,' she said, sitting up, cross-legged, on the bed.

'What is?' William asked.

'I've just remembered . . . As the mirror smashed in my hands and I heard Phoebe ranting behind me . . .' Then she shook her head. 'It was probably only my imagination.'

'What?' William yelled. It drove him mad sometimes, the way Mary never came to the point.

'Well . . . behind you both, as you looked from the mirror to the door, Phoebe was entering, there was a . . . I don't know how to describe it . . . a . . .' she shrugged, 'almost like smoke, a sort of shadow.'

William who had been gazing out of the window again, turned slowly now to look at his sister.

'What?' he gasped.

'A shadow – almost,' Mary replied weakly. 'Or. . .more than a shadow . . . smoke. I don't know how to describe it. It didn't last long. It sort of . . . blew away.'

'Like a ghost?' Alice whispered and, as she spoke, she suddenly felt very cold and she shivered.

'No! Just . . .' Mary frowned, trying hard to recreate what she had seen. 'Like I said . . . smoke.'

Then, as this new piece of information was slowly sinking in, Jack's voice was heard calling to them from the landing below and they had no more chance to discuss anything.

'What's been going on?' he asked, as he strode into the room. 'Why are you all up here?'

'Phoebe told us to stay here,' Alice said, in a dangerous voice.

'Yes,' Jack countered. 'But why? She wouldn't tell me what you'd been up to.'

'She found us up in the secret room,' William said.

'Ah!' Jack said, leaning against the chest of

drawers and studying them closely. 'How long have you known about that staircase up the back of the chimney?'

'Ages,' Alice replied, witheringly. She was against everyone at the moment and even Jack wasn't going to escape her irritable mood.

'Well, you could have told me,' he said in a grieved tone. 'I bet there are masses of things you know about this place.'

'She was really angry with us, Uncle Jack,' Mary said. 'Is she all right? Phoebe, I mean. She looks so . . . ill.'

'No, she's not all right,' Jack said, with a sigh. He walked slowly over to the small window and, leaning on the sill, looked out. For a moment he was silent then, when he next spoke, he did so with his back to them, still staring out. 'You may as well know. I've been into town to see the local estate agent. I've put Golden House on the market.'

'What?' William gasped. 'You can't!'

'You mean . . . you're going to sell Golden House?' Alice said in a shocked voice.

'Yes! That's what I mean,' Jack said, turning and looking at them. 'The chap had all the details about the house already. It's the same firm through which we originally bought the place. But he's sending someone out on Monday to see what improvements we've made. After all we've done a lot of building work – which should help with the price . . .'

'But . . . you can't!' Mary said, her words and tone precisely echoing William's reaction. 'You love it here!' She couldn't believe what she was hearing.

'Yes, I do,' Jack agreed. Then he smiled. 'But maybe that's selfish. I love Phoebe and Steph more and their happiness is far more important.'

76

'Has she made you do this?' Alice asked.

Jack frowned.

'Who exactly do you mean by "she", Alice? If you mean Phoebe, then I don't think that's a very polite way to refer to her, do you? Well, do you?' he added, sounding really angry.

'I'm sorry,' Alice said in a sulky voice.

'But Uncle Jack, you can't sell Golden House,' William pleaded.

'I can, you know,' Jack assured him mildly.

'Where will you go?'

'I don't know.'

'What about the hotel and rest-house plan?' Mary asked.

'Maybe we'll do that somewhere else,' Jack said, with a shrug.

'But you'll never find another house half as wonderful as this one.'

'Don't, Mary!' Jack said. 'You'll have me in tears if you go on like that,' and he grinned at her reassuringly.

'Have you told Phoebe yet?' William asked.

'No, not yet,' Jack said, 'I will when the time is right.'

'Uncle Jack, please, please don't do this,' Mary said, crossing over to him.

'Don't be sad,' Jack said, putting an arm round her shoulder. 'It's only a house! A falling down house! I expect it'll take ages to sell. Though the agent said he thought he might know of someone who would be interested in it.'

'What will happen to Meg?' William asked, grasping at any problem in the hope of changing Jack's mind.

'She'll find somewhere else to live. After all, she's

got all the land up round the lake to sell, thanks to you lot!'

'But the Crawdens will buy it back,' William exclaimed.

'And they'll build their leisure park,' Mary added.

'Well, if they do, a lot of people in the area will be mightily pleased,' Jack said, crossing towards the door. 'We were most unpopular when we tried to prevent all that.'

'Is that why you're going to sell up?' William asked, his voice full of disappointment. 'Because you've been unpopular?'

'No, William,' Jack replied, looking at him squarely. 'I'm going to sell up because Phoebe is unhappy here and because, if I don't, I think she will leave me and go somewhere else and take Stephanie with her. I don't think a house is worth all that, do you?'

'This house is,' Mary said firmly, 'and all you'd planned to do with it. It was the best!'

'Well,' Jack said, with a brief, sad smile, 'that's all over now. The sooner we can get away from here and start living properly again, the happier I'll be.' He went out on to the landing. 'In fact the happier we'll all be . . .' and they heard his footsteps disappearing down the stone steps.

Left alone, the children stared at each other with disbelief, and a stunned silence settled over the room. Each of their minds was racing, all of their thoughts were confused.

'He can't,' Alice whispered to herself. 'He just can't!'

'He will, though,' William sighed.

'We've got to stop him,' Mary said.

'How?' Alice asked.

'By making her want to stay,' Mary replied, deep in thought.

'And how d'you suggest we do that?' William asked, his voice mocking and full of doubt.

'By stopping Morden once and for all,' Mary replied and, as she spoke, she produced the Magician's pendulum from her jeans pocket and stared at it thoughtfully.

'Morden? You think this is Morden's doing?'

'I'm sure of it,' Mary replied. 'He'll soon be master of the house in his own time. He must be really glad that Mr Tyler is dying. . . . Yes, we have to say that word. He is dying . . . and soon Morden will take over the house. We know that happens. Miss Prewett told us and Sir Henry Crawden did. It's part of history. It can't be changed. Morden will become the master here and, after his death, his family will continue to have control over the place off and on through the years right up until now. But what he wasn't prepared for is that Phoebe should be here in this time. . . . Because Phoebe is a Tyler as well and Stephanie is the new generation and Stephen Tyler hoped that one day Stephanie, when she's grown-up, would somehow carry on his work . . . and would live at Golden House . . .'

'You mean Stephanie will become a magician?' Alice asked.

'That's a bit far-fetched, Mary,' William said.

'But that's what this is all about, isn't it?' Mary said, rounding on them both and losing her temper.

'But you don't get magicians today, Mary,' William mocked her.

'And anyway, magicians are men,' Alice added.

'Are you trying to say that one day Stephanie will be a witch?' She started to giggle at the thought.

'That's why Stephen Tyler wanted her to be born a boy,' Mary said, still angry with them. 'And that's quite a sexist remark, Alice, you know. If you can have men magicians why can't you have women ones? And what does "being a magician" mean? As far as Stephen Tyler is concerned it doesn't mean magic spells and things . . .'

'So what does it mean?' William asked and, when Mary sighed and looked at her feet and didn't answer him, he continued, 'He didn't tell us, did he? We've never really known what all this is about. And until we know, it's like wandering about in the dark.'

'That's why we've got to go to him,' Mary said, staring at the pendulum, as it swayed gently from side to side suspended from her thumb and finger.

'Quite right!' a voice said, making them all jump.

'Who was that?' Alice whispered.

'It was me, little girl!' Rattus Rattus announced, running silently along the beam that crossed the room, just above their heads.

'Oh! You gave me such a shock!' Mary said.

'Not half so much of a shock as you have caused in my own time,' the rat hissed, looking down at them.

'We have?' William asked. 'What have we done?'

'Only transported Matthew Morden, the Magician's assistant, to this time.'

'What?' William exclaimed. 'Where is he?'

'Somewhere in the house, I shouldn't wonder,' Rattus Rattus replied. 'The Master is anxious to see you. The time has come, I think, for you to do some time travelling of your own. Meet me tomorrow, up at Goldenwater, by the standing stone.'

'But what about Morden?' Alice exclaimed. 'Won't it be dangerous with him wandering about here?'

'Well, it's more complicated than that,' the rat hissed. 'It seems that his body is still in his own time, but his mind has . . . wandered.'

'What does that mean?' William asked.

'Simply that – his mind is here, his body is there. It may be a little difficult to get the two of them back together, as it were! The Master will explain.'

'But shouldn't we go to him now?' Mary asked urgently.

'No. I have much to attend to before I take you back. Meet me at the hour of two in the afternoon. Be there! Things have started to get out of control. We don't have much time. Until then, please, all of you, don't try any more experiments! You are closer to understanding than you know and understanding without true knowledge can be a dangerous weapon. You can point it at your adversary, as a cannon is aimed at the foe, and have it backfire into your own face, if you are not very careful!'

9
A Ghost Hunt

The night was dark. There was no moon. The wind
moaned round the house. Up in the children's bedrooms, their heavy breathing was punctuated by
the creaking boards of the old house. Below them,
in Phoebe and Jack's room, a lamp was alight.
Stephanie was whimpering quietly and Jack, wearing a dressing-gown, was walking up and down,
rocking the baby in his arms. Phoebe was lying in
the large double bed, watching him. Her face was
tear-stained, but she was no longer crying.

'I wish none of this had happened!' she said.
'Truly I do. Jack, you can't sell this place. You love
it too much.'

'We can't go on like this.'

'It's all my fault . . .'

'It's no one's fault. It just hasn't worked out
for us, that's all. Living here, I mean. We'll find
somewhere else . . .'

'And yet . . . I feel we're running away, and that
is my fault, whatever you say.' She frowned and
shook her head, as if she couldn't believe her
thoughts. 'I really believed I'd come home, when
we found this place. I felt so . . . . calm here, so sure.
That was at the beginning, of course. Now it's as
though someone, or something more like, is trying

82

to drive me away. I feel . . . watched all the time. I feel . . . not wanted. My father, when he was alive, used to talk about living in a house like this. It was his dream. He had this theory, you see, that in the past, some time, long ago, our family had a position. . . . You know what I mean? That we were "someones". He was a good man, Dad. I wish you'd known him. He was convinced that we came from a special line! Mother and I used to mock him. Apparently, years back, the Taylors had been yeoman farmers, from somewhere over near Stratford. But by our time we were living in a council house in Coventry. I'd like to know what's so special about that!'

'Everyone is special, Phoebe. Houses don't make people. People make houses.'

'I know. I know. But, when we found this place, when we worked out that we could . . . just . . . afford it,' she smiled, remembering, 'I was so . . . excited! I honestly felt as though it was some sort of fate – as though we'd been drawn here! You must admit, it was odd the way we found it.'

'You never were very good at map-reading!' Jack said, gently.

'But just to arrive here by mistake and find it all empty. . . ! And then to go into the town and discover the place was actually for sale . . . !' She shivered and shook her head.

'There,' Jack whispered, 'she's sleeping now.' Laying Stephanie gently on her side in her cot, he took off his dressing-gown, climbed back into bed and switched off the lamp.

'Try to get some sleep,' he said, snuggling down under the covers. 'That's what we need, both of us.

Our nerves are on edge, just because we haven't had any sleep.'

'Jack,' Phoebe's voice whispered in the dark. 'When I found the children, up in that room . . . there was such a cold feel to the place . . . I know I lost my temper. That's another of my faults. I do have this dreadful temper . . . but I was so afraid for them, Jack. There is something bad here . . .'

'You have an over-developed imagination, that's the problem. Now go to sleep, darling,' and, as he spoke, he put his arm round her and drew her towards him.

On the landing outside their door, a floorboard creaked.

Down in the kitchen below them, Spot raised his head, pricking his ears. Stealthily he rose from his bed beside the kitchen range and padded over to the hall door. There he paused again, with his nose to the ground, near the crack, sniffing intently. Vaguely, from under the door, he could smell an unfamiliar smell, part-human, part-earthy; a sour, bitter smell.

'Morden?' he growled.

The door was closed; a ridiculous precaution, he had always thought. If he was to guard the house and the baby, how was he supposed to do so with a slab of solid oak between him and the rest of the house? The back door, however, posed no problem to him. Here, there was a latch that he could lift with a flick of his paw. He had done so on many occasions. Sometimes the humans turned the key when they went to bed, but usually they didn't bother. They knew that any intruder would have to deal with him before they got any further.

Spot hooked the door open with his free paw and

crept out into the dark night. As soon as he was in the yard, he trotted across to the walled garden and ran swiftly up the centre path towards the dovecote.

He barked once. 'Jasper!' he called.

The owl was having a tasty morsel of vole, high up on a ledge of the dovecote. It was one of his favourite feeding spots. When he heard the dog bark, he was at first irritated. The night was young. He'd planned a trip up to the Four Fields area. Since Meg had abandoned the farm up there, the rabbits and mice had taken over. Jasper was intent on feeding himself up as much as possible before the winter finally came. Already the wind had the scent of snow on it and there was the edge of crackling frost on the morning dew.

'What?' he hooted.

'I don't know,' Spot growled. 'Something . . . Morden. In the house.'

'In the house?' the owl trilled mournfully. 'His rats again?'

'No,' Spot barked. 'Stronger than that! Human!'

The owl was suddenly alert. He sat up, hunching his shoulders, and looked from right to left, blinking his huge eyes.

'Human?' he hooted. 'He's here?'

'I think so,' Spot growled. 'And yet not so very strong. Odd! Here and yet not here.' He growled quietly. 'I can't work it out, and, as I can't get into the rest of the house because the door is closed, I can't check it.'

Jasper surveyed the dark outline of the house, spread across the black sky on the other side of the garden wall.

'The round window is open,' he said, more to

85

himself. 'Strange! It's usually closed when the Master isn't here.'

'You could get in that way,' Spot called. 'But first, wake the children! They can open the kitchen door for me.'

Mary woke with a start. A sound that she couldn't at first distinguish had disturbed her in the middle of a dream that was forgotten as soon as her eyes opened. The room was in darkness. Raising herself up off the pillow, she peered across to the window. There it was again! A strange, urgent tapping coming from the other side of the glass. Then a low, fluting whistle told her it was Jasper.

She crawled out of bed and hurried to the window. As soon as it was open, the owl appeared and settled on the sill.

'Something's happened!' he trilled quietly. 'Spot can smell Morden, here in the house.'

'We know,' Mary whispered.

'You know?' The owl blinked disapprovingly.

'Rattus Rattus told us.'

'He should have told me. Why didn't he tell me? This is most irregular. Where is he now – the rat?'

'I don't know,' Mary said, feeling rather guilty. 'We thought he would have told all of you.'

'Well, he certainly hasn't told me!' Jasper replied. His voice was haughty now. He was clearly not pleased.

'He said he had a lot to do,' Mary said.

'Without me? When the Master comes, I am the first to be told. Who is this Rattus Rattus?'

'The Magician's rat,' Mary said.

'Yes! Sirius told me. So far as I am aware, the Master has no rat. I eat rat. I should very much like to meet this rat. I think the whole thing sounds highly suspect.'

'I'm sorry,' Mary said, wishing he wasn't so upset.

'So am I! Did he say how Morden has arrived here?'

Mary explained as briefly as she could. Telling the story to Jasper made her feel horribly responsible for everything that had happened.

'His mind is here? Only his mind?'

'That's what Rattus Rattus said.'

'But his mind has travelled here in the creatures on many occasions.'

'But this is more like . . . a ghost, I think,' Mary said.

'A ghost?' Jasper wailed. 'Then we must chase this ghost away. I'll go and check the secret room. The windows are open.'

'That's our fault, I'm afraid,' Mary said and she started to explain but Jasper interrupted her.

'Dear me!' he said. 'You seem to have been quite uncontrolled in my absence! Wake the others and go down to Sirius in the kitchen. A ghost indeed . . .' he hooted, as he flew away across the roof to the circular window of the secret room.

As soon as all the children were dressed, they went down to the kitchen. They had to creep across the gallery, but they were still in too much of a hurry to notice the pale shadow in the corner beside Jack and Phoebe's door. Only Mary, as she descended the steps, passing close to this strange phantom, shivered momentarily. The cold she felt was intense. But she put it down to the night air and didn't really think about it at the time.

Spot jumped out at them, as soon as they opened

the door. He stood, with one paw poised above the ground, sniffing the air. Then his head swung round in the direction of the staircase and, without even greeting them, he ran past them and padded quietly up the stairs.

At the same moment Jasper appeared out of the chimney, having flown down from the secret room. As he sailed into the high hallway, his sharp eyes saw the pale, misty shape of the man up on the gallery.

'Mary!' he whistled.

Mary looked up and, as she did so, she felt herself rise up off the ground. Seeing now through Jasper's eyes, the figure of Morden instantly became clear to her.

'He's quite young,' she whispered, staring down at the startled face that watched with alarm as the owl darted out of the darkness towards him.

'But dangerous!' the owl hooted, extending his claws towards the man's face. At the final moment, as the claws slashed out at the man's cheek, the image beneath them faded and nothing solid remained; only swirling mist and a terrible cold, that struck Mary's heart.

'A ghost,' she whispered.

Spot felt the cold, like a breeze, run along the length of his back. He spun round, following the scent as it travelled from one end of the gallery to the other. When it reached the door into the first of the two rooms on the Georgian side of the house, it disappeared.

'Through here,' Spot grunted.

Alice and William had climbed uncertainly up the stairs, not wanting to get too near, both of them afraid and excited at the same time. Now, with

Spot impatiently egging them on, William hurried forward and opened the door for him.

Jasper and Mary flew in just ahead of the dog. The room was empty. It had recently been decorated and the smell of paint obliterated the strange, musky scent of the ghost.

'Gone!' Jasper said mournfully.

'Where?' Mary whispered.

Spot was sniffing the wainscot.

'Rat!' he exclaimed, growling bad-temperedly. 'I hate rats!'

'Me too!' Alice said, with feeling, from a position as near to the door as possible.

The rat appeared a moment later, on top of the mantelshelf. Its tail was twitching and its little eyes pierced the dark.

'There!' Jasper squealed, flying at the creature.

The rat jumped clear, down on to the ground, and then swerved to avoid Spot who leaped forward, barking, front paws splayed out and all the hair on the back of his neck standing up.

Alice saw the rat darting towards her and gasped. At the same moment Jack and Phoebe's door, across the wide high hall, on the other side of the square that the gallery formed, flew open and, in the light that spilled out from the room, Jack appeared.

'What the hell is going on?' he yelled. 'We're trying to get some sleep here!'

As he spoke Stephanie started to wail noisily in the background.

The rat ran down the stairs, with Spot racing after it. Jasper sailed out over the banister rail and flew for the fireplace.

The three children pulled back into the room,

89

and half closed the door, so that they could just see Jack leaning over the railing opposite them.

'What's happening?' Phoebe asked, appearing behind him.

'That bloody dog's got out of the kitchen, somehow!' Jack replied.

But – what's he doing?' Phoebe asked.

Down in the hall the rat had made its getaway through a crack in the wainscot near the kitchen door. Spot was furiously barking and scratching at the stone flagged floor as though he wanted to tear it up.

'Shut up!' Jack yelled. 'Shut up, Spot! What the hell has got into you?'

'Jack!' Phoebe whispered. 'You'll wake the children!'

'Get back in that kitchen,' Jack said, striding down the stairs and throwing open the kitchen door. 'You wretched animal!'

Spot slunk into the kitchen, with his tail between his legs.

Up on the gallery Phoebe shivered. She felt that terrible cold again.

The rat crept silently through narrow cracks between the stones of the wall and the wainscot until he reached the fireplace. Then, climbing swiftly, he made for the canopy. Reaching the wooden beam that supported the chimney breast, he ran swiftly towards the back wall of the hall and the maze of tunnels through the masonry that comprised his own secret world.

'Thank you, my rat,' Morden's mind whispered in his head. But there was despair in the voice. 'I must somehow get back,' he sighed.

90

The rat paused, in a dark tunnel, and scratched himself.

'Easy!' he thought. 'We'll just trick one of the children. The little one, probably. She is the most vulnerable to my ways.'

'But she won't know how to time travel. No one knows except the old man.'

'And yet you are here.'

'Only partly. I was . . . working to achieve the ability. I was nearly there. It's those children! They are meddling in things that they know nothing about.'

'They are the old man's creatures,' the rat hissed. 'Soon they will learn to time travel! And when they learn, we will use them; we will accompany them.'

10
The First Journey

Although the following day was bright and sunny, a keen wind was blowing from the west and the children were glad of their anoraks as they climbed the steep bank through the forest towards the yew tree and the upper plateau where Goldenwater lay. The trees around them were in the full glory of their autumn colours. As the wind blew, the leaves filled the air like golden rain and carpeted the ground with a rich pattern of reds and browns.

It was good to be out in the fresh, clear air and the children's spirits were high as they passed the badger sett and caught their first glimpse of the yew.

They had spent the morning collecting kindling and chopping wood, in preparation for the coming winter.

'We haven't much hope of selling the house before the spring,' Jack had told them, 'and if it's another winter like last year, we'll need all the fuel we can lay our hands on.'

Spot had seemed exhausted after the excitement of the previous night and had settled down in the hall. In fact he chose that position because from it he was able to keep an eye on most of the comings and goings in the house. He could still smell rat in the wainscot and was on his guard, in case the creature reappeared.

'He won't get away from me twice,' he growled, more to himself than to anyone else.

Phoebe had come down, bringing Stephanie with her. Although she still looked pale and drawn, she was obviously in a better temper and she told Meg that she was going to make a scratch lunch, and that they'd have a special supper to celebrate the children coming to stay.

The lunch turned out to be delicious home-made soup, with warm bread straight from the oven, followed by an apricot tart with sweet, golden custard that contrasted perfectly with the sharp flavour of the fruit.

The children had second helpings of everything and Alice told Phoebe that she should never be ill again because she was the best cook in the world and that one of the nicest things about being at Golden House was the meals she made. Then, seeing Meg looking at her, she blushed and said that she was sure that Meg was a good cook as well, but that Phoebe was extra special.

Meg laughed and agreed with her whole-heartedly. 'I'm a basic cook, dear! None of your fancy work with me. Sausages and mash, that's my staple.'

'Alice's favourite food!' Phoebe said, with a smile.

'No, that's not true any more,' Alice said, scooping the last of the custard off her plate. 'I'm practically a vegetable myself, now.'

It was a happy meal. Jack and Phoebe seemed much more relaxed and Stephanie didn't cry once but banged a spoon on the table so loudly that it made them all laugh.

After it was over, Mary announced that she and William and Alice were going for a walk and that they might be a bit late getting back. Phoebe seemed quite happy about this, but said not to be out after dark and that there'd be tea and ginger-bread waiting for them when they returned. Then, after getting their anoraks and changing their shoes, the children set off at a quick pace. It was already half-past one and they'd promised to meet Rattus Rattus at two.

They reached the standing stone just as the rays of the brilliant sunshine cut through the racing clouds and turned the surface of the lake into glitter-ing light. The broadleaf woodlands on the right of the lake, towards Four Fields, were the colour of honey and burnt toffee; a stark contrast to the dull green of the fir forests on the other side of the water. Distantly, the waterfall of Goldenspring sparkled through the branches of the trees and bushes that crowded up the hillside to the V-shaped break at the top and the higher mountains beyond.

'Isn't it heaven!' Mary exclaimed, looking at the scene. 'I love this place. It's the most home-like view I've ever known.'

'But it isn't our home, is it?' Alice said sadly. 'When Mum and Dad get back from Africa we'll be in London for the holidays and when Uncle Jack sells Golden House we'll never come here again.'

'This might be our last time,' William said, dig-ging his hands into his jeans pockets and kicking a stone down the slope towards the waters of the lake.

This thought made them look around with renewed eagerness, as if they were trying to capture for ever in the mind's eye all the details of the view that they'd grown to love and treasure.

'I think I shall cry for ever if they sell the house,' Alice said quietly, and, although it seemed an excessive statement, neither of the other two disagreed with her.

Their moods, which moments before had been elated by the fresh breeze and the exercise, turned sad and thoughtful. William wandered away towards the edge of the lake and flicked pebbles in a half-hearted way. Mary leaned against the standing stone, with her hands in her pockets and Alice crouched down on her haunches and then sat on the ground, with her knees up under her chin.

'So,' a voice hissed, 'here you all are!'

Rattus Rattus was sitting up on his hind legs, on top of the standing stone. He was so high above them that they had to stand at a distance from the stone to be able to see him. William turned first and hurried back from the shore. Alice looked over her shoulder and then rose and crossed to stand by her brother. Only Mary, standing immediately below the rat, was unable to see him.

'Where is he?' she whispered.

'Here!' he said and, as he spoke, he jumped down and landed with a thud on her shoulder.

'Ugh!' Alice exclaimed, then she clapped her hand over her mouth. 'Sorry,' she said.

Mary looked gingerly at her shoulder. The rat's eyes were in a direct line with her own. He was so close to her that she could feel his whiskers tickling her nose. She swallowed nervously.

'Hello!' she said, in a small trembling voice.

'Good afternoon, Mary!' the rat said and she felt his sharp little claws digging into her shoulder. 'Did you bring the Master's pendulum?'

'Yes,' she answered in a nervous whisper.

'Good! Give it to me, please.' He held out a claw towards her.

Mary hesitated, for a moment uncertain what was the wisest thing to do. She glanced at William and Alice, as if asking them to help her decide. They all still had such vivid memories of the battle over Goldenwater during the summer holidays, when Morden's crow had stolen the pendulum and they thought they had lost it for ever.

'Mary!' Rattus Rattus said, with dangerous patience in his voice. 'If you don't trust me, we shall get nowhere. If you don't trust me, we may as well all go to our homes and leave the world to the Master's assistant. If you don't trust me, I shall be very cross. Now, give me the pendulum! It isn't, after all, your property. You simply have it on loan.'

'Here,' Mary said, without looking at William and Alice again. She put her hand into her jeans pocket and produced the nugget of gold and held it towards the rat's outstretched claw.

Rattus Rattus watched the pendulum as it dangled and swung before his eyes.

'That's better,' he said. 'Now we know who our friends are! You may put it away again.'

'You don't want it?' Mary asked, surprised.

'Certainly not! Where would I keep it? You have pockets!' and he grinned. 'Let us begin, shall we? For your first journey you will, of course, have to borrow the bodies and minds of other creatures. To transport the body requires a great deal of concentration. But to project yourself forward in time is easier than to go backwards. You are going backwards! You require the bodies of creatures from the time you will be travelling to. You have me, of course,' and, as he said those words, he bowed

96

formally like a gentleman. 'Now, allow me to introduce two more of the Master's good friends,' and, jumping down off Mary's shoulder he dodged round behind the standing stone.

A moment later a squirrel appeared, as if from nowhere, and scampered up the stone, laughing and chattering cheerfully.

'This,' said Rattus Rattus, appearing with a flourish, like a conjurer performing a trick, 'is Rus, the Master's squirrel.'

The squirrel turned and grinned at them. He was quite unlike any of the other squirrels they had seen in the forest. The others were all grey, but Rus was a wonderful warm reddy-brown colour.

'Like the Magician's hair!' Mary thought.

'And now,' Rattus Rattus continued, 'you must meet a very special animal,' and round from behind the standing stone stepped a tall and elegant red deer. 'This is Cervus, the Master's deer. You will notice that she has no antlers – because she is a female. The Master loves her, I think, more than any other creature in the forest.'

Cervus wore round her neck a broad halter of golden metal.

'The band of gold,' explained Rattus Rattus, in a hushed tone as though he was imparting a secret, 'is to warn off the hunters. Woe betide anyone, be it Her Majesty herself, who brings down Cervus in the chase!'

'Does the Queen come here?' Mary asked eagerly, her love of history for a moment overcoming all other interests.

'Oh yes!' replied Rattus Rattus. 'When she was younger she came quite often. But now not so much. It is a long journey from London and although she is still one of the finest riders in the land, there has to be a good reason for her to cover such a distance these days – and, of course, to come here by coach involves many days' travelling.'

'I'd really like to meet Elizabeth the First,' Mary said. 'There's a lot I'd like her to explain.'

'A sentiment shared by most of her subjects, I suspect! But one doesn't ask Queen Bess questions, Mary, one waits to be told!' the rat said, with a twinkle in his eye. 'Now, how about a race?' he continued, changing the subject. 'Who will reach the Golden House first?'

* * *

As the rat spoke, Mary turned and darted through the tall grass, her tiny claws scarcely touching the ground as she sped towards the brink of the hill. The grasses around her were as tall as trees; they closed over her head, all but blocking out the daylight.

'I know a short cut,' Rattus Rattus whispered in her head. 'We'll be there long before the others!' As he spoke, ahead of them, Mary saw a round opening in the side of the hill.

The tunnel they entered was dark and descended steeply into the earth. Mary could feel the soil and jagged rocks pressing in on all sides of her as Rattus's body dodged and turned through the dark passageway.

'What is this place?' she asked nervously.

'Rabbit warren,' the rat replied, breathlessly. 'The rabbits are no friends of mine. Or rather, they think of me as an enemy. But, if we hurry, we'll be through before they know we're here.'

'Where does it lead?' Mary thought.

'Straight through the top of the ridge!' Rattus

said, his voice triumphant. 'Poor Cervus! To be confined to the upper ground. Dark tunnels can reduce distances most effectively.'

The rat swerved round a sharp corner and they came out into a wider space. Here the ground was covered with bits of grass and straw. The smell of dank earth was overpowering and water dripped and seeped from the roof above them.

'I don't like it here,' she thought.

Rattus Rattus paused, turning his head from side to side. In front of them, through the shadowy half-light, Mary could see three separate openings.

'Trouble with rabbits,' complained the rat, 'is that they're always extending! Which way? That is the question.' His nose twitched as he scented each hole in turn. From the first came a warm, milky smell, almost sweet; unpleasant, but not unbearable. 'Rabbit quarters,' he announced. Turning swiftly, he sniffed the entrance to the second hole. Here the smell was distinctly soily; like wet mud mixed with rotting leaves. 'Mole!' Rattus said with disgust. 'Moles are all very well, but they block the entire passage, move painfully slowly, and have powerful claws and nasty tempers when roused. A mole makes a good ally, but only if you're planning a long campaign. Moles take their time. I find such behaviour intensely irritating. But then, we rats have never been known to dawdle!' He turned his attention to the third opening. Mary at once caught a whiff of a familiar, but at first unrecognizable scent. It was sharp and musky. The sort of smell that attacks the back of your throat and makes you cough. 'This is it!' Rattus exclaimed, darting into the tunnel. 'Badger smell! This leads to the sett and, once through the sett, we're halfway down the hill on the other side and well on our way to Golden House!'

With a squeak of pleasure and excitement they both, together as one, pushed on through the damp, cloying earth and were soon in a broad underground chamber. Ahead of them a badger lay, fast asleep. Rattus put a front claw to his mouth and then, tiptoeing on all four claws, they crept past the huge, slowly breathing body.

They had almost made their escape from the badger's bedchamber when a deep, rumbling voice, seemingly very close to their ear, said,

'Rattus Rattus, I have told you before, you should ask before you come into our sett. You may be the Master's rat, but it is still an impertinence . . .' Then the voice hesitated, and there was a sound of heavy and enquiring sniffing, followed by a wet pad of a nose suddenly appearing out of the dark and thrusting itself right up against the rat's face. 'Who's that you've got with you?' the badger growled.

'Friend of the Master's, on urgent business!' Rattus Rattus hissed and, before the badger had time to ask any further questions, he dodged the nose, leaped over the head, streaked nimbly along the length of the thick hairy body and, slithering down the the plump rear, he dashed up a sloping tunnel towards the distant light.

'Whew!' exclaimed the rat, as they ran up a well-worn entrance tunnel and slithered down the other side into the bright day. 'That was a near thing! Meles can get quite touchy sometimes!' And, laughing gaily, the rat set off downhill through the ferns and grasses towards the forest track behind Golden House.

100

As soon as the rat issued his challenge Rus, the squirrel, jumped down off the standing stone and turned his head towards the yew tree at the top of the slope.

'Who's coming with me, then?' he yelled. 'You, little girl, come on! You want to be the winner, don't you?'

'Yes,' Alice replied, 'I suppose so!' Everything was happening so fast that she was only just managing to keep up with events.

'Poor rat!' Rus whispered in her head. 'He thinks, because he can go underground, that he has the advantage! We shall see!'

As he spoke, Alice saw her front claws pounding the earth in front of her. They raced up the hill, passing the yew tree on their left.

'Good tree that,' Rus said. 'The Master sometimes goes there and lives like one of us!'

'I've been in the tree house,' Alice said breathlessly. They were going at such a speed that she was finding it hard to speak.

'Good! Good! Save your breath! We haven't started yet!' the squirrel told her. They slithered down the steep bank on the other side of the yew and were soon in the familiar area of the sett. As they passed one hole a badger looked out, surprised to hear them.

'What is going on?' he said. 'I've just had the Master's rat run straight through my bedroom! Rus! What's to do?'

'No time, Meles!' the squirrel chattered. 'If Rattus is already through, we must put on a bit of a spurt!' and he dashed away down the hill.

'Silly creatures!' yawned the badger, as he withdrew once more into his hole. 'Rushing about in the middle of the day when all respectable animals are tucked up in bed!'

'We'll never catch him,' Alice called. 'He'll already be halfway there.'

'Yes!' agreed Rus. 'But, poor creature, he's earth-bound!' and, as he spoke, the squirrel shot straight up the trunk of a beech tree.

'Oooh!' screamed Alice looking down and seeing the ground disappearing below her.

'Won't be long now!' exclaimed the squirrel. 'From here to the bottom is no more than a jump or two!'

He ran out on to a high branch, that waved in the wind, showering its leaves in every direction. Out at the very end of the branch where it dwindled into no more than a cluster of dried leaves, Rus leaped for the tip of the tree in front of them. Grabbing hold of a twig with his strong front claws, he swung down and across from branch to branch and from tree to tree. The motion was extraordinary. The wind blew about them and the trees tossed and moved. It was as if they were flying and climbing and swinging all at the same time. It was as if they were part of the wind, as if they were an autumn leaf, as if they were not only a little girl and a squirrel joined by magic, but as if they were joined by that same magic to the whole of the wood and to the air and the light that surrounded them. Alice wanted the journey never to end. She was so excited, so glad to be alive!

'There!' squealed Rus. 'The forest track. Who is the fastest of all the Master's creatures?'

'We are!' shouted Alice. 'We are, Rus! That's the best ride I've ever had. You can keep funfairs!'

Cervus looked with sad eyes at William. Then, with a sigh, she turned and started to trot up the rising ground towards the yew tree.

William ran after her for a few steps before, with a kick of his back legs, he felt the power of her body become his.

'Here we go then,' he thought, as the sound of their hooves drummed on the hard earth.

They reached the yew tree in a matter of moments and, swerving sideways, they galloped down the narrow path towards the badger sett. Ahead of them William saw Rus, the squirrel, like a streak of red, disappearing into the lower tree-line.

Cervus followed a well-trodden path. It was the path that the children always used to climb from the valley bottom to Goldenwater. But, halfway along, she turned off this track and, with steps as delicate as a dancer's, she sped down an almost sheer cliff and on through a copse of silver birch. Ahead of them an impenetrable barrier of thorny gorse crossed their path. But with a surge of extra energy William felt them kick with their back legs and, launching themselves forward, they flew over the bushes and landed lightly at the other side.

Never once during all the journey did Cervus speak to William although he several times made some comment that could have expected an answer.

At last, reaching the valley bottom, they arrived at the forest track. Ahead of them they could see Rattus Rattus running fast. Cervus quickened her steps and, with her added height and length, she was soon gaining on the rat.

As the back gate of the walled garden of Golden

House came into view, Rus, the squirrel, dropped down out of an overhanging branch and landed on Cervus's shoulders.

'That's cheating!' William exclaimed.

But then, as the deer drew level with the rat, so Mary was amazed to find that, instead of putting on extra speed, Rattus used the last of his energy to do a complicated side jump. Their body turned and flew at the same moment. Mary quite thought that they would end up doing a complete somersault. But instead, they landed with a bump on Cervus's back, just behind Rus.

'Well!' exclaimed Rattus Rattus. 'Races are silly, really!' and then, as Cervus slewed to a halt by the gate into the walled garden, he added, 'We're all the winners!'

11
The Autumn Garden

The garden was bathed in golden sunlight. Rooks were cawing in the distant forest. The paths were lined with fruit trees, some still with apples hanging on the boughs. Low, neatly-clipped box hedges bounded all the beds. Brown and white seed heads nodded in the gentle breeze. In the distance, a few late flowering roses clustered up a series of poles that formed an arbour halfway along the yard wall, facing into the sun and with the dovecote in front of it and the back of the house just visible over the wall behind it.

As Cervus, bearing Rus and Rattus Rattus, trotted down the path, the children saw that an old man was seated in the arbour, covered by a thick fur rug, and with his head drooping forward over his chest, as though he were dozing. Drawing closer, they recognized the Magician.

'Mr Tyler!' Mary called out joyfully. As she did so, her feet hit the pebbly ground of the path and she ran forward a few steps.

The sound of her voice made the old man look up, a startled expression on his face. He frowned and peered in front of him, then shook his head and, with a sigh, closed his eyes again.

Cervus pushed past Mary and went quietly up

to the Magician. Reaching him, she sat at his feet and put her head on his lap.

Rattus Rattus was busily rooting about in some bushes at the side of the path and Rus jumped off the deer's back and climbed up one of the supports of the arbour and sat on top of it, in the full, warm sunshine.

William and Alice, detached from their creatures, joined Mary, who was still standing at a distance from the arbour, watching. It was as if they all instinctively felt outsiders to the scene in front of them and as if they didn't want to intrude.

The old man reached out a hand and stroked the deer's head, lovingly.

'How there, my sweet?' he murmured. 'My Cervus! My deer!'

The deer sighed as if utterly content, and stretching out, lay in the sun at the old man's feet.

'Well, Rus! Is that you up there?' he said. 'Soon be time for your long sleep, my squirrel. Though your winter sleep will be shorter than mine, I warrant! Rattus? What news have you for me? What's to do, my rat?'

'They are here, Master,' the rat said, eating an earthworm as he spoke.

'The children?' the old man said. He sounded surprised, fearful almost. 'Where?'

'We're here!' Alice cried, stepping forward into his line of vision. But Stephen Tyler looked straight through her, searching the distant spaces of the garden with his eyes. 'He can't see me,' she said sadly, looking back at Mary and William.

On an impulse, Mary felt in her jeans pocket and produced the pendulum. Holding it up, it glittered and flashed in the sunlight.

At once the Magician shielded his eyes, as though he were being dazzled. Then he gasped and half rose from his chair.

'My dear children!' he said. 'You are well met!'

'We thought you'd never come back to us,' Mary said, crossing towards him. Then she stopped in her tracks and looked round. The garden was so neat and tended. The scent of roses mingled with the woody tang of bonfire smoke and the last of the lavender. 'It's all somehow different,' she said in a puzzled voice. Then, looking first at William and Alice, standing with the sun behind them so that they were ringed with light, and then at the old man, seated in his chair with the beams bathing his face, she slowly sighed. 'We're here, aren't we?' she asked, in a low voice.

'You are certainly here,' the Magician replied, with a smile.

'I mean in your time. We've come back to you!'

'Let us say that you are nearer to me than you have ever been before!' He stretched out his arms, as though he were embracing them and the entire walled garden. 'This is my world; my garden; my life.' He said the last words wistfully. 'Dear children, I have missed you! I am so confoundedly decrepit that I have been unable to visit you; though I have had word of you and you have been constantly in my mind. But now you are here! You are so very welcome!'

'Can he see us now?' Alice whispered.

'Minimus,' the old man whispered back, 'I can see every inch of you.'

With a cry of joy, Alice ran towards him and threw her arms round his neck.

'Oh, we've missed you!' she said, and she kissed him on the cheek.

'Alice, be careful!' Mary remonstrated with her. 'He's not well,' and she could feel a lump of tears forming in the back of her throat.

'I am very well now you are all here!' the old man said, his voice sounding stronger. 'But you must not stay long. To time travel so early, albeit with the aid of the creatures, is remarkable. But we shouldn't over-tire you.'

'I don't feel tired at all,' Alice gasped. 'I went with Rus, all through the trees. It was fabulous. You have no idea what it was like.'

'Rattus and I went through a rabbit warren and right through the badger sett,' Mary said, not wanting to be outdone.

'And you, William?' Stephen Tyler asked. 'You are strangely silent, my thinker.'

William shrugged. He felt shy suddenly and out of place. He didn't know why.

'I was with Cervus,' he said. 'She didn't talk to me once. I think maybe she didn't really want me with her.'

'My Cervus,' the old man said, his voice full of love. At once the deer raised her head and put it on his lap again. Stephen Tyler fondled her ear. 'I found Cervus in a thicket when she was only a few months old. She had watched the hounds bring down her mother and the huntsman slit her throat. Cervus was in a state of trembling misery. It was terrible to see. The rest of the herd came back for her and would have taken her with them, but she was too shocked and frightened to move. For the first weeks I took food to her and, little by little, she grew to trust me. In time she followed me back here. She has stayed with me ever since, She is my loyal and most-loved friend. Oh, my Cervus, who will care for you when I am gone?' he said sadly, and he sighed again.

'We all will, Master,' Rattus Rattus squeaked. 'That's what you taught us – that we are all responsible for ourselves first and then for each other.'

'But . . .' the old man began, and then he shook his head, as if he were too tired, or perhaps too sad, to argue.

'I'll look after her,' William said and, as he spoke, he hurried forward and knelt beside the deer, putting an arm round her shoulders. The deer turned and looked at him closely, a sad, enquiring gaze, but she didn't draw away.

'You two belong in different times, my dear!' Stephen Tyler said, laying his other hand on William's head.

'Different times?' William said, frowning. 'You mean . . .'

'Yes, William!' Mary exclaimed. 'I just told you!'

William turned and looked slowly round the garden.

'I didn't . . . believe you,' he said quietly. 'I thought . . .' He shook his head. 'I thought we'd know when it happened.'

'It happened up at the standing stone,' Rattus Rattus announced, coming forward and sounding almost tetchy. Then, with a jump, he landed on the arm of the Magician's chair and settled down, facing them.

'How?' William asked, his voice made desperate by the desire to understand.

'The line of energy, William,' the old man said. 'You recall? I mentioned it to you once. It is strongest around the standing stone. You must remember this. One day it may be vital to you. The line runs, straight as an arrow's flight, cutting this whole vale down the middle: from the vantage place in the west to the vantage place in the east. It passes through the tunnel behind the waterfall, down the centre of Goldenwater, through the tree house, and the dovecote over there.' He nodded, as he spoke, in the direction of the dovecote, standing in the centre of the garden and casting long shadows over the beds and the fruit bushes. 'We are on the line now,' the Magician continued. 'Then, behind me, it severs my house in twain! That is why I put the two circular windows at the front and back of my study room at the top of the steps up the chimney. They are a symbol to show the passing of the ley through the house, and a pointer to help the journeying pilgrim, who seeks the true path, to recognize the place and know that he or she has arrived at the right place. Finally, the energy line passes out of the Golden Valley through the eastern approach, where the sun first pierces the rim of the hills at the autumnal equinox; that moment in late September when the length of the day equals the length of the night and the light and the dark are in perfect balance.'

'The silver path and the golden path!' Mary said, remembering.

'That is correct,' Stephen Tyler replied enthusiastically. 'You are good pupils! And what is a pupil? A student and yet, at the same time, that mysterious dark centre of the eye, through which the light enters the mind!' He laughed, delight overwhelming him. 'There is so much that can be understood, if we are only perfectly tuned – as the string of a viol is tuned to the correct harmonic tension.' He shook his head, chuckling with happiness. Then he frowned. 'I have lost the thread now,' he said. 'What were we talking about?'

'You were telling us about the energy line,' William prompted him.

'Ah, yes! The lie of the ley! As I say, it cuts straight across the estate here. That is why the Golden Vale is so essential to my work! But it is at the point where the great ancestors – the original people of this valley, the creators and dreamers of all this harmony – it is where they placed the standing stone that the energy is at its most powerful. It is there, more than anywhere else in this magical domain, that one may cross, as if on a bridge through the clouds of time, from one layer of existence to the next.'

'So – that's how it's done?' William asked. 'Just by stepping across the line?'

'No, William! No!' the Magician exclaimed. 'Not by crossing over the line. No, no! By being perfectly in tune while on it.'

'So, when we experimented with the two mirrors, up in the secret room . . . ?' William continued, trying desperately to understand.

'When you did that,' Stephen Tyler said, 'you chanced upon a very potent symbol indeed. You saw, through the mirrors' multiple reflection, those same layers of time about which we have spoken. And, when you produced the pendulum, the power was so great, that poor Morden's mind was dragged from the safety of his today into your dangerous tomorrow.'

'Dangerous?' Mary asked, alarmed. 'Is our time so dangerous?'

'It certainly is for Morden! He doesn't belong there and, as he has happened there by chance – or, to put it less kindly, by your meddling – and, as he has no idea how to get back to here, he is in a very dangerous state indeed.'

'But we didn't do it on purpose!' Mary protested. 'We didn't know he was there . . . sort of on the other side of the mirror, if you see what I mean . . . We were trying to reach you, that's all.'

'No one is blaming you, Mary,' Stephen Tyler said, more kindly. 'I am simply telling you what took place.'

'Well anyway, Morden's a horrible person!' Alice said. 'He deserves whatever happens to him. He makes rats appear and I hate rats!'

Rattus Rattus turned his head in her direction and hissed and spat viciously.

'Oh, not you!' she said crossly. 'You're different. You're not vile and ratty like Morden's rats.'

'You wait,' Rattus Rattus hissed. 'When the time comes you will discover that I can be more ratty than all Morden's rats put together! I am, after all, the quintessential rat! I am the Master's rat!'

Alice shivered and pulled back a little, so that she was half-hidden from his view by Mary.

'You think poor Morden is to blame, Minimus. Is that it?' Stephen Tyler said, looking at her closely.

'Yes!' she replied firmly. 'He does vile things all the time. He's made Phoebe so unhappy that she wants to leave Golden House – and she'll take the baby with her. Everthing's spoilt, because of him.'

'Our baby!' the Magician exclaimed, some of his old vigour and unexpected anger coming out as he spoke. 'They are going to take our baby away?

This must not be allowed to happen! He belongs to Golden House!'

'She!' Mary prompted him.

'Very well then, she!' the old man said petulantly. 'Take her away? What nonsense! The child will stay in Golden House and one day she will marry and have children and they will grow up there and the blood of the Tylers will flow through the line of the inhabitants once more. Then wisdom and understanding and harmony will return to the vale. The silver path and the golden path will be held in place by the pilgrims' way; the sun and the moon will be separated by the staff of knowledge and they will reflect each other in perfect harmony. That is your task! That has always been your task! To restore the balance and protect the valley for the future. That is why I visited you; why I found you. What are your names?' He barked this question at them so loudly, that it made each of them jump with surprise.

'William, Mary and Alice,' Mary replied nervously.

'No, not your given names. What is the name of your family? Is it not Constant? Well then, be so! Be constant and true! Live up to your destinies!'

They were all silent. The children felt they had been rebuked, but they weren't quite sure what it was they were supposed to have done wrong. Rattus Rattus picked his teeth with one of his front claws. Cervus curled up at the old man's feet, with her eyes closed, and Rus combed his long plumed tail, biting it gently with his teeth.

'Where is Morden now?' William asked after a moment.

'In his room,' the old man replied.

113

'What is he doing?'

'He sits. He stares. He shakes his head.'

'Does he know what has happened to him?'

'There is no mind there to know, William. He is out of his mind. Or, to be more precise, his mind has left him!'

'Is that what happens, when someone goes mad?' Mary asked.

'Mad?' The old man shrugged. 'We are, perhaps, all a little mad. No, Morden is not mad, as you call it. In some ways he is more sane than most. It is just that his mind has wandered and he doesn't know how to get it back.'

'Will he have to be without it for ever, then?' Alice asked.

'For ever is a very long time.'

'Only, in our time, it's sort of haunting Golden House like a ghost, at the moment,' Mary said, 'and I don't think that will help us in our task at all.'

'I don't suppose it is helping Morden very much either!' the Magician observed quietly.

'But he's a bad man,' Alice insisted. 'Why do we have to help him?'

'Not to help him, Minimus, would be to condemn him to a life of permanent "badness', as you call it. His only hope is your help.'

'But I don't want to help him.'

'Minimus,' Stephen Tyler leaned forward towards her and whispered, 'helping him will be a great boon to you. Never overlook the power of true charity! Charity is love! It is very easy to love the ones you like; but the power of love, the immense, transforming energy of love, comes when personal preference is not involved. With that energy you, yourself, may be transformed.'

'You mean,' William said, suddenly understanding what he was saying, 'that Morden is the . . . whatever it is you call it . . . the tin, the rubbish . . .'

'The dross,' the Magician prompted him, quietly.

'The dross that, through alchemy, can be turned into gold?'

'That's it precisely, William. Did I not tell you that Morden is vital to the scheme? You cannot have light, without there be darkness; you cannot have gold, without there be dross. Neither the dark nor the light is better; neither the dross nor the gold . . .'

'But he's evil!' Mary almost shouted the words, she felt so frustrated by what was being said.

'And he does horrible things all the time,' Alice added, speaking almost at the same time as her sister.

'Excellent!' exclaimed Stephen Tyler. 'All the more power to the transformation!'

'We know what happens to him at his death,' Alice said, quickly, as if trying one last desperate attempt to make the Magician see things from her point of view.

'Do you?' he asked, quietly, his brows creased in a deep frown.

'He's so bad, that his family have to change their name – from Morden to Crawden. And he's put to death, isn't he, Mare? We were told, weren't we?'

'We were,' Mary agreed.

'Poor Matthew Morden! It will be a terrible thing if he dies in vain. For die he will, and in just the way that you say. Your history cannot be changed. But, you know, saints are put to death, as well as sinners. With your help, he can die a good man, whatever the world may make of him.'

115

'But he isn't good!' William cried, joining in the argument. 'You know he isn't.'

'Good? Or gold?' the old man asked. 'With your help he can be transformed.' Then, his voice becoming much more business-like, he added, 'But first you will have to get his mind back here and into his body.'

'We have to?' William exclaimed.

'Certainly. You did, after all, detach them in the first place, did you not?'

'But how?' William asked.

Stephen Tyler shrugged and then winced.

'Oh! This confounded arm!' he groaned. 'You did this to me as well! You and your badgers!' Then he smiled. 'When you have brought Morden back to his senses here in this time, you will be almost there! The next step will be the making of gold!'

'But *how*?' William repeated again, an agony of uncertainty in his voice.

'Usually one has to do very little. Remember that! I have often found that too much doing gets in the way of arriving at a result. When in doubt, do nothing!'

Again, there was a long silence. The sun was sinking slowly behind the trees at the top of the forest bank behind them. With its passing, the breeze felt chill and the light in the garden lost its sparkle.

'I'm cold now,' the old man said. 'I must go in by the fire and you must go to your own time. I have been most happy to see you here. Next time I will show you the house.'

'Will we come again?' Alice asked.

'I hope so. But make it soon. I do not know how much time there is left. Time is a substance with a

116

durable existence . . . it has a beginning and an end . . . it can run out!' He looked at them sadly, then he smiled. 'So, come soon! But remember; never travel without the pendulum. Keep it with you always. The pendulum acts like a magnet. It will draw the energy, focusing it into a pin-point of power. This is very important. The focusing of energy is the essential secret of alchemy. It is the energy that does the work. It is the energy that concentrates the mind; that makes the magic. The pendulum is the conductor, the magic wand of fairy tales. With the pendulum in the right hands, all things are possible.'

'Where did it come from?' William asked thoughtfully.

'Out of the mud of my land!' Stephen Tyler replied, with a smile. 'It is the only piece of material gold that I managed to make that I decided to keep. The alchemist's gold is not for spending. It merely represents a step on the way. The journey is all important. But the pendulum is powerful. It is a great gift that I have given you.'

'Won't you need it yourself?' Mary asked, drawing closer and squatting down beside the old man.

'My travelling days are over, Mary. My time is near. But don't be sad. We'll have a few adventures yet!' Then, as he patted her gently on the head, his mood changed and he became decisive. 'Rattus, you and Rus must go with them. But Cervus, you stay here and comfort an old man! I get lonely when you have all gone away. You stay this side of the standing stone, my deer, and let the rat and the squirrel go on together. All right! Be off, now! 'Tis almost supper time!'

They left him, sitting in the gathering dusk, and,

117

when they looked back before disappearing round the dovecote, they saw an old woman, in a long black dress and apron, hobble into the garden through the yard gate.

'Master Tyler!' they heard her call. 'Come in! Come in! Would you add the rheum to your troubles?'

12
Doubts and Divisions

The night after their first journey through time the children slept long and soundly. They had left Rattus and Rus up by the standing stone. But Cervus had disappeared before there'd been time for any words of farewell, which particularly seemed to upset William, who had travelled in her and become very attached to her.

'Where's Cervus?' he'd asked, looking round, as they all emerged from behind the stone.

'She didn't come with us,' Rattus had said. 'The Master told you she wouldn't.'

He and Rus had soon left them also. They had, as Rattus had explained, a great deal to do before they would all meet again. 'When that time comes,' he'd said, 'there'll be a battle royal in the Golden Vale, the like of which has never been seen before! But remember, until I come for you, you're not to do anything. We can't have two captains on board so, for the moment, I must be in command! Never fear, your time will come! Until then, rest! Wait! But do nothing!' Then he and Rus scampered away into the undergrowth in the direction of Four Fields.

The following day was dull and although it didn't rain the atmosphere was oppressive.

A woman from the estate agent's office came out

from the town to update the particulars of the house. She spent a long time looking over the property with Jack, then she went outside and took photographs of the house from different angles.

'It's a pity it's not more sunny,' she said to Mary, who passed her when she was standing out on the front lawn. Mary said nothing, but was secretly glad that the sun wasn't shining. She hoped all the photographs were useless; anything to put poeple off buying the place. But in her heart Mary suspected that anyone coming to look at Golden House would fall in love with it at once, just as she had the first time she'd seen it.

Later the agent went with Jack to talk to Meg, who was waiting for them in her room on the ground floor of the Tudor wing. Apparently the idea was for Meg to sell all the land she owned – Goldenwater, and the woods as far as the summit above Goldenspring; the Four Fields and all the woodland and hillside between the Forestry Commission land to the south and the piece of woodland belonging to Mr Jenkins to the north – at the same time as Jack sold the house, and then the money would be divided between them afterwards.

The children were in the hall when the agent and Jack came back out of the Tudor wing and went towards the front door.

'For the right buyer,' the agent was saying, 'I think the place will be irresistible. With all that land it will make quite a country estate. I have one or two people on my books already who are looking for this sort of property. But, anyway, I'm sure it should attract a lot of interest. Which is the nearest hunt, Mr Green? D'you know? I can see the place being particularly attractive to a sporting family.

Hunting with the local hounds, shooting in your own woods and fishing in your own lake! Ideal! Indeed, for the right person, absolutely idyllic, I'd say!'

'Oh, yes!' William fumed, as the door closed behind them. 'It's just the sort of place for murderers to come and live!'

'How will we ever stop them?' Mary gasped.

'We could set fire to the house,' Alice said thoughtfully.

'Oh, Alice! Be sensible! How would that help?'

'Well, I'd rather no one lived here than people like that,' Alice replied.

'What are you children up to today?' Phoebe asked, appearing at the top of the stairs and coming down towards them. Although she was still pale, she seemed more calm since the decision had been taken to sell the house.

'Phoebe,' Mary pleaded, as she crossed towards her. 'Please! You mustn't let this happen. You can't let Golden House be sold. Not after all the work you and Jack have done here and all the dreams you've had for the place. Please, Phoebe, please!'

'It's too big for us, Mary,' Phoebe told her, speaking gently but firmly.

'But not if you run it as a hotel – like you wanted to,' Alice protested.

'And how long is it going to take us to be ready to open this famous hotel, let alone build up a clientele to start earning an income from it? There's still masses of building work to be done . . . We haven't even started to furnish the guest rooms . . . and we're already short of money. Soon there won't be any left for us to live on. When we bought the place we didn't know how difficult the financial

121

situation was going to become. It's no use. We couldn't afford to stay here, even if we wanted to.'

'That's not the reason!' Alice said, losing her temper. 'It's because you don't like it here. It's got nothing to do with money. It's only because of you!'

'Alice!' Phoebe said, her voice immediately becoming sharper. 'I don't want to lose my temper with you.'

'Just go away, Phoebe, and leave Uncle Jack here!' Alice shouted, turning on her. 'And Stephanie. Uncle Jack has as much right to her as you have. And she loves it here. This is her home. It's where she belongs. But you don't seem to care about her. Well, just leave her with Uncle Jack. They don't need you here. Jack really loves this place – and you're forcing him to leave. It isn't fair . . .' She was so near to tears now that she could scarcely speak. 'If you don't like it – you go away on your own,' she sobbed. 'There's no reason for you to ruin everyone else's life as well.'

'Ally!' William whispered. 'Let it go!'

'I don't care! I hate her!' Alice shouted. 'You, I mean, Phoebe! I hate you!' and, pushing past them, she ran up the stairs to her room.

During this outburst Phoebe had remained standing at the back of the hall, a shocked and wounded expression on her face. Now she turned and hurried into the kitchen without looking at either William or Mary. Once she was inside and the door was closed, she leaned against it and, if the children had been there, they would have seen tears streaming down her cheeks as she wept bitterly and silently.

Alice, meanwhile, was sorry she'd said as much as she had but she wouldn't go and apologize.

'I can't help it,' she said. 'I told the truth really. I never did like her.'

During the afternoon, the unfamiliar sound of the telephone ringing brought them into the hall. Jack, who had been doing complicated sums at the kitchen table, hurried to answer it. His voice sounded surprised when he spoke to whoever it was at the other end and when he'd finished the call he looked genuinely amazed.

'That was Jenny Minton, the estate agent! We've got somebody coming out to look at the house tomorrow!'

'So soon?' Phoebe exclaimed. 'That's wonderful, Jack!'

But the children welcomed the news with anything but enthusiasm. That night, when they were going to bed, William came into the girls' room.

'Can't we do anything?' he asked, for the hundredth time since the telephone call.

'No,' Mary shook her head. 'Rattus told us to wait for him to contact us.'

'But where is he? Shouldn't we at least try to find him? He won't know what's happened. If this person comes tomorrow and likes the house, Uncle Jack might agree to sell it straight away. . . . Then, when Rattus comes, it'll be too late . . .' They'd never seen William so agitated. He wasn't behaving at all like himself. 'Who said he was in control anyway? I don't remember Stephen Tyler telling him he was to take charge. I'm not sure that I trust that rat.'

'I do know what William means,' Alice said. 'Maybe we should ask Spot or Jasper. I mean they're our real friends. I was never sure about joining up with a rat in the first place.'

'*No!*' Mary insisted, loudly. 'We have to wait.'

'Oh, Mary!' William snapped. 'Well, you can wait, if you want to, but I'm certainly not going to,' and, turning he hurried out of the room.

'What are you going to do, Will?' Alice asked, running after him.

William sat down on his bed, with his hands in his pockets and frowned.

'That's the problem. I don't really know,' he said.

'I'm going to go and get Spot,' Alice said, 'he'll tell us,' and she ran quickly out of William's room and down the spiral staircase.

'Where's Alice gone?' Mary said, coming into William's room.

'To get Spot.'

'He won't be able to help.'

'Why d'you say that? It's as though you're turning your back on all our friends.'

'I'm not, Will. Only this is what the Magician told us to do . . .'

'What is?' William cried, all his frustration and anger seething up once more.

'Nothing!' Mary replied. 'He told us, when in doubt, to do nothing. Rattus said it as well.'

'Oh, terrific!' William jeered at her. 'While you're hanging about doing nothing, the house'll probably be sold and Morden will win and Phoebe'll go off somewhere, taking Stephanie with her. So much for doing nothing, Mary! We'll lose everything – and we won't even have tried to stop it.'

'All right then, William Constant!' Mary rounded on him. Now she was losing her temper as well. 'If you're so clever, tell me what we should be doing? Go on! How do you propose we should persuade Jack not to sell the house and make Phoebe want

124

to go on living here and stop Morden causing all this trouble? Well? Go on, tell me! I'm waiting, William!'

'We could use the pendulum,' William said, grasping at straws.

'To do what?'

'I don't know,' William shrugged. 'Some magic.'

'The last time we did some magic, as you call it, without really knowing what we were doing, we brought Morden here.'

'We didn't. We only brought his mind,' William snapped sulkily.

'Don't be so precise! You know what I mean. All right then, we brought his mind here, William. But we did it – by our meddling, as the Magician called it. It was our fault – and now it's up to us to get him and his mind back together again. That's what you should be thinking about, if you must do something – how do we get his mind back? That's what we were told our next job should be.'

'I suppose we have to find it first,' William said more calmly and obviously thinking more clearly about the problem. They both stopped speaking and an uneasy silence settled over the room. When Spot came in, followed by Alice, he found them both sitting on William's bed, with glum faces.

'Here we are!' Alice said brightly as she plumped down on the floor next to the dog and put an arm round his neck. 'Now, Spot,' she continued. 'As you are, without doubt, the most brilliant animal in the entire world, we expect you to tell us what to do.'

'About what?' Spot asked and then he yawned and scratched behind an ear with one of his back paws.

125

'About what!' William exploded into agitated temper again.

'Well, I don't know what you've been talking about, do I?' the dog growled, and he yawned again. 'I was in the middle of a sleep when Alice came in.'

'Spot!' Mary exclaimed irritably. 'You know what we're talking about! Somebody's coming tomorrow to look at the house. They may buy it! Then we'd all have to go away. We have to stop them . . .'

'I thought you said we had to do nothing, Mary,' William said, his voice petty and irritable still.

'Well,' Mary said, rounding on her brother, 'better nothing than something without having thought it through and making everything worse, like we did last time.'

'What do you think, Spot?' Alice said, hugging him closely.

'I think,' the dog said, 'that if you fall out amongst yourselves, you haven't a hope of getting anywhere. But Mary is right. Better to do nothing than to do the wrong thing.'

'But what about the right thing?' William exclaimed. 'Isn't the right thing worth doing?'

'Yes. If you know what that is,' the dog said.

'We won't know if we don't try to find it out,' William said.

'Well, if you're asking me,' Spot said slowly, 'then I must tell you that unless I'm told what to do – usually by the Master – I just get on with being a dog. Sorry. That's the way I am.'

'That's not true,' Alice said. 'Look how brave you were when the badger-baiters were in the valley. Mr Tyler wasn't anywhere near, but you didn't wait to be told then.'

'I knew what I had to do then,' Spot said.

'How?'

'The Master had already told us to help you. He didn't really desert you. He never does. And, besides, the badgers are our friends. Of course we had to help them.'

'But you mean that until you're told what to do, you do nothing?' William asked.

'With the big things, yes,' Spot replied. 'I'll chase a rabbit without thinking much about it; or something like that. But, with the big things, I wait till I'm told.'

'But how d'you get told?' Mary asked.

The dog looked slowly round at the three faces.

'That,' he said, 'is a very good question!'

'So what's the answer?' Alice asked. Even she was beginning to find his attitude a bit irritating.

The dog put his head on one side and then on the other. He was obviously deep in thought.

'My heart tells me,' he said at last.

'Your heart?' William exclaimed.

'I think that's what happens. I haven't really thought about it before. But, I think, when something needs doing, the idea comes into my mind from my heart.' The dog yawned again and ran the back of his paw down his nose. Then he sneezed and shook his head a few times. 'If you've no more questions,' he said, 'I think we should get some sleep. When that rat comes back for us, we'll probably need all our strength. According to Jasper, he's been rushing round seeing all our creatures.'

'What?' William exclaimed. 'Well, why didn't you say so?'

'You didn't ask,' the dog growled.

'I just thought no one was getting on with any-thing,' William complained.

'Why did you think that?' Spot demanded.

'I don't know,' William shrugged.

'I'll tell you why, shall I? Because you only believe things are being done when you're doing them yourself. I'm right, aren't I? But there are other people concerned as well, you know, William.'

William sighed and looked at his feet.

'Don't be cross with him, Spot!' Mary said. 'We're all just trying to do the right thing.'

'Be like Alice, then,' the dog said, 'go to sleep!' And William and Mary turned and found that Alice had curled up on the bed behind them and was fast asleep.

13
A Potential Buyer

The following afternoon the children and Spot were out on the front lawn playing a noisy and extremely violent game, known in the family as 'Constant Death'. This was a version of tag mixed with football – the object being to score goals while your opponents tried to get the ball away from you and score for themselves. It was suitable for any number of players who didn't mind being tripped up, knocked over or generally mutilated. Spot had taken to it at once and was by far the best player, being virtually impossible to trip up or knock over. It was the third time they'd played since they'd arrived for the half term holiday and although the children weren't in the mood for games, Spot had persuaded them, saying that it would stop them all brooding. But his excited yelping and barking showed that he'd mainly wanted to play simply for his own enjoyment.

'How can you, Spot?' Alice said, picking herself up off the damp grass yet again and rubbing a bruised knee. 'We've got much more important things to worry about! And, besides, that really hurt!'

'No point worrying,' Spot barked. 'What good does worrying do?' Then he swerved to avoid Mary,

129

who was running to intercept him, and lost the ball
to William who came in from the other side and
scored a goal.

'That's my fourth,' he yelled, picking up the ball.

'No it isn't, William! It's your third!' Alice
shouted, running back into the middle of the lawn
and waiting for him to kick off again.

'All right then,' William conceded. 'Though I
still think that other one went in.' Taking a couple
of steps, he kicked the ball so that it flew in a high
arc over Mary's and Alice's heads. Spot, watching
intently, turned on his heels and scampered across
the lawn, judging perfectly where it would land.
Then, just as it bounced in front of him, he leaped
into the air, hitting it with his head. The ball went
off at an angle, in the direction of the front of the
house. Alice, with her arms outspread, was running
in to receive it when her attention was distracted
by the sound of a car approaching along the drive.

'Someone's coming,' she yelled, and they all
turned to watch as an old but gleaming Rolls Royce
slid into view. As it drew level with them and came
to a halt outside the front door, they all remembered, at the same moment, where and when they'd
seen it before.

'It's the car the Crawdens came in, when they
met Meg and all of us up at Four Fields last
summer,' Mary whispered.

The children and Spot gathered together in a
tight group, as though they had felt a sudden surge
of nervous anticipation and were seeking support
from each other. At this same moment, as if to
reflect their change of mood, darker clouds blew in
from the west and the light faded, making the day
feel threatening and dangerous.

The car was driven by a chauffeur. In the back sat an old man and a young child. The children recognized the man as Sir Henry Crawden, but the child – who, as he scrambled out of the car, turned out to be a young boy, no more than six or seven years old – they had never seen before. As soon as the boy saw the children staring at him, he stopped in his tracks and hung his head with a guilty expression on his face, as if he had been caught doing something he shouldn't. Behind him, the chauffeur produced a folded wheelchair from the passenger side of the front of the car. Opening it up beside the rear door, he removed a rug from the old man's knees and helped him out of the car and into the chair.

'What's the matter, Mark?' Sir Henry called to the boy.

'People, grandfather,' the boy replied.

'Well, greet them, you duffer!' the old man said and he raised a hand in the direction of the children and waved. 'You must forgive my grandson! People think that he's rude; but in fact he is only shy. We have met before, I think. It's the young, aspiring lawyer, isn't it?'

'He means you, William,' Alice whispered. 'You speak!'

'We met up at Four Fields, during the summer,' William said, trying to steady his voice so that he didn't betray how nervous he felt.

'Yes, yes! I remember! My son was quite put out by your legal manoeuvring. It really spiked his guns! Ruined his plans! No matter. So,' he said, with a beaming smile, 'Golden House is back on the market! We should never have let it go. Now, no doubt, it will cost me money to get it back! Ring the bell, Summers. We are expected, I think,' and, as he spoke, he rotated the wheels of the chair, so that it swung round, and turned his back on the children.

They continued to watch in silence as the chauffeur crossed to the porch and pulled the bell rope. The boy hurried to join his grandfather in front of the door, but, as he did so, he stole another glance over his shoulder at the group on the lawn and then, to their surprise, he stuck his tongue out.

'The little brat!' Mary gasped.

Alice immediately stuck hers out in return and made her face into such a hideous scowl that the child was obviously shocked and pulled his tongue back into his mouth and looked away quickly.

Beside them, on the grass, Spot growled quietly to himself.

After what appeared a very long time during which the two groups, the one by the porch and the other on the lawn, seemed held in suspension, the front door opened and Meg came out. At once she registered surprise.

'You?' she said.

'Good afternoon, Miss Lewis,' the old man said, in a clear voice. 'We have come to inspect the property.'

'You, Henry?' Meg said. 'But . . .' she was clearly overcome with a mixture of emotions and it seemed almost as though she might faint. Reaching out with a hand, she leaned against the stone wall beside her for support.

'It is, I understand, back on the market. I am correct, am I not?' Sir Henry asked.

'Well, yes. But . . .'

'But, Meg?' he enquired, in a softer voice. 'But not on the market to me? Is that it?'

'Well, I never thought . . . it was your family that sold it to Mr Green. Why on earth would you want to buy it back now?'

'Family home, my dear! Sentimental attachment! We Crawdens go back to Elizabethan times here. I hope, one day, that my grandchild will be the master of Golden House.'

Meg looked at the small boy standing in front of her with his hands in his pockets and his head lowered.

'You have grandchildren, Henry?' she said, quietly.

'Three! This one is the youngest. He is my son's offspring from his second marriage. The other two, a boy and a girl, I never see. Their mother took them with her when she ran away from the Crawdens! Poor girl! I think she found us a difficult family to marry into!' All the time he was speaking, the old man was staring intently at Meg. It was as though the words he was using were a substitute for what he really wanted to say. 'But Mark, here, Mark I see quite often. His mother – my son's second wife – travels a great deal. I must admit that I fear the signs are not good! She is a woman looking for escape! Meanwhile her husband – my son, Mark's father – wheels and deals and is rarely at home. Consequently Mark is as lonely as I am lonely. We are a comfort to each other. Aren't we, child?' Sir Henry reached out and ruffled the boy's hair. Mark pulled away and continued to stare at the floor.

'You are lonely, Henry?' Meg said. Her voice bore no bitterness.

133

'You should never have turned me away,' Sir Henry said, quietly and slowly.

'That was all a long time ago, Henry,' Meg replied. 'It is a sign of old age, to dwell in the past. I'll go and get Mr Green, he is looking after all the business.'

She turned and was going back into the hall when the old man spoke again, stopping her in her tracks.

'Will you mind me moving back into Golden House, Miss Lewis?'

'It will make little difference to me. I shall not be here!'

'Where will you go?'

'A long way away.'

'But with the money you receive you could repair the house at Four Fields . . .'

Meg looked at him and smiled.

'When I leave this place, Henry, I will go as far away from it as I possibly can. I will never look back. You say you are lonely?' Now her voice began to shake and the children, listening and watching from a distance, realized that she was fighting back tears. 'You are lonely?' she emphasized the words, shaking her head. 'I have been alone most of my life.' Then she turned and hurried away into the hall, saying, 'Excuse me!'

The children glanced at each other. They felt embarrassed. It was the sort of scene that you felt you shouldn't have watched. It was too personal and too painful.

At the front door, the old man was obviously upset by what had taken place.

'Put me back in the car, Summers,' they heard him say. 'Mark, get in! We are going!'

The boy turned and looked at the three Constant children for a moment.

'Do you live here?' he called to them.

'They are just visiting, Mark. Get into the car!' Sir Henry said. The chauffeur was pushing the wheelchair back and then the complicated exercise of returning the old man to the back seat began.

'Will they come and see us if we live here, Grandfather?' they heard Mark ask.

At that moment Jack appeared at the front door. He had been chopping wood out in the yard and was sweating and dishevelled.

'Sir Henry, I'm sorry. I didn't hear the bell,' he said, hurrying towards the car.

Summers, the chauffeur, had by now installed the old man into the seat and was covering his knees with a rug.

'I will match any offer that may have already been made to you, Mr Green. Golden House is returning to the ownership of the Crawdens! It was a mistake ever to have let it go.'

'I see . . . but . . .' Jack was obviously very surprised by this speech.

'But? You also but me? There are no buts! Either the house is for sale or it isn't! If it is – then I shall have it. This house, I will have you know, has been in my family off and on since Matthew Morden, my ancestor, acquired it from a certain Stephen Tyler in 1590. I have, I think, a priority claim. Now where are your buts?'

'I was only going to say . . .' Jack began, when Sir Henry interrupted him impatiently.

'Well, is the house for sale, or isn't it?' he snapped.

135

'Yes,' Jack said, an irritable note creeping into his own voice, 'but . . .'

'But what?' the old man cried, losing his temper completely.

'It will be sold when we are ready,' Jack replied, now coldly controlled. 'We have only just contacted an agent. We have not, as yet, even fixed a price. We haven't discussed any of the details with our solicitor. We have yet to decide where we will move to ourselves. You are here too soon, Sir Henry.'

'Well, don't take too long. I am a very old man.'

'I will certainly bear you in mind as a potential buyer . . .'

'I am not a potential buyer. I will have this house. . . . Do you understand me? I must have it – and I will tell you why.' He leaned towards the window of the car as he spoke. 'This isn't a happy place. But the unhappiness is a Crawden legacy. We understand it. We can live with it. It is part of our make-up. Perhaps, one day, we will even disperse it.'

'I don't agree with you, Sir Henry,' Jack said firmly. 'I find it an entirely happy place.'

'Then why are you moving from it, boy?' Sir Henry asked. 'Answer me that! Why are you moving?' Jack and the old man stared at each other. But the conversation was at an end. 'Drive on, Summers!' Sir Henry called.

The car moved slowly away, round the circle of the drive. Sir Henry remained with his eyes staring in front of him. But his grandchild, Mark Crawden, turned his head, watching the three children on the law until they were lost from sight.

'That man!' Jack muttered. 'Why did he have to come?'

'You won't sell it to him, will you?' Mary asked, as the children crossed towards him.

'We're not ready to do any deal yet,' Jack said irritably. 'We've only just thought about putting it on the market. It beats me how he knew so soon that it was going to be for sale again. I'll have to get on to the agent. We haven't even agreed a price yet.' And, still grumbling irritably, he went back inside.

'The Crawdens!' William groaned, echoing all their feelings.

'We'll have to do something now,' Mary whispered.

'I'll go and find the others,' Spot said and he turned and raced away round the back of the house in the direction of the walled garden and Golden-water.

14
Rattus Returns

Meg's room was on the ground floor of the Tudor wing. One day, if the plans Jack and Phoebe had drawn up for the house were to come to fruition, it would be part of the hotel dining room. Until such a time came, Meg lived there. She had moved in after the fire up at Four Fields had forced her out of her own home. Two of her cats, Cindy and Flanders, shared the room with her. The others had joined the dogs in the outhouse across the yard, which they all found more like home. The house at Four Fields had never been a place of comfort.

Meg didn't come to supper that evening so, after it was over, the children went to see her. They found her, sitting in the dark, with the curtains still open. Cindy was asleep on her knee and Flanders was curled up on the bed. When they knocked on the door there had been no reply and it was only after pushing it open and switching on the light that they discovered she was there.

'Sorry, Meg!' William said. 'Are we disturbing you?'

'You should have something to eat, Meg,' Mary suggested. 'Shall we bring you something?'

Meg remained silently staring into the distance.

It was almost as though she hadn't heard them, as though she didn't even realize they were there.

'Phoebe made vegetable curry,' Alice said. 'It was really good. We had rice and chutney and there were nuts and bananas in it . . .'

'Meg?' Mary said, louder. 'Meg, please say something . . .'

The old woman slowly turned her head and looked at them. Then she smiled; a sad, wistful expression.

'So,' she said, 'that's how things will end!' and she shook her head.

'How?' Mary asked, really more to fill in the silence than for any other reason.

'Why – you heard, didn't you? Henry will come here to live. He'll end his days, like his uncle did before him . . . going slowly mad, I shouldn't wonder! Only difference will be that I won't be up in the tree house, watching. Did he really believe that I'd go back to Four Fields? What fools some men can be! I suppose he also thought that I would be glad to see him back; that all this time I have been waiting for him!' She shook her head and absentmindedly stroked the cat on her lap. 'I have not been waiting for him. I watched him walk away from our door after Father had sent him packing. And I watched him again – a frightened man in his uniform – back from the war, hoping to make amends.' Her head was shaking violently now, as though she was trying to rid her memory of the visions. 'Sooner this whole business is over, the better. Sooner we're all free of this place . . .'

'Don't sell the land to him, please Meg!' William urged her. 'And stop Uncle Jack from selling the house!'

139

'No, dear!' she said. 'It's for the best, I think.'

'But what about Jack and Phoebe and the baby?' Mary cried. 'Where will they go? They'll split up. Is that what you want?'

'Split up?' Meg said, her voice sounding bitter. 'What ugly words you youngsters use! Ugly words for ugly deeds! Split up! Well, let them do just that! It happened to me. Why should I care? Henry and I . . . we "split up" – if you can do that without ever having really been together in the first place! I thought he loved me. I thought one day we would be married; that I would be his wife; that that was what he wanted as much as I did. I hoped that we would have grandchildren to comfort us in our old age! But no! All he was after was the land. The Crawdens didn't want the house without the land. I suppose that was it. So, first hint that the land and the house were back together on the market – and guess who comes running! Oh, Henry!' she sounded so disappointed, 'Henry!' Then she turned and looked closely at the children again. 'I'd have had him back!' she whispered. 'I'd have had him back once. He'd have got his land . . . Oh! I must stop thinking . . . I didn't come all this way to be unhappy again.' She searched in the pocket of her cardigan and pulled out a handkerchief. With it she blew her nose loudly. 'Will you do me a favour, before you go back at the end of the week? Will you?'

'Oh, Meg! Of course we will,' Mary said, putting an arm round the old woman's shoulders.

'Take me up to see my badgers,' Meg said, tears beginning to trickle down her cheeks. 'They were my only friends through all those years. I wish he hadn't come back, that man. Henry Crawden! I wish . . .'

She would not be consoled. They left her sitting in the chair, with the cat still on her lap, all the memories of her past going round and round in her head.

As they were going out of the door she murmured; 'Switch the light off, will you, deary? I prefer the dark. Never could get used to the electric . . .'

Out in the narrow passageway, they were about to turn back towards the front hall, when one of the doors in the other direction creaked on its hinge, making them all look round.

'Oh! It scared me half to death!' Alice whispered.

'Let's get back to the hall, Will!' Mary said. 'This part of the house is so spooky.'

'It's all right!' William said with false bravado. 'There are lights everywhere.'

'I know,' Mary shrugged. Then the door creaked again.

'What's making it do that?' William said, walking towards the door. 'There isn't any breeze or anything.'

'Will!' Mary pleaded.

'You go back, if you want to,' William said.

'I'll come with you, Mare!' Alice said.

'It's the door down to the cellar,' William remarked, pushing it open. 'Funny!' he shook his head, deep in thought. Then he seemed to make some decision. 'There's a light here,' he whispered, pressing a switch on the wall beside him. A pale glimmer appeared from lower down the stairs, illuminating his face and casting shadows on the passage wall behind him. The girls saw him take a deep breath as though he was preparing himself for an unpleasant act. Then he looked back to where they were still standing near Meg's door. 'Come with me, will you?' he said, and they realized that he was as scared as they were.

'We don't have to go at all,' Mary said.

'I know,' William agreed. 'Only . . .'

'What?' Mary whispered.

'I don't know,' William replied, sounding puzzled. 'I just. . . . Listen!'

He said the word so urgently that Alice had to stifle back a scream.

'What is it, Will?' Mary gasped.

'Come here, quickly!' he urged them. 'Mary, have you brought the pendulum?'

Mary felt in her pocket and her hand closed round the nugget and chain. Beside her she could feel Alice shaking. She took her hand, trying to reassure her.

'Come on,' she whispered. 'We'll go back to the hall!'

'No!' Alice wailed. 'We'd better go with him. He'll only go on his own.'

The two girls went slowly along the passage and joined William at the open door. In front of them a flight of stone steps led down into the cellars beneath the house. One single electric light bulb was glowing halfway down. Below and beyond it, the darkness closed in again; an impenetrable barrier. Now they could hear what it was that had caught William's attention. It was a sound as gentle as a breeze, although no breeze was blowing; a soft, indistinguishable chattering, like massed voices, all whispering excitedly at a great distance from them, as though in a far-off room.

'What is it?' Alice mouthed.

'I don't know,' William murmured. 'I wish I'd brought a torch.' And, as he spoke, he tiptoed down the first steps.

'We could go back for one,' Mary hissed.

William swung round, his finger to his lips. Then he beckoned to them. Mary's fingers tightened round the pendulum in her pocket. Then, still holding on to Alice's hand, she started down the stone steps, following William.

At the bottom, a long stone corridor led past several doors to the entrance to the underground crypt that lay below the central hall of Golden House – the original, medieval tower round which the house had been constructed.

Dimly along the dark corridor pale light shimmered from this opening and now, as they drew closer, the noise that had first attracted William's attention was becoming more distinct. It was as if a great company were secretly chanting. And the word, the single word, that all the many voices were repeating over and over again made the children stop and gasp.

'Morden! Morden! Morden!'

'Let's go home!' William whispered, taking a step backwards. As he did so, one of the side doors flew open and a rat ran out and swerved round in front of them.

'In here!' Rattus Rattus ordered in a voice that was no louder than a breath of air but had all the command and the urgency of a shout. Without hesitating, the children scrambled into the room and the rat followed them, pushing the door almost closed behind him with his backside.

'So!' Rattus Rattus hissed. 'You are well met! Since you're here, you may as well come with me!'

'Where are we going?' Alice asked in a terrified whisper.

'Into the enemy camp,' he replied. 'We need to know their plans – and that would seem to be the best way of finding out, don't you agree?'

Alice swallowed hard and did not reply.

15
Into the Enemy Camp

The room they had entered was in darkness. At first, they could see nothing at all. But, little by little, as their eyes grew accustomed, and with the aid of the small amount of light that spilled in from the passage through the crack in the door, they began to distinguish vague shapes.

Rattus was standing on his hindlegs, staring at them. Behind him, looking extremely small and nervous, was a mouse.

'Alice,' Rattus hissed, 'this is Timrous – my name for her! She's a good little creature, but scared. Try and stiffen her up, will you?'

'Me?' Alice asked, surprised that she should be chosen for this job. 'How? What d'you mean?'

'Just stop her flapping while you're with her.'

'With her? Am I going with her?'

'Certainly! You don't think you can walk into Morden's camp looking like yourself, do you?'

'But . . .' Alice started. She wanted to say that she had no intention of walking into Morden's camp in any guise whatsoever. But before she could say another word, Timrous, the mouse, jumped towards her and the next thing Alice knew, she was landing on four tiny claws and twitching her nose excitedly.

'I don't want to go at all!' Timrous squeaked in her head.

'Me neither!' Alice assured her.

'Trouble is,' Timrous explained, 'they need me. I know every inch of this house and I'm known by most of the rats. They'll only accept these other creatures if I'm with them. That's what the rat said, anyway.'

'We'll have to go then,' Alice thought in a resigned voice.

'What d'you make of it all?' Timrous squeaked. 'The rat seems to know what he's doing – but he's a bit too bossy for my liking. Still, to be fair, I was going to have to move out. So I may as well go along with him! The old woman's cats were no problem! This is a big house and I'm used to coping with cats . . . but Morden's rats!' The mouse shuddered. 'It's been hell since they moved back in. So many of them! And the trouble with them is if you don't join them, your life isn't worth living! Lots of my friends have gone over to their side. Fear! Sheer fear! If you don't join them, they think you're against them – and they bother you all the time. So I keep in with them. Doesn't pay to make an enemy of a rat. But I'm certainly not one of them, whatever they may think. Horrible, uncouth louts! They'll ruin everything for us, you know. They'll drive the humans away from here – and without humans, you have to really work at making a living. . . .'

'Shut up, mouse! Stop your squeaking!' Mary hissed and then she gasped, realizing that it was Rattus who had spoken through her.

'You'd better be with me,' Rattus explained in her head. 'You have the pendulum. William, there's a weasel called Mustel over there. Now I'm not partial to weasels myself, but if we're in for a spat, they're good fighters. Mustel?'

'What, your honour?' the weasel said, wriggling out of the darkness towards them.

'You heard what I said,' Rattus snapped. 'You take William!'

'Take him, your honour?'

'Yes. Do pay attention, all of you! You really must!' Rattus sighed. 'I should have been given much longer to prepare! It's taken me all my time to recruit them – and they really need several weeks training before they venture into the field.'

He and Mary shrugged. She was rather enjoying this new-found authority. 'Is this all we've got?' she asked, looking through the thin light at the half-dozen assorted mice, the weasel and an almost white rat.

'The rat I have called Albus, because of his colour,' Rattus explained. 'He knows the escape routes and being so pale he'll stand out in a crowd. If we get into trouble, we're to follow him. He'll show us the nearest exit! Well, go on, William!'

'What?' William demanded. He was feeling left out and his nerves were making him jumpy.

'I think, your honour,' hissed the weasel, 'that we're supposed to be going as one!' and, as he finished speaking, William turned, like a fur snake, and, rising up on his tiny back legs, he stared through glinting eyes at Rattus.

'We're ready,' the weasel squeaked.

'I suppose we are,' Timrous whispered doubtfully.

'Good!' hissed Rattus. 'Now we three must stay together. We are carrying the Master's children. No harm must come to them. First sign of trouble and we get out, is that understood?'

'I won't want to stay,' Timrous assured him. 'I'm not keen on going at all.'

'No, well, we've got to,' Alice said firmly. The mouse's cowardice was beginning to irritate her. 'I mean, we're all scared – but we mustn't go on about it!'

'Sorry!' Timrous sighed.

'Is this our entire army?' Mary asked.

'Lord's blood, no!' Rattus replied. 'Rus is up top rallying the troops. We've got a good showing. The owl, Jasper, and the fox, Cinnabar, are good lads. I've often heard the Master talk about them. I've always wanted to meet them . . .'

'You're enjoying this!' William exclaimed.

'Can't deny it!' Rattus Rattus said, with a grin. 'I'm a fighter! Been in dry dock too long. Amorous verses and philosophy are all very well, but once in a while I miss the beat of the drum and the cannon's roar. Pity you're not sea-folk. Most of all I want a south-westerly in my whiskers and the distant scent of tropic shores. No matter!' He shook his head and Mary marvelled at the taut muscles and the surging energy in their body.

'Now,' Rattus said, 'if all goes to plan and – more importantly – if that shower in there manages to get Morden's mind to attend the meeting, then the big idea is to lure Morden into Albus and then for us four to hot foot it back to the Master as quick as a flash.'

'You mean . . .'

'Wait! Wait! Wait, William! Don't interrupt, lad! This is going to take some planning. We've got the pendulum, which will enable us to time travel, and,

148

if Morden knows we're about, he'll be attracted. Don't forget, he'll be desperate himself. He never meant to get into this pickle he's in! I think he'll enter easily enough, because Albus will allow him to . . . but whether he'll want to stay in Albus, once he discovers that he's the Master's rat, is quite a different matter. It may be necessary for you two, Alice and William, to hold him there . . .'

'How?' William cried.

Rattus twitched his tail, thinking.

'Albus, what say you?'

'This is all new to me,' the white rat said. 'I've only vaguely heard of the Master before. The creatures I belonged with were past such hope. That's why I escaped . . .'

'From where?' Alice asked.

'I was in a circus. Sideshow attraction! I did several tricks with hoops and a few balancing acts. It was a doddle, really! I was well fed. My human was quite kind to me . . . but the call of the wild is very strong, you know.'

'We don't want your history now, Albus!' Rattus snapped.

'Actually, my human called me Chalky . . .' the rat said.

'Humans,' said Rattus, 'have very little poetry! Come on, or we'll miss the fun..!'

'But what do we do once we get Morden's mind into Albus?' William insisted.

'Get out! Depart! Au revoir, mes amis!' Rattus replied, with a grin. 'We must make for the tunnel behind the waterfall. It's a powerful place – and we'll need all the magic we can muster.'

'But what if Morden doesn't want to come with us?' William asked, pressing home his point.

'We'll . . . improvise,' Rattus replied. 'One of the great secret weapons is improvization! It counters the unexpected! Timrous, you lead the way!'

'Oh dear!' the mouse squeaked in Alice's head. 'Here we go, then!'

'And you lot, follow after us,' Rattus said to the other mice. 'And all stick together! Once we're in the camp, I don't want any of you straying! Which way, Timrous?'

'Just follow me,' the mouse replied.

Alice and Timrous ran nimbly to the door and squeezed out into the passageway. Then, turning in the direction of the crypt, they scampered along the stone flags.

'Bit of a climb now,' the mouse whispered in Alice's head and, swerving to the left, they ran up the side of a door frame and along its upper edge. Ahead of them Alice could see a large hole in the mortar between two stones. Once beyond it, they entered a maze of tunnels that twisted and turned through a darkness so profound that even Timrous's sharp eyes couldn't see further than their immediate surroundings. The sound of the chanting had completely disappeared and the silence and the darkness pressed in on all sides. Alice felt panic rising in her with every step they took.

'Where are we going?' she whispered in her head.

'I call this place The Devil's Trip!' the mouse replied. 'I give all my walks a name. Needless to say, I don't come on this one very often! In fact it was a pure fluke that I ever found it. I was on my way back from an outing, and took a wrong turning in one of the tunnels. Trouble is . . . there are so many of them . . .' as she spoke, she slowed down, her nose twitching, her ears straining.

'What's to do?' Rattus whispered, coming up behind them.

'Just checking!' Timrous squeaked. 'Ah!' she exclaimed, running forward again. 'Can you smell it?'

Alice got a sudden whiff of a damp, rotten odour.

'What is it?' she complained. 'It's horrible!'

'Drains,' replied the mouse. 'Don't worry! We won't be going that way. That was the outing I was on my way back from, the time I discovered this place. I usually go to the drains from quite a different direction.'

'You go to the drains?' Alice exclaimed. 'Whatever for?'

'Whatever for?' whispered Timrous excitedly. 'You humans are a funny lot. You miss out on all the best things in life! Come on! We now start some serious climbing!'

But not upwards. Down they went, by a series of steps and slopes and sheer drops. At one place the tunnel opened out into a wider space. Here there were metal pipes that were cold to the touch.

'But not when the hot water is flowing,' Timrous explained. 'Then it can get a bit dodgy! I've had quite a nasty burn off these pipes. Hang on!' and as she spoke, she gripped hold of the pipe and jumped. Down, down they slid, with the pipe clamped between their front feet.

Behind them Alice heard Rattus squeak out cheerfully.

'Lovely!' he exclaimed. 'Just like being up in the rigging!'

At the bottom they had to navigate an awkward jumble of pipes and loose stone. Now the air felt much colder and when they paused for a moment

151

Alice thought she could hear the sound of running water.

'There's a stream that runs right under here,' Timrous explained. 'It feeds the well of the house.'

'I know. We've been there,' Alice whispered. 'That's how we got into the Magician's laboratory.'

'You've been there?' Timrous asked. 'Well, why didn't you say? You could have led the way.'

'Is that where we're going?' Mary asked as she and Rattus drew level and she overheard the end of the conversation.

'Yes,' Timrous whispered. 'Morden's lot use the room as their meeting place. They have done for years, I think.'

'Stop talking, you two!' Rattus commanded. 'We must be nearly there.'

'There's a way through the solid rock along here. It's just a cleft in the ground, really,' Timrous explained. 'It brings us out at the back of the room.'

'Right. I'll go first now,' Rattus said and he and Mary pushed past the mouse and took the lead. 'Albus, you next! Then Mustel, you and William bring up the rear! You other mice, stay in line behind Mustel. . .! and when we're in the room, all keep together! Albus, once inside, you'll have to be the guide! The mouse doesn't know the waterway . . . and that's going to be our line of escape . . .'

'Just a minute!' William interrupted him. 'D'you mind if I ask..?'

'What is it now?' Rattus exclaimed.

'Just that, if we're going by water, I want to be sure that Mustel can swim,' William said.

'Don't you worry about that, your honour!' the weasel said. 'I swim like a fish, if I have to. I'm not keen on climbing trees – but water's no problem. No problem at all . . .' then, still shaking his head, he nosed the mouse behind him and licked his lips . . .

'No! Mustel, no!' William exclaimed. 'We mustn't eat that mouse – he's one of our friends.'

'Oh, all right, your honour!' the weasel said grudgingly. 'But just you warn them – once we're out of this business, I'll be looking for a nice meal . . .'

'Right! If everyone is quite happy, can we get on?' Rattus demanded irritably. 'Sooner this is finished, sooner we can all have a meal.'

Mary shuddered and made a mental note to part company with the rat before he started foraging. Ahead of them she could see the cleft that Timrous had mentioned. It was no more than a narrow crack, running through the solid rock wall that they were facing. With a quick look over their shoulder, Rattus and she led the way into it.

The journey through the cleft was long and difficult. It led deeper and deeper into the rock. Mary could feel the cold stone scraping against her body. She hoped that Albus wouldn't be too large to squeeze through and that Alice and Timrous, behind them, were not panicking.

Eventually Rattus paused again, lifting a claw to stop the line of creatures following behind. The sound of the running water was muffled now and in its place they all heard once again the low, insistent chanting that they had first noticed up in the cellar passageway.

'Morden! Morden! Morden!' the voices repeated, over and over again. The sound was coming from somewhere ahead of them, out in the dark.

'Nearly there!' Rattus whispered.

'You'll find the wall of the room first,' Timrous whispered in the rat's ear. 'Then, almost at once, there's a beam of wood. It's been badly burned at some time and it's possible to run along the top of it. It brings you out on a big flat stone halfway up the other side of the wall. Once there, you're in the room. The blocked-up doorway to the well shaft is opposite to you . . .'

Rattus nodded, taking in all that the mouse was telling him, then, with a long wave of his claw, he beckoned the others to follow and he and Mary set off again into the dark.

The chanting grew steadily louder. They found the stone slabs of the wall and the burned beam, exactly as Timrous had said they would.

'Morden! Morden! Morden!' the chanting continued, louder with every step they took. Inch by inch Rattus and Mary edged their way along the beam, followed closely by the rest of their company.

'Morden! Morden! Morden!' the united squeaking of a hundred rats and other, unknown creatures chanted. The sound was growing in intensity until it was almost deafening.

Then, with a terrible 'AAAH!' of excited, delighted welcome, the chanting stopped. At the very same moment Rattus emerged from the wall on to a large flat stone followed by Timrous and Albus, with Mustel and the other mice crowding in behind them.

In front of them the whole of the dark, subterranean room was filled with rats, stoats, ferrets, weasels, a polecat or two and even some foreign creatures – mink and coypu. They were all staring at the flat rock where Rattus and the others had appeared.

Then, a big, solid brown rat pushed his way to the front of the ranks and stood on his back legs with his nose and whiskers twitching, staring up at them.

'You lot!' he shouted. 'What the hell are you doing there?'

16
A Voice in the Dark

'More of your company,' Rattus hissed, stepping forward. 'I found them lost in the passages back there.'

'This is most irregular! They haven't been checked,' the brown rat squeaked. 'They should have come in through the yard tunnel.'

'The mouse is known to us,' one of the other rats said.

'You, mouse!' the brown rat bellowed. 'Name? Rank?'

'I'm only a poor house mouse,' Timrous whimpered.

'But what's your name and number?' the brown rat insisted and, as he spoke, he jerked his head. Several large rats sprang out of the crowd and up on to the flat stone, surrounding Rattus and his company.

'My n-n-name and n-n-number?' Timrous stammered. 'Oh dear!'

A big, vicious-looking stoat pushed through the crowd and went up to the brown rat.

'We're wasting time!' the stoat barked. 'Are we taking the house, or aren't we? I could be spending my time much more usefully up in the woods . . .'

'You lot, get down here!' the brown rat

commanded and, as he spoke, his rats edged the company off the flat rock down into the main body of the hall.

'And you, stoat,' the brown rat continued, turning on the creature savagely, 'get back in the ranks and don't speak unless you're spoken to!'

Rattus and Albus remained close together but Timrous, being so small, was soon separated from them, and Mustel, the weasel, deliberately turned his back and squeezed through the rows of animals, making for the back wall.

'Where are we going?' William whispered nervously.

'I never like being near the front, your honour!' Mustel replied. 'Near the front, you get chosen for things. I prefer a bit of cover, a bit of obscurity.'

'But we were all supposed to keep together,' William said.

'Right! Pay attention all of you,' Morden's rat shouted. He had jumped up on to the flat rock and was facing his troops. 'Now, we all know why we're here, don't we?'

'Yes!' the company roared in unison.

'Yes!' Timrous squeaked, to Alice's surprise.

'Yes!' Mustel hissed, making William jump.

'Morden's time has nearly come! Soon the valley and the house will be ours! The humans will come with their lovely rubbish and their drains! Our life will be changed! There will be houses for us all to live in. Rich pickings! We'll be able to live like our town brothers! We won't be the forgotten poor relations any more!'

'I must say, it does sound attractive, when he puts it like that!' Timrous thought. 'Of course, I only considered them driving the present humans

157

out. I never thought about others coming . . . in their place. And more of them! Life could be quite pleasant . . .'

'Shut up!' Alice interrupted the voice in her head. 'Try and get back near to Rattus and the white rat, Timrous!'

'Oh, all right!' the mouse whined, and she started to squeeze her way between the big rats that surrounded her.

'But in order for the great dream to become a reality,' Morden's rat was now saying, continuing his rallying speech, 'we have to make one last great push. Not only here in the house, but up in the woods as well . . . One last battle! A battle to the death! Are you with me?'

'Yes!' the crowd roared.

'Will we win?'

'Yes!' they squeaked.

'Who is our leader?'

'Morden!'

'Who do we honour and obey?'

'Morden!'

And then the chant started again. The whole room took it up. Low and earnestly, the incessant sound drummed in the dark:

'Morden! Morden! Morden!'

'I think we should be with the others, Mustel!' William whispered.

'Morden! Morden! Morden!' Mustel muttered, catching the rhythm and the intensity.

'Stop it!' William commanded him.

'What, your honour?' Mustel asked, surprised by William's tone.

'Just saying his name binds you a little bit to him. Come on!' and, without waiting for Mustel to agree, William slipped his long. thin, furry body back through the crowd making for Albus who, thanks to his white coat, was easily distinguishable, standing further along, near the blocked-up doorway.

'What kept you?' Rattus whispered.

'Sorry!' William replied. 'Bit of trouble with the weasel.'

'Morden! Morden! Morden!' Mustel chanted in his head.

'Stop it!' William insisted.

'Oh! Sorry your honour! Was I doing it again? It sort of gets hold of you . . .'

'Where are our other mice?' Mary asked.

'They're all here, beside me,' Albus said. 'But I hope we don't have to wait too long. They're not the bravest of creatures!'

Which was true. The mice were all pressed together in a tight little group on the other side of the white rat and were shaking so much that it made their tiny teeth rattle.

'What now?' Albus asked.

'We wait,' Rattus replied.

'What for?' Timrous and Alice asked in unison.

'For the Master's assistant!'

'Morden! Morden! Morden!' the chant continued until, with a sudden twist of his body, the big brown rat, who was still standing up on the flat stone, silenced them.

'Help me!' a voice whispered through the room.

'What is it you ask?' the brown rat said.

'A safe journey.'

'Where would you go?' the rat asked.

'Back to my time,' the voice replied.

'Now, Mary!' Rattus hissed. 'The pendulum!'

159

As he spoke, Mary felt in her pocket and produced the piece of gold. But, as she did so, she realized that she was no longer in the black rat. She was standing alone in the dark room, with all those creatures, crawling round her feet.

'William! Alice!' she gasped.

'You? Here?' Morden's voice cried out.

'Where is he?' William yelled, appearing beside Mary.

'There are rats all over my feet!' Alice screamed and she reached out towards William and Mary for support. 'I can't bear it! I can't. . . .'

'*You* . . . little children! You have done this to me!' Morden's voice howled.

'Well, come with us,' Mary shouted, her nerve almost cracking. 'But come . . . *now!*' and, as she said the word, she lifted up the Magician's pendulum, holding it dangling in front of her face, where it shone with a mysterious luminosity, as though it were lit from within.

'Get the gold!' the voice shrieked.

A rat near Mary's feet leaped up at her hand. Mary, taken completely by surprise, swung her hand away and, in doing so, the chain slipped from her fingers.

Alice saw the golden nugget spiralling through the dark towards her with the chain shimmering after it like a tail. She reached out a hand, and caught it.

'You, little girl!' the voice screamed. 'I will have you!'

'Rattus!' William pleaded. 'Do something!'

Alice took a deep breath and, gripping the pendulum in her hand for courage, she tried not to think about the vermin crawling at her feet.

'Mr Morden,' she said, 'we're really sorry for what we've done . . . and . . . we've come to take you home!'

'You?' the voice sobbed. 'You will take me home?'

'No!' Albus, the white rat, called. 'I will!' And jumping high and turning a somersault at the same time – a trick he had learned in the circus – he flicked the pendulum out of Alice's hand and darted away into the shadows.

'Come on, you lot!' Rattus commanded. 'We mustn't lose him now!' And, much to the relief of each of them, William, Mary and Alice rejoined their hosts and quickly followed the white shape of Albus as he disappeared through a hole low down in the stone wall that had been used to block up the entrance to the room.

'Get me that gold!' they heard the voice cry and then, behind them, the crowd in the room erupted into loud and angry squeaks and hisses.

'After them!' the brown rat hissed. 'Stop them!'

The hole led to a sheer drop. The sound of water dripping and flowing surrounded them. Each of the creatures slid and fell down slimy cold stones until, reaching the bottom, they went deep into the icy stream that flowed through the dark.

'Have you got him?' Rattus asked Albus, gasping for breath as he spoke.

'Not yet!' Albus answered. 'But I've got the gold, and that seems to be what he's after.'

'Oh, hurry! Please! They're following us,' Timrous and Alice said together.

'Which way, honoured sir?' Mustel asked, with an unusual urgency in his voice.

'Straight up the stream and into the mines!' Albus replied.

'The mines?' William asked. But there was no time for further discussion.

Albus led the way through the stinging water. It was hard work for them all, for they were swimming against the flow. Timrous soon tired and Rattus stuck his tail in her mouth and pulled her and Alice along.

'I never thought I could like a rat,' Alice thought. But she found that she not only liked Rattus at that moment, she really loved him.

Reaching a waterfall, Albus scrambled on to a shelf of dry rock. Here he waited to give each of the others a helping hand. Two of the mice were missing.

'Pity!' exclaimed Rattus, seeming to care less about their welfare than the difference their disappearance might make to his plans. 'Right! I want two volunteers – you and you!' he signalled to two of the remaining mice. 'You stay here and make sure the others follow us.'

'You want them to follow us?' Alice exclaimed.

'I want the Magician's assistant to, yes!' the rat replied.

'But what about all the others?' William asked.

'No time! Come on,' Albus whispered and, as he spoke, they saw the first of Morden's rats swimming towards them.

Turning, they raced off into the dark.

'All this tearing about!' Timrous exclaimed.

The sound of flowing water grew louder until it was almost deafening.

'What is it?' Mary had to shout to be heard.

'The locals call it Blackwater Sluice,' Albus yelled. 'It's a no-go area, I'm afraid. The flow is far

162

too strong for anyone to survive it. It's where the water leaves Goldenwater . . .'

'Yes,' William said. 'We've been there.'

Alice shuddered.

'I didn't like that much, either,' she thought.

'You've had a lot of adventures!' Timrous said.

'I suppose we have!' Alice agreed, 'but I'm not sure they're the sort of adventures I like really. I prefer watching television . . . that way you can always switch it off if things get too frightening. . . .'

'Would you mind being quiet for a bit?' Timrous asked her. 'I think we need to concentrate. . . .'

They were now climbing a great cliff. The darkness that surrounded them was so intense that even their keen, animal eyes found it difficult to penetrate. Tiny claws gripped the cracks and fissures in the rock, hanging sometimes to the under-side of ledges and at other times balancing along knife-edged chasms.

'It's just as well we can't see,' William thought. 'If we could our nerves would snap.'

Sometimes they had to leap across gaping voids, sometimes to squeeze through minute gaps. Then they entered a series of passages that were broad and high.

'The old mines,' Albus explained. 'Even I can get lost here.'

'Where are we making for?' Mary asked.

'The Dream Place,' Rattus replied.

'But I thought Morden's creatures didn't know it existed,' William said.

'That's why we're going there,' Rattus replied. 'How far now, Albus?'

'To the tunnel behind the waterfall?' Albus asked, then he paused, his nose twitching. 'Almost there.'

'Mary,' Rattus whispered.

'What?' Mary thought.

'Someone has to wait for Morden's mind.'

'What?' she asked, feeling panic rising.

'That's my job,' Albus said.

'But we need you to show us to The Dream Place,' the rat said.

'No problem,' Albus replied. 'You're there.'

'Where?' Rattus asked, puzzled.

'Straight down!' Albus said, pointing to a thin crack in the rock.

'We're above it?' Rattus asked, surprised.

'We're nearly at the top of the mountain,' Albus said. 'I'll wait here.'

'You can't keep the pendulum. Mary and I must have it, in order to cross time.'

'He'll think I've still got it,' the white rat said, passing Rattus the pendulum. 'But I won't be able to fool him for long. As soon as I come to you. . . . You must go at once!' Then he paused and shivered. 'Will he hurt me, Rattus?'

'No, old lad! Don't you worry!' the Magician's rat replied, but none of them really believed him. 'You other mice can hop it now,' he continued. 'Come on, you children!'

'Can we go, then?' Timrous asked.

'Well, not till you've safely delivered the Master's children to The Dream Place. They'd be a bit big for this crack!' Rattus said and, taking Mary with him, he slipped through the narrow opening in the rock.

164

17
The Second Journey

The sound of the waterfall at the end of the tunnel was deafening after the oppressive silence of the underworld. The cave was in darkness but, as their eyes grew accustomed to their new surroundings, so a faint silver glow pierced the gloom, shining down from an opening in the rock ceiling, way above their heads.

'Moonlight!' Rattus whispered. 'Phoebe is on her throne!'

'Phoebe?' Alice asked, puzzled by his words.

'Phoebe! The Moon!' Rattus explained. 'Don't you children know anything?'

'I thought he meant our Phoebe!' Alice muttered.

'Can I go now?' Timrous asked. She looked so small, sitting up on her hind legs beside one of Alice's feet.

'Yes, off you go, mouse!' Rattus exclaimed. 'Well done! You've served us well.'

'Oh, thank you!' Timrous squeaked joyfully and she ran towards the tunnel's mouth and the waterfall beyond.

'Poor creature!' Rattus said, watching her. 'It must be terrible to be born fearful.'

'Your honour?' the weasel whined, curling himself round one of William's legs.

'Yes, you as well,' Rattus said, anticipating his request.

'Thank you, your honour!' Mustel said. 'Always glad to be of service.'

'Good!' Rattus said. 'Then I'll expect to see you by the yew tree when we raise our standard for the great battle . . .'

But Mustel wasn't listening. He was already half-way along the tunnel, running fast.

'They say rats leave sinking ships!' Rattus grumbled to himself. 'Strikes me that we're the only ones you can really rely on!'

'Now what do we do, Rattus?' William asked.

'We wait,' the rat replied. 'You've got the pendulum, have you, Mary?'

Mary felt in her jeans pocket and was surprised to feel the familiar lump of gold and the thin chain.

'Yes,' she told him.

'Good,' Rattus said. 'If all goes to plan we'll need it.'

Then they all relapsed into silence. Rattus paced up and down, his long tail twitching impatiently. William crouched on the floor, leaning back against the wall of the cave. Mary sat near to him, on a boulder and Alice wandered towards the tunnel, looking through the dark towards the distant water-fall. It was bitterly cold and none of them had brought coats because they hadn't known that they would be going outside.

'We only went along to Meg's room to talk to her for a bit,' Mary said, speaking her thoughts out loud. It seemed such ages ago that she could hardly believe that it was still the same night.

'I'm frozen!' Alice said, wrapping her arms round her body for warmth.

166

'So am I,' Mary agreed, sounding really miserable.

Rattus sighed, his mind far away. Then turning to look at them, he put his head on one side and smiled.

'Don't be down-hearted,' he said. 'Bit of a singsong, that's what we need.' Standing up on his back legs, he spat on his front claws and rubbed them together. 'Nothing like a song to raise the spirits!' he added and, taking a deep breath, he started to sing:

'I am a rat from Bristol town,
I've sailed the seven seas.
But when it's time to settle down,
It's home to dock for me . . .
I am my Master's rat
And a very good rat, that's me.
I share my Master's mat,
And I keep him company..y..y,
Yes, I keep him company!'

Then, still humming the shanty tune, he skipped away across the floor and turned, looking up at the children.

Alice yawned.

'I wonder what time it is?' she said.

William looked at his watch, holding it carefully so that the face was illuminated by the thin ray of moonlight that fell from above. Raising it to his ear, he listened carefully.

'Stopped!' he said, talking to himself. 'Must have forgotten to wind it.' Then he also yawned. It felt to him as though it must be long after bedtime and he suddenly longed for warm blankets and a pillow for his head.

'I am a famous fighter,'
Rattus sang:
'I'll fight in any affray.
But I think it far politer
To go to the foe and say:
You men, you men, you naughty men
You're foolish here to stay.
So off you go while I count to ten
Or else I'll make you pay..ay..ay,
Or else I'll make you pay!'

Suddenly, as if out of nowhere, came the sounds of hundreds of tiny scampering feet.

Rattus stopped singing and his body tensed.

'Here they come!' he whispered, his voice urgent, 'Take each other's hands now and, Mary, when I say the word, hold the pendulum where we can all see it. . . ! Then concentrate on it, all of you! Concentrate as though your lives depended on it!' He finished speaking in a shout, for the noise of the approaching horde had grown so loud and fearsome that it drowned not only his voice but also the sound of the rushing waterfall.

Tumbling into the cave down the walls from the hidden opening came rats and stoats and ferrets; weasels, spiders, flies; a frog slithered down the rock face; an adder, woken from slumber, fell to the ground; and, in the middle of this writhing, squeaking, hissing and surging melée appeared Albus, pursued so closely by Morden's hideous brown rat that the creature was actually clinging to his pink tail with its two front claws.

'Aaaah!' shrieked the white rat, jumping towards them. 'Help me, Rattus. Help me!'

'Stay still, rat!' Morden's voice screamed out,

seeming to come from Albus's mouth. 'I will be satisfied!'

'Take my claw, Albus!' Rattus shouted, stretching out a front leg. But at that moment a group of big rats descended on him, their eyes flashing, their teeth chattering excitedly and, pushing between Rattus and Albus, they swept them further apart.

'Now we've got you,' one of Morden's rats hissed, licking its lips and staring coldly at Rattus.

Meanwhile the children were being attacked on all sides.

'Rattus!' William screamed as a stoat started to claw its way up his leg.

Mary was kicking out at a group of sharp-toothed little mice and Alice was jumping up and down, trying to avoid a particularly nasty ferret with evil, glinting eyes and a cruel smile, when a noise made her look over her shoulder.

'Mary, William! Behind us!' she shouted and, looking round, her brother and sister saw what had caused her such dismay. Flying into the cave from the tunnel behind the waterfall was a crowd of crows and starlings and, amongst them, even a big, grey heron.

'Reinforcements!' Morden's rat bragged, releasing his hold on Albus. 'Now you're completely surrounded! Surrender! Give yourselves up! Where are your friends? Where is your army? Admit it, Morden is the winner!'

'Morden! Morden! Morden!' chanted his creatures as they moved in a slow circle round the children and Rattus and Albus. The breath from their mouths smoked in the pale light and they grinned and squeaked delightedly, as if in anticipation of some treat to come.

169

'Are they going to eat us?' Alice whispered, her voice so tight with fear that it came out as a squeak as well.

'Who knows, little girl?' Morden's rat answered, with a hideous grin on his face. 'Who knows how we're going to deal with you?' and, as he finished speaking, he lunged at her, his teeth bared and his eyes gleaming.

'Rattus!' Alice screamed. 'Rattus, help me!'

'Now, Mary!' Rattus yelled and as he did so Mary pulled the pendulum out of her pocket and holding it firmly, with the chain wound round a finger, she allowed it to swing in front of her, where they could all see it.

Morden's rat slewed to a standstill in front of them.

'The Magician's gold!' Morden's voice howled through the cave and, as they all heard it, Albus suddenly leaped into the air, as if he had been kicked, and then fell back on to the ground, trembling . . .

'Where is he, Albus?' Rattus shouted.

'I don't know,' gasped the white rat. 'I don't know. But, thank God he's left me. For pity's sake, Rattus, don't let him come in me again . . .'

'Now, little girl,' the terrible voice whispered in Alice's head. 'Do as I tell you, and I won't hurt you. Disobey me and . . .'

'Oh!' Alice cried out, wincing as a terrible jab of pain stabbed through her head, near one of her eyes.

'What's the matter, Alice?' William gasped.

'Nothing,' Alice said quickly, knowing that if she told them what had happened the pain would come again. 'Mary,' she added, turning towards her sister with an unfamiliar note of cunning in her voice, 'give me the pendulum! I'll look after it. Please, Mary . . .'

'Quickly, now!' Rattus exclaimed, cutting in before Mary had the chance to answer her sister. 'You know what we have to do . . .'

'Alice!' the voice hissed in her head. 'Do as I tell you! Get me the pendulum! I want that gold! At once, Alice . . . Or else . . .'

The terrible pain started in her head again, but Alice forced herself not to listen to the voice and not to feel the pain and she stared with all her powers of concentration at the golden pendulum flashing in the light, as it hung from Mary's finger by its glittering chain.

'Alice!' shouted the voice. 'I will be obeyed, child. . .!'

'No, Morden,' she said, in a trembling voice. 'I am not afraid of you. Don't hurt me any more. . .! There's really no need . . . We're going to take you with us. . . . *Now*!'

'Now!' shouted Rattus.

'Now!' said Mary and William in unison.

'Now?' asked Morden's voice with a note of surprise, speaking through Alice's lips.

* * *

'Follow me,' whispered Rattus Rattus and, as they walked slowly along the tunnel towards the waterfall, none of them noticed that all the birds and the insects and the terrible seething mass of rats and stoats and other creatures had completely disappeared.

The moon was shining on the cascading water, making it sparkle. The air was fresh and smelt of peat and damp earth and rotting leaves. An owl hooted somewhere not far away and then, as they edged their way off the ledge on to the steep, spongy ground beside the falls, a deer suddenly appeared out of the shadows and trotted towards them, a golden collar glinting round her neck.

'Here's Cervus to greet us!' Rattus squeaked gladly.

'But I thought she never came to our time!' William said.

'No more she does, William,' the rat replied. 'So instead we must welcome you all to ours!'

'You mean . . . we've travelled back in time?' William asked in amazement. 'But how. . .?'

'No discussion now!' Rattus commanded. .'We must make haste. Cervus will carry the little one.'

Alice didn't protest, and climbed gladly on to the deer's back. As soon as she was safely in place Cervus set off at a good pace down the steep bank towards the lake and on along the shore in the direction of Golden Valley, with William, Mary and Rattus running beside her.

The moon was floating in the dark dome of the sky, surrounded by clouds like thin silver threads. Further back, pinpricks of light danced and dazzled from the depths of space. Goldenwater reflected the heavens like a mirror. Around it, the trees moved restlessly in the cold breeze. Somewhere an owl hooted and then another screeched, as it flew low across the ground, hunting for food.

Reaching the far end of the lake, Cervus trotted up the slope towards the darker mass of the yew tree, silhouetted against the night sky. As they passed the standing stone, they were reassured by the familiarity of all that they saw but, pausing for a moment at the edge of the valley before dropping down the steep bank into its depths, Mary, who had gone a little ahead of the others, gasped.

'The house!' she exclaimed. 'Look at the house!'

Below them, at the valley's bottom, Golden House was brilliantly lit by the silver rays of the moon.

'It's different!' Mary said. 'It hasn't got the new bit.'

To the right of the centre tower, where the stone Georgian wing stood in their own time, was a black and white beamed edifice that matched the Tudor wing on the other side.

'It looks much better like that!' William said. 'Whoever changed it must have been mad.'

There was a light burning softly in the circular window under the chimney and, between them and the house, the silver discs on the weather vane of the dovecote flashed in the moonlight.

'We really have gone back,' William said, speaking to himself. 'We're really there!'

'Tut, William!' Rattus hissed from the dark. 'Did you doubt me?' Then the view of the house disappeared as they dropped down into the trees, passing the badger sett on the way.

On all the length of the journey Alice remained silent. Her mind was a terrible jumble of thoughts. Some were her own, but others belonged to Morden. These were dark, troubled imaginings that, later, she would find very hard to recall.

'You're home now,' she whispered in her head, trying to reassure him. But Morden would not be comforted.

'I will suffer for this,' he kept whispering. 'The old man will make me suffer.'

'No!' Alice told him. 'I'll speak for you. I'll ask Mr Tyler not to be cross with you.'

'You will?' Morden sneered. 'Why would you speak on my behalf, little girl?'

'Because it wasn't your fault that you came to our time. We did it to you.'

'You? How could you, ignorant children, achieve what I have been unable to do after years of trial?' he spat at her.

'Well – how else do you think your mind and your body became separated?' Alice asked him.

'An error on my part, child. It had nothing to do with you.'

'Oh, well!' Alice said with a shrug. 'Have it your way, if it makes you feel better!' And, releasing her grip on the deer's fur, she wiped her nose with the back of her hand.

They reached Golden House just as the moon was sinking behind the trees. Cervus went right round the house and approached it from the front. There was no drive but in its place the ground in front of the house was divided into a series of small flowerbeds, edged with low hedges. The beds were all different shapes and sizes and had narrow paths running between them, forming an intricate pattern. In summer these beds would have been filled with sweet-smelling flowers, but now, as winter approached, they were empty of any plants and the soil was raked as though they had recently been cleared.

Rattus went up to the front door and stopped.

'Here you are!' he whispered. 'The Master is waiting for you. You, Alice, have been a brave soldier! Very brave indeed.'

'Alice has?' Mary asked, surprised that her sister

should have been singled out for his praise. 'What's she done that's so special?'

'Why, Mary!' the rat replied. 'You mean you don't know? Tell them, Alice.'

'I've got Morden,' Alice said in a low voice. But before they could make any further comment the front door opened and Stephen Tyler stepped out from the light behind him into the dark of the night.

'Here you all are!' he exclaimed, stroking the deer's nose lovingly. 'You are most welcome to my house.'

18
As It Was

'Master Tyler! Master Tyler! Come in at once!' a voice called behind him.

'I'm coming, Kate,' the old man said, not taking his eyes off the children. Then, raising a finger to his lips, he ushered them into the hall.

There was a huge fire burning in the grate and the air was thick with wood smoke. Candles were alight in many sconces, but the room was filled with shadows and dark corners.

Stephen Tyler walked heavily and slowly, leaning on a stick and with his other arm in a sling. His long, black coat was stained and matted with dirt. His red hair was flecked with silver and there was a stubble of beard on his chin.

The children followed him in and, as they did so, an old woman came out of the shadows and closed the door with a slam.

'Letting the night air in!' she grumbled. 'What are you thinking on? 'Twill be the rheum that will carry you off – and then who will be blamed?'

'No one will blame you, Kate, that I promise you.'

'If you require nothing more, Master. . . .'

'Go to bed, Kate. Sleep sound! I will see you in the morning . . .'

'God willing!' the old woman said and she disappeared back into the shadows and through the door that led, in the children's time, to the kitchen.

As soon as she had gone Stephen Tyler turned towards the children.

'You have brought what is desired?'

Rattus jumped up on a table near to the old man.

'The youngest has it,' he said.

'My Minimus!' the Magician said. 'The bravest of the brave. Come! We must go at once! It takes me so long to move now, confound the day, that the merest effort is like a trip to Jerusalem! Up the stairs, come now!' and, still speaking, he started to haul himself up the staircase towards the galleried landing above.

Morden was in one of the rooms that would later be converted into the Georgian wing of the house. But now it was a small, low-ceilinged chamber, sparsely furnished with a bed, a stool and a large cupboard against one wall. There was an uncurtained, leaded window looking out on to the dark night. A candle was alight on the stool beside the bed. In the bed lay a young man. His face was deathly pale and his eyes were open, staring, unseeing, into some distant place.

'He has been like this since it happened,' Stephen Tyler explained to them. 'Sometimes he mutters unintelligible words. Poor boy!' As he spoke the old man gently mopped the younger man's brow. 'I knew we were on dangerous work. But I would not have had it come to this!' Then he turned and looked at Alice. 'Well, Minimus,' he said quietly. 'Discharge your burden!'

'How?' Alice asked.

177

The old man shrugged and leaned against the foot of the bed.

'You are the bearer!' he said. 'I hoped that you would know.'

'But I didn't choose to be,' Alice said. 'I was . . . chosen.'

'What does the mind say?' the old man asked.

Alice shrugged.

'It doesn't say anything,' she explained. 'It's still there – but it's . . . sort of . . . muddled. You mustn't be cross with him . . . ,' she began and then she shook her head, suddenly and inexplicably very close to tears.

Mary put an arm round her shoulder.

On the bed the young man made a slight movement.

'Help him!' Alice whispered.

'I don't know how to,' Mary told her. 'Will?' she asked, looking at her brother.

'What?' William asked. His hands were in the pockets of his jeans and he stared at the floor. For some reason he felt embarrassed. 'I don't know what we're supposed to do.'

'Maybe Morden would know?' Mary said, walking over to the bed and kneeling down in front of the young man. 'Oh, the poor man!' she said, staring at his face. 'He seems so lost and. . . .'

Morden's face was covered with fine beads of perspiration. His black hair was matted to his forehead. His eyes stared.

'I thought he'd be horrible and ugly,' Mary said quietly. 'He's not!' She looked up at Stephen Tyler. 'He doesn't look evil.'

'No?'

She shook her head.

178

'He looks frightened.'

'Perhaps,' said the old man, 'you have just learned the most important lesson of all. Fear can lead us into dark places. And what do you suppose can bring light to the dark, Mary?'

Mary shook her head, not able to take her eyes away from the old man's gaze.

'You above all my Constant children should know the answer to that. Alice has the courage. William has the intelligence. What is your gift, Mary?'

'I don't have one,' she mumbled.

'No?' the old man asked her gently. 'Are you so sure?'

'Quite sure,' she replied. He made her feel rather silly, staring at her and speaking so personally to her when the others were also in the room. She wanted him to stop. 'You could have helped him,' she said, dragging her eyes away from the Magician and looking once more at his sad, suffering assistant. 'You could have helped us all.'

'Do you attack me, Mary?' the old man asked, in a whisper.

'No, Mary, don't attack him!' Alice said, her voice coming out of the darkness behind her.

'But look at poor Morden!' Mary said, her voice louder and stronger. 'He isn't some horrible person . . . he's just . . . a person. I think he looks rather nice, really. He looks as though he wants to be understood. Oh! I know that's always used as an excuse – that people don't understand you – but, sometimes, it's the truth. And it's so horrible! Not all of us are as clever as William! Not all of us are as brave as Alice! I know that. I know they're better at all this than I am. I can't help it. It's the way I

179

am . . . Well, maybe that's the way Morden is, as well. Maybe all he wants is to be . . . able to . . . not feel alone and separate and . . . lost all the time. Yes, I'm sure he's greedy and ambitious. . . . But maybe all of us make him like that. You said, Mr Tyler, you said that he was the dark to your light . . . well maybe he wants to be the light – and it's you who is stopping him. Maybe it's your light that is making him dark. Maybe . . .' and she started to cry.

The tears that came scalded her cheeks and the sobs shook her whole body. She remained kneeling beside the bed in front of Morden and buried her head in the crook of her arm.

William stared at his feet and Alice folded her arms. She wanted to go and comfort Mary but, as she thought of doing so, Stephen Tyler raised a hand and motioned to her to stay still.

All the while the old man remained leaning against the foot of the bed. He was so close to Mary that he could have reached out and touched her but he refrained from doing so. Both Alice and William were drawn into watching him and were stopped from going to Mary themselves by the intensity of his attention on her. But it was hard to stand by, doing nothing, while she shook and sobbed quietly, kneeling on the ground in front of them.

'I don't care what you think, any of you,' she continued. 'I think what's happened to Morden is our fault and Mr Tyler's fault and I think that therefore all that Morden is doing in our time that's so horrible . . . the rats and the misery, the Crawdens, and Phoebe and Jack not speaking to each other . . . it's as much our fault as his. Because we've made him like he is . . . because we always have to have someone else to blame, just so that we can feel smug and satisfied with ourselves. . . .' Great gulps of tears and sobs racked her body making her gasp and shake.

'Stop, Mary! Stop!' William said quietly, unable to bear to hear and watch her any longer.

But Stephen Tyler signalled to him impatiently to be quiet.

'Oh, Morden! I'm sorry. I'm sorry on behalf of us all,' Mary whispered. 'You've got a really nice face and I bet one day some one will love you very much. Then you'll be able to forget all about us. I'm so sorry!' she said again and then the tears started once more. 'I don't even remember your other name,' she sobbed.

'Matthew,' a voice whispered. 'My Christ-given name is Matthew,' and, as Mary looked up, they all saw the figure on the bed stir and move. Slowly he reached out a hand and wiped the tears away from Mary's cheeks. 'Don't cry, strange girl. I'm all right now. It has been like a dream from which I have awoken. Don't cry any more. . . .'

'Alice?' Mary asked, in a strong voice, without looking round. 'Are you all right now?'

'Yes,' Alice said, stepping forward and putting an arm round her sister. 'You did it. You released his mind.'

'I did?' Mary asked, surprised.

'She did, didn't she, Mr Tyler?' Alice said.

'Come now,' the old man said, quietly. 'We must leave Matthew to sleep. He has been on a long journey . . . and he will be tired.'

Matthew Morden, as if in answer to his master's words, breathed deeply and closed his eyes in sleep.

'Good night, Matthew!' Mary whispered, then

William crossed and helped her to her feet. 'I'm all right,' she said and she smiled shyly. 'Trust me to go and howl my eyes out. Sorry!' and she sniffed and felt in her pocket for a handkerchief.

'You must be getting back,' the Magician said, leading them out of the room.

They walked along the dark landing towards the stairs. In the corner they passed the little turret steps that led up to their own bedrooms.

'Not that way,' the Magician said as Mary turned as if she was going to go up them.

'I'm tired,' she said.

'Soon be home,' the old man told her gently, and he put a hand on her shoulder. 'But you must go from my study. You will need all the power of my magic to return. For one person to travel is a miracle, but for three of you. . . . Come!' he said, leading them slowly down the stairs into the light of the hall.

'Can't we stay a little while?' William asked. 'There's so much I'd like to see now that we're here.'

'Time travelling takes a great deal of attention, William. It is not something to be undertaken lightly.'

But William wasn't really listening.

'Look!' he exclaimed, pointing at the chimney-breast above the hearth. It was made, as in their own time, of mellow coloured brick. But now, clearly etched on to its flat surface with a series of raised lines of bricks, there was a strange picture, or perhaps a diagram would be a more accurate description. At the bottom there were two dragons, biting each other's tails, and, between them, two snakes climbed up a stick that separated the dragons. On one side of the snake-stick there was a big, round sun and on the other side a crescent moon.

'That's the design I saw when I first discovered the steps up the chimney. So it really was on the wall once?'

'Now!' the Magician said with a smile. 'Now it is on the wall – by your time it has been removed.'

'I wonder who got rid of it,' William said.

'Morden's family. They will not like having a magician in their past. They will not approve of a magician's house. They will try to remove all trace of our art. And then, they will practise greed and chicanery and pervert the truth. . . . All in the name of respectability and church-going piety!'

'You know all this?' Mary said.

'It is how it will be,' the old man replied, reaching at last the level hall and leaning heavily against a great oak chest. 'And this, for you, is how it was. This is my house. And that,' he said, pointing again at the design over the fireplace, 'that is my art. Not only is it an alchemical symbol – forgive me, Minimus, I have to use these words!' he said, reaching out to Alice and smiling at her. 'They are not so long that you cannot understand them, if you really try.'

'It's all right,' Alice said, with a shrug. 'I work it out later, usually.'

'See the design. See it!' the old man urged them, his voice throbbing with excitement and urgency. 'And listen to me! The dragons are nature; the natural world, life and death, the eternal cycle. The snakes are energy; the quicksilver mind, looking in both directions, twisting and turning. The sun and the moon are the eternal balance, the dark and the light, the duality without end. And, down the centre, running from heaven to earth, the silent, still, unifying spirit. The I. The one. The now.' Then he sighed, as if he was suddenly very tired. 'This picture contains all you need to know. It is our work. It is our valley. It is why you were chosen. *Finis corruptionis et principio generationis.* You understand the Latin? "The end of corruption and the beginning of generation". A great corruption has been started here – and a new generation can grow out of it. Phoebe the moon, marrying Phoebus, the sun. The great marriage. A new beginning. This here,' he indicated the hall, 'is as it was. You are going to how it will be.' And, straightening up, he walked slowly towards the fireplace. 'Now! Time to see my study! Time to go home!'

19
The Magician's Glass

Stephen Tyler collected a lantern from the table in the centre of the hall and handed it to William to carry. Then, leading the way into the smoke-filled fireplace, he started to climb slowly up the slabs of stone to the ledge at the side of the hearth.

'I'll go first,' he said. 'You, William, follow with the light. I need no light. These stairs are so familiar to me they are like a part of me,' and, disappearing round the corner, he started the long ascent of the spiral staircase, through the wooden smoke door and on towards the room at the top of the chimney.

The children followed him in single file, with William holding the lantern aloft as he had been directed. None of them spoke. Each was lost in their own thoughts.

William's mind was filled with half-formed ideas and thoughts, provoked by what Stephen Tyler had said to them in the hall. It was as though he had just been given a glimpse of the finished picture of a jigsaw puzzle which, up until that moment, he had been trying to solve without any aid at all. Now suddenly pieces that had for so long seemed meaningless and unimportant were falling into place. But he knew that he wouldn't fully understand what it was he was working on until the last piece was in position and the picture was complete.

Alice, who had found that most of what the Magician had said was quite beyond her, was happy to let her brother work it all out. She was much more concerned about what would happen when they returned to their own time. Would all the Morden creatures be waiting for them? Would they have to return to the tunnel behind the waterfall? Or would they arrive back in the secret room? She thought it would be best of all if they landed up safe and warm in bed. She was, she discovered, incredibly tired. So tired that she scarcely had the strength to put one foot in front of the other as she climbed the stone steps, following the pale guttering light of the lantern.

Mary, who was the last in the line, was thinking about Morden. Now that his mind was back in his body and he had seemed to make friends with them, surely the threat that he represented in their time would be removed? Perhaps their work was done? Perhaps the task, set them by the Magician all those months ago early in the Christmas holidays, was complete? Perhaps when they returned to their own time they would find that Phoebe and Jack were happy again and Jack and Meg weren't going to sell Golden House and its land to Henry Crawden? Perhaps the rats and the other horrible creatures would have gone away . . . ? Perhaps? Perhaps?

But when they reached the Magician's study, all their hopes and fears, all their questioning and surmising were quickly brought to a halt.

The room was quite unlike the way they had seen it before.

A small fire was burning in the grate. There were

candles alight in the sconces in front of the round windows on both sides of the house. The room was packet full of objects. There were shelves crammed with books. There were books lying open on a large table. There were maps and charts and diagrams hanging from the eaves or lying in abandoned heaps, while others had been flung into dark corners, as if their usefulness had come to an end and they had long ago been forgotten. There were jars and strange instruments on every available flat surface. The stone floor was covered with dried rushes and branches of plants that smelt sweetly of lavender and rosemary as they were crushed underfoot. There was a woven tapestry covering part of the back wall and a thick woollen blanket on the floor beside an armchair, which was drawn close to the fire. There were discarded woollen scarves and a long cape; gloves and walking sticks; a pair of boots; a hat, balancing rakishly on the back of a chair; a half-eaten apple; a mug; a measuring stick. . . . The room was so crammed to overflowing with the old man's belongings that there was scarcely space to move in it.

'This,' he said with a gesture, as they stood in a group at the door, 'this is my room! A room like this is a picture of the owner's mind! See how cluttered and untidy my old mind has become! Matthew tries to order it sometimes, but I stop him. I know where everything is, I tell him. Move even the smallest object and confusion will ensue! This chaos is my right, it is my order! Touch it, he who dares! But now, come quickly, children!' He beckoned to them. 'See my glass!'

As he spoke, he led them across the room to where, hanging on the wall in exactly the position that the mirror hung in their own time, there was a circular glass bowl, framed in dull, black oak. The glass was old and misty. It was so dusty and stained that it hardly reflected at all. But, as they drew closer to it, Stephen Tyler shifted a candelabrum on the table-desk so that the light from its several candles fell across the mirror's surface.

The centre of the bowl seemed to have so much depth that it reached into infinity. The glass sides, reflecting backwards and forwards across the void, made it seem to contain volumes of space. The rim, where the wooden frame overlapped, was dark and strongly defined, like a pencilled circle on a blank sheet of paper.

'Remember the drawings on the cave wall in the Place of Dreams?' Stephen Tyler whispered, 'created out of nowhere, out of nothing, out of the sheer need and joy of the artist simply to express himself? This is the Philosopher's Glass. Here we may each create our dream; our unique, never-before-thought, never-before-seen vision. Here we may bring out from the depth of our being our own experience of creation. Every man, woman and child in this great universe has this individual talent within him or within her. It is the ultimate gift. It is the priceless pearl. It is the still centre, around which the twin snakes of mind twist and turn. This glass is mercury, held still; quicksilver, stopped in mid-motion. This glass is the greatest of all my possessions.'

The children clustered together, staring into the grey-green depths of the glass. No reflection of themselves looked back at them. But instead, as they gazed into the floating, limitless space that the bowl contained, a feeling of great calm, of silent thought, of infinite possibilities, overwhelmed each of them.

'It's magic, isn't it?' Alice whispered.

'Yes, little girl! My Minimus . . . my Minima!' Stephen Tyler murmured. 'It is undoubtedly magic.' Now his voice took on a firmer note; the tone of instruction, of command. 'I want all of you to work very hard. I want you to keep your minds free and clear, and no matter how much you want to turn and look at me, no matter how much you may want to speak, resist the temptation. You understand?'

'Before we start . . .' William said, in a rush, but the Magician interrupted him.

'No, William!' he said so firmly that he sounded almost cross. 'Stop now! Listen to me! We may not meet again . . .'

'Oh, Mr Tyler!' Mary gasped.

'Be still, Mary!' the old man commanded her. 'Listen! We may not meet again. Yours has been a privilege not given to many people. Use it well. I have been most happy in your company. And now, as my time grows near,' the old man's voice faltered, 'I fear that I may not have this pleasure again. Do your best in your own time! That is all that anyone can ask of you, or that you can ask of yourselves. If, at the end, we can say with certainty and truth that we did the best we could, then we will have fulfilled this great burden, this great gift, that is called "life". Remember: *Finis corruptionis et principio generationis*. Allow the corruption to end. It is up to all of you. Bring about the beginning of generation. The child; the little girl, Stephanie. By the by, I never thanked you for naming her after me. I do so now. She is a Tyler! My heart rejoices at that. She

189

and her mother both! Tylers living again in Golden House. That is such good news for me. One day – who knows? – Stephanie may also take up this great work, to guard the valley against those who would exploit it and destroy its particular and most unique qualities. If it comes about that Stephanie takes up the great task it will be with your guidance, you Constant children; my good and all-time friends. Stephanie Tyler! The child of my future. I regretted once that she hadn't been born a boy; I regret now not having met her myself. . . . What a foolish old man I have become! There are no regrets in this work. There is only the striving.' He paused for a moment. 'And now,' he continued, in a softer tone, 'you have all the knowledge you need . . .' Each of the children longed to turn and look at him, but there was something so soothing about the pale, limitless, featureless void into which they were focusing their attentions that they were able to over-come the desire.

'I may wish I had later,' Alice thought. 'But I won't for the moment . . .'

'Mary,' Stephen Tyler's voice whispered in her head, 'take out the pendulum.'

Mary did as she was told, feeling in her pocket and producing the now-familiar lump of gold on its chain.

'Hold it aloft in front of you. See!'

As he said the word, the pendulum started to turn slowly, swinging out on its chain from Mary's clenched finger and thumb.

Then, as the children continued to stare into the centre of the Magician's glass, a golden wheel of reflection appeared in its depths. The pendulum spun faster and faster, and the line of gold in the glass throbbed with intensity, growing brighter and brighter until the brilliance of its light, burnt into their eyes. The whole glass seemed to be suffused with golden luminosity. It filled the void with a radiance like the sun. It reached out and surrounded them, making the dark places glow and the shadows flee away. Like the dawn of time it chased away the night; it pulled them into itself. They were the light. They were the gold. They were drenched in its brilliance, they wore it like raiments of silk.

'You now know all there is to be known,' Stephen Tyler called to them. 'My tutelage is at an end!' and they knew that the separation was complete, because his voice seemed to come from far away down a corridor, from another room and another time. It echoed and faded and was lost into the golden light.

Now across the great bowl of gold that surrounded them and contained them, an arc of colour was slowly forming; dark purple at the top, through blues and greens and yellows to glowing, brilliant red at the bottom, this arch of colour seemed to span the infinite horizons of their golden world.

'It's like a bridge,' William whispered.

And, as the gold faded and the light of the bowl drained away, so the intense colours of the arch remained, momentarily across the now-cloudy glass.

'A bridge in the clouds,' Alice murmured.

'Mr Tyler,' Mary called sadly, but she knew there would be no reply. The room they were in was cold and dark and empty. 'We're back,' she said and as she spoke, the pendulum stopped swinging.

20
The Beginning of the End

When Mary awoke the first thing that she thought about was the baby. It was as though some worry had been nagging away in her head all the time she'd been asleep and only now was she able to give it proper attention.

'It doesn't fit!' she said, out loud.

'What doesn't?' a voice asked and, opening her eyes, she saw Alice sitting cross-legged on the other bed, looking out of the window.

It was broad daylight and the sun was flooding into the room.

'What time is it?' Mary asked.

'Nearly ten,' her sister replied.

'You should have woken me,' Mary said, sitting up and shivering as the cold air hit her.

'I was going to,' Alice said, then she frowned and looked out of the window again.

'It's freezing in here,' Mary said, climbing out of bed and hurrying to the bathroom.

As she was cleaning her teeth Mary thought again about the baby.

'It can't work,' her thinking voice insisted.

When she returned to the bedroom, William was

there. He and Alice were talking together in low voices, and they both looked up with worried faces when she entered.

'You know, there's something that doesn't fit,' she said, throwing her towel down on the bed and starting to get dressed. 'Mr Tyler says that, now Stephanie and Phoebe are here, there are Tylers once again living in Golden House. But that doesn't mean much, does it? Maybe Phoebe's name, Taylor, was once Tyler – but she can't be the Magician's descendant – because we know his wife died in childbirth. We were told that ages ago – so his line must have died with him, surely?'

William and Alice stared at her blankly, as though they hadn't listened to a word she'd been saying.

'But it is odd,' Mary said, pulling on a pair of jeans. 'We must remember to ask him, the next time we see . . .' then she stopped in mid-sentence, the horrible truth about the previous night coming back to her, and shook her head. 'We won't be seeing him again, will we?' she said sadly and all the depression she had felt as they'd dragged themselves wearily to bed came flooding back to her.

'There's something much more important than that to worry about,' William said urgently.

'What?' Mary asked, noticing for the first time how grim and serious the other two were looking.

'Phoebe's gone!' Alice blurted the news out as though she couldn't contain it any longer.

Mary looked at them blankly.

'Gone?' she said. 'What d'you mean, gone? Gone where?'

William shrugged.

'No one knows. She's taken the Land-Rover . . .'

193

'What about Steph?'

'She's taken Stephanie as well,' Alice said, in an agitated whisper. 'Uncle Jack's in an awful state. He says he should have guessed something like this would happen. He says Phoebe's been behaving . . . what was that word, William?'

'Irrationally,' William replied.

'Anyway,' Alice continued, 'whatever that means, he's blaming himself for not having listened to Phoebe more . . . Oh, poor Uncle Jack! I don't see why he should blame himself for Phoebe going bananas. But he is. He's been on the phone, asking people he thinks she might have gone to if she's with them . . .'

'Not that there are many' William added. 'She hasn't any family alive – nor does she have many friends, apparently.'

'I can't say I'm surprised,' Alice said. 'I'd hate to have Phoebe as a friend.'

'But . . . how? When?' Mary asked, her mind racing.

'When Jack woke up, she just wasn't there,' William explained. 'He thought she'd gone downstairs to prepare Steph's breakfast . . . but when he went to look for them, they'd completely disappeared. Then, when he went out into the yard, he discovered the Land-Rover was missing as well . . .'

'Didn't she leave a note, or anything?'

'No,' William replied, shaking his head.

'But . . . this is the worst thing that could have happened!' Mary exclaimed.

'Not really,' Alice said. 'I'm quite glad to tell the truth. I think Uncle Jack will be much happier without her . . .'

'Oh, shut up a minute, Alice!' Mary snapped,

making her sister pout. 'I don't mean Phoebe and Jack, I mean Steph! The whole point of our task was to prepare Steph for her future here at Golden House . . . Well, we can't if she's gone, can we?' Suddenly she felt a wave of anger sweep over her. It was all Phoebe's fault! She was, as usual, only thinking about herself. 'Why? Why has she gone?' she shouted, furiously.

'Because she can't stick it here,' Alice snapped, determined not to be ignored.

'But she was the one who first fell in love with the place,' Mary argued. 'She was the one who said she felt it was like coming home . . . which, in a way it was, of course – if she really is a Tyler. Maybe he had a brother. Would that work? If Mr Tyler had a brother – then Phoebe could be his descendant . . .'

'That isn't important now, Mary!' William exclaimed.

'You're getting as bad as William,' Alice said.

'What d'you mean by that?' William asked turning on his younger sister.

'You know,' Alice told him brightly. 'The way you always go rambling off, worrying about all the wrong things . . . !'

'I do not!' William snapped.

'Yes, you do, William,' Alice said in a smug voice. 'It's a well-known fact about you . . . Everyone knows . . . !'

'Oh, do shut up!' Mary exclaimed. 'This is serious!'

'Precisely!' William said. 'That's what I was trying to tell you! The only important thing is that Phoebe's gone off,' then he added, frowning. 'And she's taken Steph . . .'

'No, William!' Mary snapped, annoyed at being interrupted. 'The important thing is that we won't be able to complete the task if she isn't here . . .'

'*No!*' William shouted. 'It's what might happen to Steph that's important. This is real life, Mary!'

'And you mean the task isn't?' Mary asked, turning on him. 'You mean Mr Tyler and all the magic isn't real? Is that what you're saying, Will?'

'Steph's only a baby,' her brother replied. 'She isn't a year old yet. Her life is far more important than anything else, surely? She could be in danger. Phoebe's obviously gone bonkers. We don't know where she's taken Steph . . . you should see Uncle Jack . . . he's obviously worried stiff . . .'

'So the Magician isn't important,' Mary repeated. 'That *is* what you're saying.'

'I'm not! But . . . oh, I don't know!' William shouted. 'I don't know! I think we've got so caught up in it all that we're not seeing the real things any more. What's the point of worrying about whether Steph may one day look after this valley or not? What's the point in worrying about the future? It's the present that matters. It's *now!*'

They were all silent for a moment. Alice scratched her cheek and stared at her feet. Mary sat on the side of her bed with her hands in her pockets and William went and opened the window and leaned out, as though he was hot and breathless and wanted to feel the fresh air on his face.

'It's like one of those things you see on TV news . . .' Mary said at last, speaking to herself. 'Where a child gets kidnapped by one parent and the other one tries to get her back . . . and it all ends up in the law courts . . . tug of love, or whatever they call it.' Then another thought occurred to her. 'If Phoebe and Jack aren't married . . .'

'Which they aren't,' Alice cut in.

'. . . who has the legal right to the baby?' Mary asked.

They all considered this question for a moment.

'I think she'd have to stay with her mother,' Alice said at last.

'Why?' William demanded.

'Because a woman would know how to look after her.'

'So could a man know.'

'Well Uncle Jack certainly couldn't feed her,' Alice said, as if proving her point, 'because he hasn't got breasts!' Then she blushed and wished she hadn't said something which sounded so rude.

'Breast-feeding doesn't go on for ever, Alice,' William retorted, using his know-all voice, and making her blush more. Then, crossing and sitting on Mary's bed, he added, 'does it, Mare?'

'No, of course not!' Mary replied, without paying either of them much attention.

'I should hope not!' Alice mumbled, scratching her cheek again.

'It's like when we first came here, isn't it?' Mary said, pushing her fingers through her hair and looking out of the window. 'There's been trouble ever since before Steph was born . . . I mean, even then, it nearly didn't happen . . .' She frowned. 'You don't suppose . . .'

At that moment the other two looked at her. They had all had the idea at precisely the same moment.

'Morden!' William said. 'All this must be Morden's doing.'

'Or Morden's foul rat,' Mary said. 'Maybe he's scared Phoebe so much that that's why she's gone.'

'But I thought Morden was better now?' Alice cut in. 'I thought he was grateful to us and . . . well, he seemed quite nice when we saw him . . .'

'Morden may now wish he hadn't started things,' Mary agreed, 'he may even wish he could put things right . . . but that wouldn't mean that everything would just go back to the way it was before. I mean – it's like . . . if you squeeze the trigger on a gun and then immediately wish you hadn't . . .'

'. . . changing your mind wouldn't stop the bullet hitting its mark,' William said quietly.

'Precisely!' Mary said. 'Sometimes people change their minds too late.'

'Morden!' William repeated.

'So, in fact, the battle's still on . . .' Mary added, thoughtfully.

'. . . and we seem to be losing it completely,' a mournful voice hooted from somewhere outside the room.

'Jasper!' Mary exclaimed, running to the open window.

The owl was perching precariously further along the steep roof. As soon as he saw Mary, he fluttered over and sat on the sill.

'There you are,' he said. His voice sounded more depressed than usual. He hopped from one foot to the other and then combed his breast feathers with his beak in a distracted way.

'What's the matter, Jasper?' Mary asked, looking at him closely. He didn't look like the owl she knew. All his self-importance, all his superiority and pride seemed to have been stripped away from him. He looked . . . humbled.

'Oooh!' he trilled, blinking and seeming not to want to meet her eyes.

'Jasper?' Mary whispered. A trickle of fear ran down her back, making her shiver. 'What's happened?'

'The world has gone mad, I think,' the great owl replied. 'Nothing you can do, I'm afraid. Nothing anyone can do. Not now that the Master never comes any more. Foolish of us to have relied on him, I suppose. He used to tell us that one day we'd have to look after ourselves . . . but, for it to be now! Now . . . when he's needed so much . . .'

'What's happened?' William asked him, squeezing in next to Mary at the window.

'What hasn't happened, would be a more likely question!' the owl replied. 'There is absolute riot in the woods. None of us is safe.'

'So – it hasn't stopped?' Mary asked, her bright dream of a happy ending breaking into pieces in front of her.

'Stopped?' the owl hooted. 'No, it certainly hasn't stopped. In some respects, it's hardly begun. The creatures are fighting each other. Oh, I'm not just talking about Morden's lot – we're even fighting amongst ourselves. I've just had a distinctly awkward spat with that stuck-up . . . Oooh!' he trilled and shivered at the same time, a wave of suppressed rage sweeping over him. 'I'm all for a quiet life! That's me! Far too many of my relations have been wiped out. I believe in keeping my head down . . . and hoping to survive. But not him! Oh, no!'

'Who?' William demanded.

'He's all for organizing resistance! Resistance! We're outnumbered three to one, I shouldn't wonder.'

'Who are you talking about, Jasper?' Mary demanded.

'That rat!' Jasper replied, indignantly. 'The one who claims to be the Master's creature. All I can say is, I never remember the Master mentioning a rat before! What would be the point of his having a rat? All they're any good at is fighting . . .'

'Then – that might be the point of having one, mightn't it?' William asked, a note of hope creeping into his voice. 'Has Rattus Rattus returned?'

'Oh, yes!' trilled the owl. 'He's returned, all right. And he seems to think that he's in command. I was always the Master's favourite . . .'

'And you still are, I'm sure you are!' Mary told him, reaching out and gently stroking his chest. 'But I don't think he has any one particular favourite . . . I think he has lots of us.'

'Yes!' Jasper said, blinking at her. 'I expect that is exactly what you would think and probably, for you, it is correct. But you are a mere mortal. I am different. The Master and I have a very special relationship . . . We share a common bond. The Master has never been interested in fighting. A good discussion is always far more in his line . . .'

'But,' said William, interrupting this long, mournful tirade, 'discussions aren't going to get us anywhere with Morden's creatures, now are they, Jasper? They won't be interested in debate! Strength is the only argument they'll respect . . .'

'Just tell us what's been happening,' Mary said, 'and we'll see if there's anything we can be doing about it.'

'There are packs of stoats and ferrets scavenging through the woods. Two of our badgers were mobbed by a group of starlings and crows – in the middle of the night! I ask you! Is there no order left? One of our rabbits came upon some ferrets actually attacking one of the farm dogs! A human's animal, being attacked like that. It's unheard of! Sirius has gone to check if it's true. But it will be! It is! These are unnatural times . . . I've been to see Cinnabar. But he's keeping to himself, more's the pity. That fox would be a help. But he's expecting the human hunt any day. You can't blame the beast for being jumpy . . .'

'You haven't any idea where Phoebe and the baby have gone, have you?' William asked him.

'The motor was seen up on the moor road early this morning by Pica, the Master's magpie. I don't know where they've gone now . . .'

'The moor road?' Mary asked. 'Heading towards the town?'

'No,' the owl trilled. 'Towards the Four Fields turn . . .'

'What would she be doing up there?' William said, hurrying towards the door.

'Where are you going, Will?' Alice asked.

'To tell Jack,' William replied, disappearing out on to the landing.

'Tell him what?' Mary said, hurrying to the door after him. 'That a friendly owl has just told us where Phoebe might be?'

William's steps were heard slowing to a halt half-way down the spiral staircase.

'Come back!' Mary told him. 'We must have proper plans this time.' Then, as William followed her back into the room, she turned once more to Jasper and said; 'Where is Rattus calling the meeting?'

'How did you know he was?' Jasper trilled.

'It's obvious. He's come back to lead us into battle, hasn't he?'

'A disastrous idea!' the owl sighed. 'But, yes, that seems to be the plan. We're to meet at the yew tree at dusk. He says that until then we're to keep our heads down and out of harm's way! Which is exactly what I intend to do!' and he launched himself off the sill and sailed away over the roof in the direction of the dovecote, a favourite resting place.

'Right!' said Mary, 'that gives us the rest of the day to try to sort out Phoebe and Jack . . .'

'How are you proposing that we should do that?' William demanded.

'First, by finding her I suppose,' Mary replied. 'We'd better start up at Four Fields.'

'Then what?' Alice asked.

'We talk to her. We tell her she can't leave the Golden Valley. We tell her that this place is Stephanie's birthright.'

And, although both William and Alice doubted they had much chance of getting Phoebe to listen to them and to believe them, they neither of them said so, because Mary had that look that suggested she wasn't going to put up with arguments from anyone.

'Well!' she exclaimed, as if she were reading their thoughts. 'We haven't come all this way to be defeated by Phoebe. Have we?'

Alice and William shook their heads and remained silent.

21
The Enemy Gather

Jack was out on his bike looking for Phoebe when they went downstairs. But Meg was in the kitchen and, as Mary helped herself to a slice of bread and marmalade and a glass of milk, she kept up an endless flow of agitated conversation.

'Things have been getting steadily worse . . . I should have realized . . . What will happen to that poor little babe?'

Whenever one of the children tried to interrupt her, to comfort her, or to reason with her, she would listen for a few moments with wide, staring eyes and then set off again on another tack.

'They should have sold up ages ago . . . The Golden House is no place to bring up a young family . . . I blame Jack as much as I blame her . . . What possessed him to buy it in the first place? It has always been an unhappy house. Always. I should know. I've a good mind to telephone Henry Crawden right this minute and tell him the place is his for the taking . . . then we'll all have done with it . . .'

'No, Meg!' Mary exclaimed. 'You must promise us not to do anything of the sort. Let's find Phoebe first . . . and then make decisions like that . . .'

'Yes, dear! Of course, dear!' Meg told her, as if

she was agreeing, but her eyes still had a far-off look and her mind was already racing somewhere else. 'I thought we should tell the police, but Jack says that at the moment all we could say is that Phoebe's gone off in the motor . . . I can see it doesn't seem like an emergency . . . but it's so unlike her to leave without a word. Where is she? Why has she gone like this? What's the explanation? That's what I'd like to know . . .'

As soon as they could, the children made their escape. Pulling on their anoraks as they went out of the back door, they hurried across the yard and through the walled garden to the forest gate and the deep woods beyond.

It was a bright sunlit day after the rain and the forest smelt clean and tangy. A brisk breeze was blowing that made the air cold on their cheeks, but they felt better at once for being out of the house. They set off at a good pace along the forest track and then struck off up the narrow path that twisted and turned as it climbed the steep cliffs towards the badger sett and the yew tree at the top of the valley.

It was while they were pausing for breath about halfway up that Mary noticed how quiet it was.

'Listen!' she said, drawing William and Alice's attention to the strange, muffled stillness that surrounded them despite the strong breeze that moved through the trees.

'What?' Alice whispered.

'Nothing!' Mary replied, with a frown. 'That's just it. Nothing! No birdsong . . . no animal sounds . . . no dog barking . . . It's so quiet.'

They all listened intently.

'Maybe birds don't sing much in the autumn?' William suggested.

'But it's more than that,' Mary said, looking round at the encircling trees. 'It's as though everything is holding its breath and . . . waiting.'

Alice shivered.

'I wish Spot had come with us,' she said. She glanced nervously over her shoulder, feeling as if she were being watched from every branch and every bush. 'I don't like it much here,' she whispered. 'Let's get up to the top! These woods are a bit spooky.' And she set off again, scrambling up the steep hillside towards the summit that was just coming into view through the branches ahead of them.

'I know what she means,' Mary admitted to William as they followed her. 'It's weird, isn't it? It's such a bright morning . . . and yet there's a sort of darkness everywhere . . .' and she also looked suspiciously at the shadows that pressed in on all sides of them.

They caught Alice up just as she reached the yew tree, its evergreen branches tossing and swaying in a breeze that was much stronger now they were out of the shelter of the valley. Up above, clouds raced across the blue sky, and a big sun came and went casting shadows on the ground, as they passed in front of it.

'Can we stop for a bit?' Mary asked, puffing after the exertion of the climb.

'We'd better not,' William said, glancing at the top of the yew. 'I don't suppose there's any point going up to the tree house, is there?'

'She wouldn't have gone up there,' Mary said. 'I don't think she's ever been. Jack came with us once but, that time, Phoebe stayed down below with

Steph . . . and she's got Steph with her now . . . it'd be impossible to climb up the tree carrying a baby.'

'If she still has got Steph with her,' William said grimly.

'She wouldn't leave her on her own,' Mary protested.

'Normally she wouldn't, I know that,' William agreed. 'But I don't feel anything is very normal now!'

They were all silent as his words sank in. Then Mary shivered and hugged herself for warmth.

'We've got to find them,' she said. 'We must. It's no use us just standing around feeling gloomy!'

'We don't even know if she's gone to Four Fields,' Alice said.

'No, of course we don't!' Mary snapped. 'But where else are we going to start looking?'

As they were passing the standing stone, William asked Mary if she'd brought the pendulum.

'Yes,' she said, feeling in her pocket. 'But why?'

William shrugged.

'We could always try to go back to ask Mr Tyler . . .'

'No. We must find Phoebe and Steph first,' Mary said. 'I couldn't bear to tell him what's happened. I think the news would kill him . . .'

'It isn't as bad as that, is it?' Alice asked.

'Of course it is!' Mary exclaimed. 'For Mr Tyler it couldn't be worse. It will ruin every one of his plans . . .'

All along the edge of Goldenwater the bright autumn leaves danced on the breeze and covered the shore with a carpet of gold and red. The sky, reflecting on the choppy surface of the lake, was wrinkled and broken into flashing light by the waves, and the flat stones at its edge gleamed like shining metal. But, in spite of the splashing water and the rustling branches, there was an overwhelming silence everywhere that seemed to deaden the exuberance of the day and to blanket any sense of joy into dull depression.

Reaching the turning they walked away from the lake and took the path through the woods that led to the hedge skirting the four fields which had once been Meg's farm before her house had been burned down.

Arriving at the gate, they were about to climb over, Alice slightly in advance of the other two, when a scurrying sound made them all look round.

'What was that?' Alice whispered, her nervousness making her voice shake.

William shrugged and took a step towards a mound of dead bracken entwined with tendrils of ivy and sharp-thorned brambles. As he approached it, he picked up a piece of dead branch that had been brought down by the wind. Holding it in his hand made him feel a little more brave, though he wasn't sure how, or on what, he thought he was going to use it. But he was determined not to show the other two how scared he felt, so he prodded the mound of undergrowth a few times. Then, when nothing happened he turned his back on it with considerable relief and started to walk back to the girls.

'William!' Mary screamed. 'Behind you! William!'

Spinning round he was just in time to see a big grey squirrel leaping towards him, with its claws open wide. Taken completely by surprise, William dodged and hit out with the branch he was holding, swinging it like a cricket bat. He caught the squirrel a sharp blow on the side of its body that sent it spinning and turning through the air. It landed on its feet some distance from them and turned and skittered away into the dense bushes and out of their sight.

'I hope I didn't hurt it,' William muttered. 'It took me so by surprise.'

'It was coming straight for you!' Alice gasped.

'I don't suppose it was really,' William said but, as he reached the gate and started to climb over it, he noticed that his legs were shaking.

'You know it was!' Mary whispered, with a look of absolute terror on her face. 'What was it going to do to you?'

'Nothing!' William said, trying to make his voice sound calm. 'I expect I gave it a shock, prodding about in the undergrowth, and it just jumped the wrong way.'

But it seemed a feeble excuse and they walked in silence across the field, glad to be out in the open, away from all the trees and bushes. At least now they would be able to see any creature approaching them.

'It had such big claws,' Alice said, speaking to herself.

'They just use them to climb trees, Al!' William said, trying to reassure himself as much as her.

Reaching the next gate they were able to see the corner of the field where Meg's house stood. Its fire-blackened windows and door were now almost completely obscured by the creepers and bushes that had grown in profusion since she had been away and there had been no one there to hack at them and keep them in some kind of order.

208

'When we first came here,' Alice said, 'I remember being amazed that there was a house here at all.'

The fire had raged through the place, eating up most of the wooden beams and the furniture. But the walls were built of stone and were still standing and some of the roof was in place. Even the front door, charred and blackened as it had been by the heat of the flames, still hung by one hinge and leaned in a lop-sided manner across the opening.

'It looks so sad,' Mary said, hanging back, not wanting to go inside.

'She's not here, is she?' Alice asked.

'We'd better go in and look all the same,' William said. But he also hesitated. It was as though all of them felt some evil was waiting just across the threshold.

'I wish Mr Tyler was here now,' Alice said in a small voice. 'I wish he was here more than I've ever wished he was here before.'

'The pendulum, Mary,' William whispered. 'Maybe, if you just held it up, it'd give us a bit of . . . power?'

Mary felt in her pocket and, wrapping her fingers and thumb tightly round the chain, she pulled the lump of gold out and held it up so that it hung, glittering in the morning light.

Almost instantaneously, all around them, the sound of birds screaming and complaining excitedly broke the solid silence.

The children swung round, Mary still holding the pendulum out in front of her. Every branch of every distant tree was covered with birds, mainly crows and starlings, with some magpies and a few grim, staring sparrowhawks. The margin of the field down at ground level was thick with rabbits and rats, ferrets, stoats and weasels. Squirrels clung to the hedges. A fox crouched in some long grass.

Nothing stirred. The children were surrounded by a great wall of staring eyes. The sound the creatures made had dropped to an ominous growl. They didn't move. They simply stood their ground, staring and grumbling in low, threatening voices.

'You've seen them?' a voice behind them said and, looking back quickly, they saw Phoebe standing just inside the hall of the fallen house holding Stephanie closely in her arms.

'Phoebe!' William whispered. 'You shouldn't be here! And certainly not with Steph.'

'They followed me,' Phoebe said quietly. 'When I got up and went down to the kitchen, I heard this noise out in the yard. I thought it was you. The Land-Rover keys were on the dresser. I remember picking them up as I went towards the door. I don't know why. The idea came from somewhere . . . I went out into the yard . . . and across to the Land-Rover. I wasn't going anywhere. I just . . .' she shrugged. 'It was as if I was doing everything in a dream, as if I was sleep-walking . . . I strapped Steph into her seat in the back and then I was going back to get my coat. But . . . when I turned round . . . the yard was crammed with rats . . .' There were tears in her voice and an edge of panic. 'So I climbed in and . . . drove away. I thought I'd just go as far as the phone box on the moor road and telephone Jack . . . to warn you all. But, when I got there, there was a rat inside the box . . . I was so scared . . .' She started to shake violently, holding Stephanie in her arms and burying her head in the baby's shoulder.

'It's all right! It's all right, Phoebe,' Mary said, putting an arm round her. 'You must be brave – for Steph. We've all got to be!'

'They just sit there,' Phoebe said, looking up again and staring at the creatures. 'I thought of going back to the Land-Rover . . . but I haven't got the courage.'

'I'm not surprised,' William said grimly. 'But we're here now.'

'What can you do? What can anyone do? I've been trying to warn Jack for months . . . but he wouldn't believe me.'

'Warn him?' William asked.

'There is something very odd going on. The rats in the house . . . the feel of the place. What can we do?' Phoebe wailed.

'A lot,' Mary said determinedly, looking at the pendulum still dangling from her finger and thumb. 'We can beat them . . . somehow. We can restore order to this place. There isn't a single creature over there that is actually evil. The evil is in the way they're behaving . . .'

'But what can we do about it?' Phoebe whispered. 'I didn't want Jack to kill them . . . I still don't . . .' she shook her head. 'I'm so afraid . . .' she whispered.

As they were speaking they were not looking at each other. Their eyes were constantly fixed on the battalions of wild creatures that faced them across the field.

'If only Spot was here,' Alice sighed.

'And Rattus,' Mary said.

William frowned.

'One of us has to get away . . .'

As he said the words a tiny creature appeared

211

out of the rough grass at his feet. It came so quietly that it was a moment before any of them noticed it sitting patiently staring up at them. Then Alice glanced down and gasped with surprise.

'What is it?' Alice asked.

'A shrew,' Phoebe said, taking a step away from it. 'This place is crawling with creatures. They must outnumber us ten times over. We don't stand a chance . . .'

'But this one's so tiny,' Alice whispered.

'Yes,' William agreed, doubtfully, 'but is it one of ours or theirs?'

'It keeps staring at us . . .' Mary said, then, with a gasp, she felt the pendulum start to tug in her hand. 'Oh!' she exclaimed.

'What, Mary?' Phoebe asked, the panic coming back into her voice. 'What's happened? What's that necklace in your hand? What is going on?'

'It's OK, Phoebe, honestly it is,' Mary said, quickly closing her fist over the pendulum. 'Um . . . Alice, d'you think you and Phoebe should go inside . . .'

'What?' Alice demanded indignantly. 'Why?'

'I was just thinking, it might be a good idea to have somewhere to sit . . . out of this cold wind . . . for the sake of the baby . . .' As she spoke, Mary was glaring at Alice, willing her to understand and not to ask questions.

'I'm not going in there!' Alice said.

'Yes, you are!' William suddenly announced, realizing that Mary was trying to get rid of Phoebe. As he spoke he pushed Alice towards the doorway, whispering in her ear as he did so: 'Get her inside, Alice! We need her out of the way.'

'Oh!' Alice exclaimed, with a sudden grin. 'Yes,

212

of course! Come on, Phoebe! I'm frozen!' and she put an arm round her and steered her and Stephanie back into the hallway.

'Will,' Mary said, as soon as they were alone, 'you're fastest. You'll have to go. You need to get to the phone box on the moor road. Phone Meg at the house and explain what's happened. Then she can tell Jack where we are, when he gets back. Maybe you should ask her to phone Mr Jenkins and tell him. He could come for us if Jack is still out . . . and his dogs could be useful. If only Spot was here . . . Never mind! Have you got change for the phone?'

'Yes, but – what am I supposed to say?' William protested.

'Just tell her what's happened. Meg will believe you – it'll be up to her to convince the others. Tell her that the birds and the animals are behaving peculiarly. Tell her that we're all up at Four Fields – scared out of our wits . . .'

'Even if Meg believes us, the others will only laugh!'

'Then let them laugh,' Mary cried, her nervousness making her tremble all over, 'just make her get them to come quickly . . .' And, as she finished speaking, she handed him the Magician's pendulum. 'You'll need this. The shrew will take you . . .'

'I can't . . .' William said, sounding desperate.

'Oh, don't be such a wimp, William!'

'No! I mean . . . I can't leave you all here.'

'You can! You've got to! Now hurry . . . !' and as she said those last words, she glanced at the shrew, still sitting patiently at their feet. With a sudden movement it leaped into the air and turned in a circle. Then, without a backward glance, it darted into the tall grass of the meadow and when Mary turned back to William she found that he also had disappeared. She quickly scanned the distant trees, but none of the waiting birds, nor the squirrels, nor any of the creatures on the ground seemed to have noticed his departure. They continued to grumble and stare, hissing and squawking threateningly but, as yet, without making any move towards the house.

'Good luck, Will!' she whispered. Then, stepping backwards very slowly, as though she were afraid that the slightest movement on her part might provoke an attack, she withdrew into the house.

22
Battle Stations

William and the shrew darted through a jungle of thick, damp grass. It towered over their heads forming a roof that blotted out the sky.

The shrew was strangely quiet. William couldn't get inside its head at all. He asked it one or two questions, but the only reply that he got was a rather loud and agitated squeak. So, apart from telling the creature that he wanted to get to the moor road, he decided to save his energy for the journey.

Their movement was so light that their feet hardly seemed to touch the ground. It was more as though they were flying through the grass than walking.

Once the shrew stopped suddenly and William could feel their heart beating with fear. Listening intently he heard something moving in the undergrowth to the side of them. Whatever it was sounded heavy and large. The shrew held its breath, watching and waiting and, a moment later, a hedgehog shambled past them.

'Ours or theirs?' William thought.

The shrew gave no reply but turned again and continued its nervous, high-speed dash through the jungle. Sometimes they reached clumps of grass so thick and matted together that they had to make detours to avoid them. Once or twice William had a nasty feeling that they were running in quite the opposite direction to the one in which he thought they should be going. But they had swerved and dodged so much that it was impossible for him to keep his bearings. The only other living creature that they met was an earthworm. For a moment, to his horror, William was tempted to eat it. But then either he, or his host the shrew, realized that there wasn't time. So, with a lingering look, and a definite watering of the mouth, they let it slide past and together they forced their four claws to an even greater speed, until they were skimming along, parting the grass in front of them like a plough and feeling it swish back behind after they had passed through.

Eventually, leaping a broad ditch which was filled with water, they scrambled up a rough bank and found themselves on the forest track.

'No further!' the shrew squeaked.

Those were the only words that William was ever to hear it say. For a moment later two events occurred in quick succession.

First, William saw the Magician's pendulum in the palm of his hand where Mary had placed it and he realized that he and the shrew had separated and then, immediately after this, a magpie lunged down out of the sky and scooped the shrew up into its beak with a sickening crunch.

'Delicious!' a harsh, guttural voice declared and William swallowed hard, feeling the tiny creature sliding down his own throat.

'Oh!' he exclaimed. 'That was revolting!'

'Not to me,' the voice whispered in his head and,

stretching his wings, William took flight in the black and white bird.

'Pleased to meet you, William!' the voice whispered. 'I'm Pica, the Master's magpie. I had hoped that Mary would come. Mary and I got on very well. She was a spunky fighter in that skirmish we had over Goldenwater during the summer. But I'm afraid that today's encounter is going to be a much bigger affair . . .'

'Hang on a minute!' William exclaimed. 'That shrew was on our side!'

'It didn't really want to be on any side,' Pica said. 'It was persuaded to come and get you . . .'

'How persuaded?'

'I promised I wouldn't eat it.'

'But you did! You just have!'

'I didn't say for how long!'

'You're horrible!'

'Where d'you want to go, little boy?' the magpie squawked.

'To the phone box on the moor road . . . and then to Rattus.'

'Be my guest!' the magpie mocked and, turning in a loop, the bird and William together flew low through the trees along the side of the track.

'Don't want to break cover at the moment,' Pica whispered. 'The enemy are everywhere. Bit of luck I spotted you . . .'

'How did you?' William asked.

'The pendulum! There are scouts out all over the area looking for you. Even Cinnabar has been persuaded to show his head.'

'Cinnabar?' William said, glad to hear news of his friend. 'Is he all right?'

'As right as a fox can be at this time of year . . . So! Here's the moor road . . .'

'And there's the phone box,' William whispered as Pica and he broke the cover of the trees and flew silently along the line of the narrow lane.

'No one about, as yet,' Pica said, darting his head from side to side. 'I'll wait for you in the trees over there,' and landing on the hard surface of the road near to the telephone box, he hopped from one leg to the other and fluttered his wings.

'Thanks, Pica!' William said scrambling towards the door of the box and feeling in his pocket for some money. 'I still think it was rotten of you, eating that shrew.'

'I'm inclined to agree,' the bird replied. 'I swallowed it too fast. It's given me indigestion!' and with a squawk of cruel laughter he flew away low over the ground and in amongst the fir and pine trees that crowded the edge of the lane.

* * *

Phoebe and Alice were in the room that had once been Meg's kitchen when Mary came in. Phoebe was still carrying Stephanie, who was crying miserably. The room had once been crammed with Meg's belongings, but now the table and the old armchair, the cupboards and stools and innumerable packing boxes were only charred remains. For this was where the fire had been at its most furious after the rat had struck the match that ignited the paraffin.

'Ugh! It still smells foul, doesn't it?' Mary said, stepping in through the open doorway.

'And I'm not at all sure that it's safe,' Phoebe added, looking up at the sagging ceiling overhead. 'If that roof comes down . . .'

'Well, where else can we go?' Alice said, her nerves beginning to snap.

'We'll have to wait here . . .' Mary said.

'Where's William?' Phoebe asked.

'He's gone . . . for help,' Mary replied.

'But – if he's managed to get away, we all can!' Phoebe exclaimed, pushing past Mary and going out into the hall, carrying Stephanie with her.

'No, Phoebe!' Mary said, hurrying after her, followed by Alice.

Phoebe had already reached the front door. She stepped out into the bright sunlight.

'It's better outside, anyway!' she said, her eyes sweeping the distant hedgerow and the trees beyond it. 'They're still there,' she continued, sounding disappointed. 'What are they waiting for?'

'I don't know,' Mary said, her eyes on the mass of birds and animals that surrounded them.

'It's me, isn't it?' Phoebe said. 'It's all got something to do with me.'

'In a way,' Mary nodded.

'What is it all about?' Phoebe asked. 'You must tell me.'

'It's a bit difficult, Phoebe,' Mary said.

'You must try,' Phoebe pleaded with her as she cradled Stephanie against her, trying to calm and comfort her. The baby turned towards her, tears on her cheeks and her nose running . . . then reaching out her little hand she took hold of the necklace hanging round Phoebe's throat. It was the pendant that Jack had given her for Christmas, the one he had found in the hall fireplace at Golden House. An oval frame of dark red metal contained a golden sun and a silver moon.

219

'Of course!' Mary said in a voice no more than a whisper.

'What, Mare?' Alice asked her.

'Phoebe's necklace!' Mary said.

'What about it?' Alice asked.

'Yes, what about it?' Phoebe agreed.

'You never take it off, do you?' Mary said.

'Only at night. I love it . . .'

'Have you ever wondered about it?' Mary asked her.

'Often,' Phoebe replied. 'We've had it looked at as well. It is made of gold and silver. But the red metal is a bit of a mystery. It's apparently some sort of amalgam . . . though amalgam should usually be silver or white . . . you know, like they use for filling teeth!'

'Filling teeth?' Alice exclaimed, not hiding the fact that she obviously thought Phoebe had finally gone mad.

'I know!' Phoebe laughed. 'But the jeweller who had it analysed for us said that was the nearest he could get. Apparently the stuff they fill teeth with is made of mercury mixed with silver . . . or it used to be. I can't believe it still is! Anyway, this red metal also contains mercury, with gold and silver in it . . . But the red colour is a complete mystery . . . It might possibly be coloured with cinnabar . . .'

'Cinnabar?' Alice exclaimed. 'That's the name of our fox!'

'Your fox?' Phoebe sounded surprised. 'I didn't know you had one.'

'It's a long story,' Alice answered gravely. 'What's cinnabar?'

'You'd have to ask Jack that – he's the one who

trained as a chemist!' Phoebe replied. 'It's some sort of pigment, I think taken from a mineral . . . I don't know!'

'Can I look, Phoebe?' Mary said suddenly.

'Look? At what?' Phoebe asked, surprised.

'The pendant, would you mind?'

'Now?'

'I just want to look at it. You don't mind, do you?' and, reaching round behind Phoebe, Mary unfastened the clasp on the chain round her neck.

The necklace slipped away from Phoebe's throat and Stephanie held it in her tiny hand. Mary reached and took it from her, the baby giving no resistance. Then, holding the fine chain, she let the pendant fall and swing in front of her.

Across the field the birds started to scream and flap their wings and the animals in the hedgerow visibly reacted, jumping up and down, impatiently.

'Of course!' Mary said, staring at the pendant.

'What? What? Tell me what you're talking about!' Phoebe exclaimed.

'This pendant was made by Stephen Tyler,' Mary explained.

'Stephen who?' Phoebe asked.

'Tyler,' Mary said, irritated by how slowly Phoebe's mind worked. 'You've heard of him lots of times. He used to live at Golden House. He was a . . .' she stopped herself from saying the word "magician". '. . . a sort of chemist.'

'An alchemist,' Phoebe said, nodding. 'I remember now. Miss Prewett mentioned him . . .'

'And he was one of your ancestors, wasn't he?' Mary said, looking at Phoebe.

'Was he? Maybe. Yes, I think our family used to spell our name differently. Dad talked about it. He was quite keen on the family tree. But I wasn't into all that, so I never really listened to him. I rather wish I had now . . . Now it's too late. But I'm sure our family never lived in this area. We are supposed to have been yeoman farmers . . . from Warwickshire.'

'Yes – but they were somehow related to the man who used to live at Golden House, Stephen Tyler. When he died he left the estate to his assistant, Matthew Morden. Maybe your ancestors didn't want to give up their farm . . . or, more likely, Mr Tyler would feel that Golden House should go to Morden . . .'

'How do you know all this?' Phoebe asked, looking puzzled. Mary shrugged and dodged the question.

'A lot of it's in that book Jack borrowed from Miss Prewett,' she said.

'Oh, yes! Of course,' Phoebe nodded.

'But now, Phoebe, Golden House has a Tyler living in it again. This place is Stephanie's birthright. You mustn't take her away and let the Crawdens move back in. You mustn't, Phoebe!'

Phoebe seemed very moved by Mary's words. She shook her head and there were tears in her eyes.

'I honestly don't want to. I love the place. You know I do. It was me that first wanted to move in there. Only now – with everything that's happened . . . I feel so threatened. It's as though something . . . evil . . . or as though someone . . . doesn't want us there.'

'That's all going to change,' Mary said firmly.

'While you two are yabbering,' Alice said

urgently, 'something seems to be going on over there . . .'

They looked in the direction of the woods once more. Birds were now rising up out of the trees in swarms, flying in low circles, squawking and screaming.

'Oh, help!' Mary said quietly. 'I think it's starting!'

'I wish Spot would come,' Alice said in a whisper. 'I'd feel much safer then.'

'I wish Mr Tyler was here,' Mary said, not taking her eyes for a second off the birds.

'And I just wish that Jack and Steph and I were at home together,' Phoebe said and she knew in her heart that when she said 'home' she meant Golden House.

* * *

Jack turned into the drive and crunched to a halt outside the front door. He was exhausted and deeply troubled. He knew the time had come when he'd have to phone the police. He'd gone as far as the town and then realized that he was on a complete wild goose chase. Phoebe and Steph could be anywhere by now. They could be on one of the motorways; they could have driven to Druce Coven Halt and taken a train. He had no idea where to look, because he had no idea where or why she had gone in the first place. He blamed himself for all that had happened. For months Phoebe had been trying to tell him, to warn him that things were not as they should be and he had refused to listen to her.

The rats in the house should have brought them together; she had been insisting that there was a rat in the house ever since they'd moved in but at

223

first he hadn't believed her. Then, more recently she'd said that there were more than one and still he'd not listened. Finally, when he'd seen for himself that she was right, instead of telling her and the two of them facing the problem together, he'd put down traps in secret and hidden the facts from her. No wonder she was angry. No wonder she thought he was treating her shamefully. The rows had been getting worse . . . and it was all his fault. Yes, Stephanie hadn't been giving them much rest recently; yes, he was worried about money; yes, things had been getting on top of him, but: 'I'm to blame for all this', he told himself, 'because I haven't been sharing things with her. I've been excluding her. I've been hoping that if I close my eyes to the problems they'll go away. So, now I've pushed her too far; and she's gone, taking Steph with her . . .'

He opened the front door and went inside the house. As he did so, the telephone was ringing in the hall and Meg had come out of the kitchen and was on the point of picking up the receiver.

'Hello?' she said, speaking nervously into the headset and glancing at the front door at the same time.

'Is it her?' Jack asked, crossing the hall at a run.

'William?' Meg said, raising her voice as though she felt she had to shout to be heard. 'Where are you?'

Jack took the receiver out of Meg's hand.

'William?' he said. 'What's happened? Where are you? I can't hear you? Will? Are you there? William?' He shook the receiver and jiggled the phone rest. 'It's gone dead,' he said. Then he lifted the headset back to his mouth and ear and shouted,

'William! William! He's been cut off!' he said, his voice full of disappointment. 'The line's gone dead. What did he say, Meg?'

'Well, dear, he'd hardly started really. I answered the contraption and . . . I heard his voice. He said, "We've found them" . . . and then I didn't hear any more and you took the machine out of my hand.'

'He's found them?' Jack said, relief flooding his voice. 'Thank God for that! Where? Where did the children say they were going?'

'I don't know dear. They just went out for a walk. I don't think they said where . . .'

'They can't just have gone out for a walk. They must have been looking for Steph and Phoebe. Which is the nearest phone box?'

'It depends which direction you're taking, dear. There's the one near the Jenkins' farm and the one up near my turning . . . I can't think of any others.'

'I'll have to go and look in both places,' Jack said, hurrying across the hall, 'I'll try the Jenkins first.' Then, as he reached the front door and went outside, Meg heard him exclaim, 'What the hell's he doing here?'

'Who, dear?' Meg called, hurrying after him.

'You'll have to cope, Meg. I can't stop now,' and, by the time she'd reached the front door he was already on his bike with the engine revving.

'No, wait, dear . . . !' she called after him, fear and agitation sweeping over her, for there, coming up the drive, was the Crawden's Rolls Royce and the last thing she wanted was to have to face Henry Crawden on her own. But Jack had already turned his bike and swinging wide to avoid the car, he drove away fast.

* * *

'Nothing!' William shouted. 'Nothing!' He could feel tears welling up in his throat, strangling his voice. 'The line went dead! Now what do I do?'

'We go find Rattus Rattus,' Pica the Magician's magpie croaked hopping down on to the road in front of him.

'No!' William said, losing his temper and fighting back tears at the same time. 'I wanted Jack to know . . .'

'We go find Rattus Rattus,' Pica insisted. 'He's running this show. He'll be livid if we don't. Now, no arguments, little boy! You trust me! Come on!' and before William had a chance to protest he felt himself being overwhelmed by the magpie and forced to spread his wings.

'Is it far?' he whispered.

'Not as the crow flies!' Pica answered and squawked a harsh laugh.

* * *

The rat eased himself down off the ledge. It had been easy biting through the wires. Now the humans couldn't talk to each other. Humans relied on talking, it was the only way they seemed to manage to communicate. Poor humans! The sooner they were beaten into submission the better.

As he sidled across the floor towards the door he could see the old woman on the front step. She was talking to a man in a wheelchair.

The rat paused, judging his distance, and then with a surge of energy he launched himself towards the door and ran between the old woman's legs. On the other side of her, standing beside the old man's wheelchair, was a small boy.

The child screamed.

'A rat!' he wailed. 'It ran between your feet!'

226

'Pull yourself together, Mark!' the old man said. 'Summers,' he called and the chauffeur, who was lounging against the side of the car, moved towards him, 'wheel me back! And you, Meg, come with us. We must find them . . .'

'No,' Meg said, taking a step backwards. But the old man stopped her with a look.

'Meg,' he said gently. 'Time to bury the past! We can't undo what has happened, but we don't need to live in its shadow for the rest of our lives, do we?'

Meg stared solemnly at Henry Crawden. For a moment she could see his young face, the face that had broken her heart, the face she still loved.

'We haven't much of our lives left, you and I, Henry!' she said with a glimmer of a smile.

'Then let's make the most of what we have,' Henry Crawden told her. Then his voice became very businesslike. 'But first let us resolve this affair.'

'How?' Meg gasped.

'Find the children and tell Mr Green and his lady that a few rats shouldn't drive them away from this place. Golden House needs a young family. It needs love and care . . . it needs them. Summers! Get me out of this confounded chair and into the car, man!'

As the chauffeur and the old man negotiated the complicated but familiar manoeuvre, the small boy turned to Meg.

'Can I come and play with them sometimes?' he asked.

'The children aren't often here, dear. They go away to school.'

'I meant during the holidays,' Mark Crawden told her.

'I expect so, dear,' Meg said, following him into the car. 'But you'd have to ask them about that.'

'Where to, Meg?' Henry Crawden asked her.

'Four Fields, dear,' Meg said quietly. 'We'll start up at Four Fields.'

As the Rolls Royce turned on the drive, the rat was already heading up the steep cliffs behind the house on the way to his army.

* * *

Rattus Rattus had miscalculated badly. All the signs suggested that the enemy was going to attack in daylight. He hadn't thought they'd dare. He had issued orders for the troops to muster at the yew tree in the late afternoon. Now he'd had to send out scouts to call them in early.

It was a hopeless situation – and it was all his fault.

He paced backwards and forwards, fretting and fuming. He was still waiting for news of the children. The dog, Sirius, had brought word that the mother and child were missing. It was all getting out of control.

'I must steady myself,' he thought. 'You can't lead an army into battle with panic in your heart!'

He had been getting ominous rumours all morning. A hedgehog had been sighted. A hedgehog at this time of year! It should be starting its winter sleep, not out and about. Two squirrels had been found fighting to the death; squirrel against squirrel!

'It's civil war!' he thought, turning and pacing in the other direction. 'Civil war is the worst. If brother is against brother, then who can one trust?'

He turned and paced away again.

'You'll wear a rut in my floor,' Trish, the badger told him.

The badgers had let him billet in their sett.

228

Although they were naturally nervous of a rat, this one was after all the Master's rat.

'If only the Master could come,' Trish said.

'Not possible,' Rattus said, gravely. 'This is one fight we'll have to do on our own.'

'Oh dear!' said Trish, 'I don't know about that.'

'That's why I'm here,' Rattus told her. 'I'm in command.'

'Yes?' Trish said and silently wondered why, if he was in command, he seemed in such a nervous state.

'Because, badger,' the rat answered her thoughts sternly, 'I'm really a sea-going rat. Put me in charge of a boarding party and you couldn't ask for a better leader.'

'Well,' Trish said, 'pretend you're at sea, dear. Whatever "sea" is!' Trish had never seen any water broader than Goldenwater and had never ventured further than Blackscar Quarry.

'Haven't you anything you should be getting on with?' Rattus asked, stifling his irritation.

The badger closed her eyes.

'I suppose I could sleep,' she said. 'It is, after all daytime. It's just that your pacing keeps me awake.'

'Go to sleep, good animal!' Rattus said more kindly. 'Only the captain never sleeps! And I am the captain of this ship . . .' As he spoke he felt in his imagination the salt spray on his whiskers and he heard the boards creak and the rigging slap. For a moment he was on the prow of the *Revenge* with the gale at his back as God's mighty wind blew the Spanish fleet round the Eddystone and up towards Start Point and his captain, the mighty Drake, with Hawkins in the *Victory* and Frobisher in the *Triumph*

229

closed on the *San Juan de Portugal* and the first blood of the great Armada was drawn.

'Happy days!' Rattus sighed and then he began to sing quietly:

'Drake is in his hammock,
And a thousand miles away . . .'

And his pacing steps became lighter until he almost skipped with pleasure and twirled with excitement.

Trish, the badger, half opened her eyes and watched him. Then she smiled. Better let him be, she thought, he's got a big day ahead of him.

* * *

Cinnabar saw the black and white bird dropping out of the sky towards him as he was racing up the steep bank towards the badger sett.

'The battle's starting!' Pica called. 'We can see the enemy massing round Four Fields! That's where the woman is with the baby and the girls . . .'

'Where's the boy?' Cinnabar asked.

'I'm here, Cinnabar,' William said in a whisper and, as he spoke he separated from Pica and stood in front of the fox.

They looked at each other deeply. The fox's eyes smouldered like burnt toffee, deep and penetrating.

'Hello, little boy!' he said.

'Hello, Cinnabar!'

'I'm going to tell Rattus Rattus where the battle will be,' Pica squawked. 'You two meet us at Four Fields. We'll need every body we can muster . . .' and the magpie flew away towards the yew tree and the badger sett.

'I thought you were going to be my friend,' Cinnabar said, his breath smoking on the bright air.

'I am,' William gasped.

230

'You never come to see me,' the fox said.

'I'm always so busy,' William mumbled.

'I've never had a human friend. Don't really like humans. Apart from the Master – but he's different. I thought you and I . . . D'you remember when we chased through the snow? When the baby was being born?'

'Of course I do!' William said. 'You saved my life that day.'

'Didn't.'

'You did. I'd have frozen to death in that blizzard.'

'I thought . . .' the fox suddenly stopped speaking and raised his head. 'Listen!'

'What?' William asked.

'Listen!'

William strained forward trying hard to pick up the sound that had so obviously affected Cinnabar.

'I can't hear anything,' he said at last . . . but then, a moment later, he heard what it was that had captured the fox's attention.

A long clear note blown on a horn.

'The Hunt is up!' Cinnabar said. Then he turned once more and searched deep into William's eyes. 'Well, boy. Will you be hunted with me, or must we part again?'

'I'll stay with you,' William replied without a moment's hesitation.

'Right!' a voice whispered in his head. 'Let's lead those hounds a merry dance, shall we? You and I? Let's show them the Golden Vale!' and, with a bark of defiance, he and William together plunged downhill towards the sound of the horn.

'But you're going towards them!' William gasped.

'Certainly!' Cinnabar yapped. 'They need to know where we are in order to hunt us, don't they?'

'Do we want to be hunted?'

'Wait and see!' the voice whispered.

23
The Battle Royal

Mary led the way, running fast through the long grass. Behind her Phoebe moved more slowly, afraid of dropping the baby. Alice kept up the rear, as she'd agreed to do when they'd been standing in the doorway of the ruined house. It had been a simple plan. Mary would get to the Land-Rover first. She'd open the driving door for Phoebe and put the key in the ignition. Then she'd climb into the back of the motor so that, when Phoebe and Stephanie arrived, she'd be there to take the baby from Phoebe and to strap her into her seat while Phoebe started the engine. Meanwhile Alice would go round to the passenger side and get in the front beside Phoebe.

That had been the plan and that was what they were now trying to do. But once they were out of the cover of the house it seemed a pretty flimsy scheme.

As soon as Mary appeared, the noise of the birds rose to a deafening roar and the chattering and squeaking of the creatures on the ground added a strange and ominous counter-melody.

Then a crow separated from the main group and with a terrible, squawking ferocity it lunged down out of the sky screaming and flapping. Mary put her hands over her head and didn't allow herself to falter. But, behind her, Phoebe's steps slowed as she watched in disbelief the bird fly at Mary, it's beak snapping and its claws outstretched.

'Look out!' she gasped but then behind her she heard Alice's desperate voice hurrying her forward once more.

'Go on, Phoebe!' Alice yelled. 'Run! We can't turn back now! They've cut us off from behind . . .'

'What?' Phoebe gasped, looking round.

The grass behind Alice was moving as though a scythe was swishing through it. But Alice's desperate and determined face made her turn back in the direction of the forest track.

'Mary's nearly there!' Alice shouted, encouraging the older woman on and wanting to believe it herself.

Meanwhile ahead of them they could see Mary flapping her arms, warding off the bird's attack.

'Go away, crow!' she snarled. 'You and I have no argument. Just go away!'

The Land-Rover was in sight now. But over to her right she could see a squirrel prancing towards her, its delicate steps skimming across the surface of the ground. It had a far greater speed than she and was cutting off her line of escape.

'Hell!' she exclaimed aloud.

'What?' Phoebe asked.

'It's all right!' Mary panted.

'They're all coming!' Alice exclaimed, panic rising in her voice. What she had seen that prompted this outcry was a wave of scurrying, snapping stoats tumbling over each other in excitement as they hurled themselves towards the humans.

'Run, Mary! Please! Run!' Alice screamed as the panting, squeaking, chattering horde grew closer.

Now, in front of her, the squirrel turned to face Mary. It was standing between her and the Land-Rover, completely blocking her way. Its front claws were raised and its tail swished threateningly.

'Oh, come on!' Mary thought, 'it's only a squirrel!' and as the vicious creature leaped at her, she ducked quickly to the side, dodging past it, and running fast for the Land-Rover.

The squirrel landed on the ground immediately in front of Phoebe and the baby. As both Phoebe's hands were engaged in holding Stephanie securely, there was nothing she could possibly do to ward it off if it decided to jump at her. She cried out, instinctively covering the baby's face and began running in an arc to avoid it.

'Keep going, Phoebe,' a tense voice whispered just behind her. 'I've seen it!' and, as the squirrel jumped again, Alice leaped at it with a bloodcurdling scream that took her by surprise and sent the squirrel jibbering with fear back to the safety of its friends.

'Well done, Al!' Phoebe shouted, running forward once more.

'Well, honestly!' Alice exclaimed. 'I've had enough of all this . . .' and swinging round she ran straight at the line of stoats hoping to scare them in the same way. But they had the security of the group on their side. There were so many of them that they hardly seemed to notice her. Instead they came leaping and snapping around her legs.

'Oh!' screamed Alice. 'Wrong!' and she turned, kicking out with her legs and ran as fast as she could in pursuit of Phoebe. As she did so, a stoat at the head of the pack leaped at her arm, sinking its claws and teeth into the material of her anorak. 'Oh, get off me!' she screamed, trying to shake it away. 'Get off me! Get off me!'

Just when it seemed that this final attack would break her courage a movement in the grass beside her made her look round.

With a terrible savage snarling, a black and white dog appeared.

'Spot!' Alice shouted. 'Oh, thank God!'

'Not now, Al!' the dog barked. 'Save all the talk for after. Get to the Land-Rover and leave me to sort this lot out . . .' Then his voice turned into a furious barking and when Alice next looked back he was rolling over and over, snapping and snarling, as he went in amongst the stoat brigade.

When Mary reached the Land-Rover and was opening the door she heard Phoebe, behind her, call out her name. Feeling in her pocket for the ignition key, she turned and held out her other hand to pull the woman and the baby towards her.

'In, in!' she insisted, bundling them both into the Land-Rover. Then, slamming the door, she ran back to where Alice was running towards her, still fighting off the stoat on her sleeve.

'Here, Al! Let me!' she yelled and she grabbed at the creature with her bare hands and dragged it away kicking and squealing.

'Oh, Mare!' Alice wailed. 'It's so vile!'

'Don't give in now!' Mary shouted, flinging the creature away into the grass and grabbing hold of Alice's hand.

Together they covered the short distance to the Land-Rover and scrambled into the passenger side.

Then slamming the door behind them, they collapsed into an exhausted, puffing heap.

'Give me the key, Mary!' Phoebe said tensely.

'The key!' Mary wailed. Both her hands were empty. 'I had it when I dragged that horrible ratty thing off Alice . . . Oh, no!' she groaned.

'What?' Alice sobbed.

'I haven't got it. It must have . . . I must have . . .' she stared desperately out of the window.

'Must have what?' Alice whispered.

'Thrown it away when I was getting the animal off you,' Mary said quietly.

'Now what do we do?' Phoebe whispered, rocking Stephanie backwards and forwards as she wailed miserably.

'We'll just have to wait,' Mary said. 'I am sorry . . .'

'Wasn't your fault,' Alice told her, putting an arm through hers and holding her close for courage and warmth. 'At least they can't get in here. Can they?'

'Shouldn't think so,' Mary replied as she continued to search her pockets hoping to find the key. Her fingers closed round an unfamiliar object. 'I've still got your necklace, Phoebe,' she said, producing the pendant.

'Don't worry about that now,' Phoebe told her. 'Just keep it safe for me.'

'Oh, Mr Tyler!' Mary thought, gripping it in her clenched hand. 'I wish you were here now.'

* * *

'Cervus!' the old man called. 'Come to me, my deer. We must have one last try.'

He was standing by the forest gate. The first frost

237

of winter was hanging late on the boughs. The air crackled with cold.

'Master Tyler,' Kate called from the house. 'Come in! Come in!'

'A moment Kate,' the old man shouted. 'It is such a . . . bonny morning. Give me a moment longer. Who knows when I will see another morning like this one?'

'All right!' he heard the voice reply. 'But not for too long mind.'

'Dear Kate!' he murmured and then Cervus appeared, her golden collar gleaming in the autumn sunlight.

'My Cervus,' he sighed, reaching out a loving hand as the red deer nuzzled towards him. 'We must go, my dear,' he whispered. 'The last great battle is being fought. Our place is there, beside our good friends.'

* * *

Jack called in at the Jenkins' farm when he failed to find Phoebe and the children at the phone box. Mrs Jenkins was there but her husband was out in the fields.

'Always in a bad mood when the Hunt is out, is Thomas. We once had the hounds across our land. Only the once, mind! You never did see anyone as angry as Thomas! He believes in shooting foxes. Quick, neat and tidy! All those hounds . . . hunting them. That's terrible, that is. And they make such a mess of everything . . .'

Jack explained why he was there; that Phoebe and the children were missing. . .

'As soon as Thomas comes back, we'll go looking,' Mrs Jenkins told him.

Jack said that he was going up to the Four Fields

phone box to see if William were there. He was pretty sure that was where he must have telephoned from since he wasn't here.

'I'm sure you'll find them,' Mrs Jenkins said walking back with him across the farmyard to his bike. 'The world's gone mad at the moment. My hens are attacking each other. Never seen anything like it! I've had to separate half of them. Put them in different pens. They were like fiends! One old bantam actually turned on me. Look!' she said, showing Jack the back of a hand where an ugly red, scratch gleamed with antiseptic cream.

Jack promised to let her know if Phoebe and the children turned up, then he got on to the bike and started the engine.

'You see that, now!' Mrs Jenkins exclaimed, pointing towards the distant forest. Clouds of birds were wheeling in the sky, making it dark with their bodies as they flapped and dived. 'I do believe they're fighting each other! There is something strange afoot. I blame it on the fall-out, from that Russian disaster. You remember? We've still got sheep that are not cleared of the radiation, you know. Chernobyl – sounds like a foreign place, doesn't it? And here we are in the Golden Valley living the result of their disaster, as if it had just taken place next door!'

Jack turned his bike towards the forest and looked up grimly at the sky. Mrs Jenkins was right, he thought. There was something most odd going on. But it wasn't just at Golden House. It was here at the Jenkins' farm as well. He found the knowledge strangely comforting.

* * *

Pica was bleeding in one wing and Falco, the

239

kestrel, had a gash on the side of his head but between them they had organized their airborne divisions into some sort of order and the battle was going well for them. This was partly due to the courage of their birds, inspired as they had been by the Master's years of training. But it was also a strategic quirk that was giving them the upper hand and it was irritating for both Pica and Falco to admit that Rattus Rattus, (who in any normal circumstances would have been eaten by either one of them within moments of his arrival), had told them it would be so. Their size would work for them, that's what he'd said, and it looked as if he were going to be proved right. For the most part the Master's birds were all small; tits, finches, blackbirds, thrushes, with some owls and a heron or two. Singly, most of them wouldn't have stood a chance in combat against Morden's troops. Morden's birds were big thugs: crows and magpies, pigeons, a few renegade kestrels and with a sturdy back-up of starlings. But in massed combat, the smaller birds were proving much more effective. They could get in under the wings of their opponents, they could twist and turn and dive for freedom with greater agility. Although their beaks were not nearly so strong nor their claws so large as their adversaries', it was their ability to get in close and hit the vulnerable, soft areas that was winning them the day.

Rattus had told Falco and Pica it would be like this when he had been briefing the two birds after giving them joint command of the air forces.

'Your battle will be closest to the kind of fight I'm used to,' he'd told them. 'Flying must be very like sailing, I shouldn't wonder. One of the reasons why we beat the Spaniards was because their galleons were too big and cumbersome. The English ships slipped in under their guns. They were firing too high. We got in and pelted them and then got out quick. It'll be the same for you. You mark my words! See if I'm not right! But, you boys, don't ever forget – down on the ground it will be a very different story . . .'

*   *   *

And so it was proving to be. Morden's land forces outnumbered and outstripped the Master's ten times over.

The rats made up the main body of his army but the ferrets, stoats and weasels had gone over to his side in huge numbers.

Mustel, the weasel, had told Rattus that his brothers and sisters were all fighting with Morden.

'They've been wanting something like this, your honour,' he'd said. 'They're a very vicious lot, but they've not had the opportunity to show their colours till now.'

Rattus had managed, with Rus the Master's red squirrel, to win the loyalty of a number of squirrels but as many had gone to Morden, and the strange foreign creatures, the mink and the coypu – of which there were a few in the area – had joined Morden on the grounds that they were already outsiders and if they won this battle they could claim the land as their own.

'That's what that varlet has told them all,' Rattus fumed. 'A lot of lies! Promising them heaven knows what benefits if they only fight under his banner. I never did like the brown rat as a type and this one takes the ship's biscuit. 'Course with the Master's assistant training him he's become the lowest of the low.'

So, by the time Rattus Rattus had reached Four Fields the fighting had already begun and it looked as though Morden's side were winning the day.

'It broke out as soon as the humans left the house,' Mustel told him. 'There was no stopping the other side. They were in there at once. We held back, waiting for you, but eventually we had to join in.'

'Where are the humans now?' Rattus asked.

'In the motor-thing,' Mustel told him. 'Sirius, the dog, is guarding them and a few of our squirrels and a couple of badgers have gone to help him. Bloody good fighters, badgers! I'm really impressed!'

'I would be more impressed if you started doing something yourself, Mustel!' Rattus snapped.

'Yes, your honour,' the weasel said, feeling slighted. He'd already killed three stoats and had himself, personally, taken on the squirrel that had attacked the human children. 'That's what's so rotten about this world,' he grumbled. 'You do things and you get no praise . . . No praise . . .'

But Rattus Rattus wasn't listening. In fact, he was no longer there. He was right in the middle of the fray fighting off assaults from left and right.

* * *

Morden's rat was deeply alarmed. Although the battle on the ground seemed to be going well – though it was a little difficult to judge because there was a lack of order which displeased him – the battle in the sky – which should have been an easy victory considering their vastly superior forces – was not going at all as he had hoped. All around him crows and starlings were flapping on the ground, wounded or near to death. Even the heron

242

he had persuaded to join them had beaten a hasty retreat like an arrant coward.

The rat, overcome with anger, bit the head off a vole and only then realized the creature belonged to his own side.

'Typical!' he fumed and he turned to enter the fray once more when, out of a heaving mass of bodies immediately ahead of him emerged the one animal that he had sworn would be his prize of the day.

'You, rat!' he screamed. 'You black filth! Here I am! Take me, if you dare!'

Rattus Rattus spun round. He was wounded in his left shoulder where a rabbit had bitten him and there was blood over one eye from a scratch caused by a ferret's claw. He blinked, clearing his vision. Morden's rat was standing a short distance away from him, apparently unscathed, his brown fur glowing in the autumn sunlight.

'You're losing this day,' Rattus shouted. 'Call off your troops. Surrender, rat! Admit defeat!'

'Never!' Morden's rat hissed. 'We have you. Look around you. I can count your supporters on one claw. We have hundreds. You'll never win. You surrender . . .'

At that moment one of the mink ran towards Rattus, its teeth bared.

'Back, creature!' the brown rat screamed. 'This one is mine,' and without another word he hurled himself on to Rattus, kicking and scratching and biting at his body with the fury of a mad creature.

Rattus twisted and turned, fighting for his life. Sinking his teeth deep into the other rat's neck, he felt a stab of pain in one of his own front legs at the same moment. As blood from both their bodies

243

started to flow and mingle, they squirmed and turned in the mud of the field, fighting to the death.

* * *

'There they are!' exclaimed Meg, as the Rolls Royce bumped up the forest track and the Land-Rover came into view.

'What's that dog doing?' Henry Crawden asked.

'It's my Gypsy!' Meg cried. 'He's bleeding all over . . .'

* * *

Spot was exhausted. He had stood guard on the Land-Rover from the moment Alice and the others were safely inside. He had fought off squirrels and a whole host of stoats and weasels. He had killed some and wounded others. In the process he had had his body ripped and torn and his fur pulled out in tufts. He was tired and terribly thirsty. He wanted more than anything to lie down . . .

* * *

'Here's a car coming!' Phoebe cried excitedly.

'It's Henry Crawden,' Mary said with disgust. 'Come to gloat, I suppose . . .'

'He's got Meg with him,' Alice whispered as the car drew up beside them.'

'Are you all right?' Henry Crawden asked, lowering the window and calling.

'Oh!' Phoebe exclaimed, and tears began to run unchecked down her cheeks as she climbed out of the car. 'Thank God you've come!'

At the same moment Spot started to bark excitedly.

* * *

In the Master's study Matthew Morden stared and stared into the glass, willing his mind to be still, willing his body to travel.

'I want to be there!' he whispered. 'I want to be part of it!'

Then, holding up the piece of gold on its fine chain, he forced all his attention on to its shining surface. He had made the gold. It was his secret accomplishment. He had managed to make gold – so now, surely, he could time travel . . . ?

'I want it! I want it! I want it!' his mind whispered greedily as the pendulum hung heavy and motionless in front of him.

'Stop, mind!' Morden cried out in an agony of disappointment. 'Am I never to succeed?'

'I want it! I want it! I want it!' his mind whispered, over and over again.

Morden let the pendulum fall to the ground and covered his face with his hands.

'I have started something that I cannot stop,' he cried. 'Lord God in heaven, forgive and protect me!' and great painful sobs racked his body.

* * *

Cinnabar and William raced up the steep escarpment. The hounds were terribly near. William could hear them baying and panting through the trees behind them.

'The hunters will be furious!' Cinnabar whispered. 'They like to chase us across open fields.'

'Where are we going?' William gasped. They were already exhausted and their breathing hurt his lungs.

'To a battle,' Cinnabar gasped. 'We're going to join a battle.'

* * *

As Jack turned off the forest road and on to the track he could hear the din of the birds and he was suddenly terrified of what he might discover.

245

'Just let them be all right,' he whispered in his heart. 'Any other problems can be solved. But, please, let Steph and Phoebe and the children be all right . . .'

Then, as he swung round the corner, driving hard, he had to swerve to avoid crashing into the Rolls Royce and the Land-Rover.

* * *

Rattus pulled himself out from under the dead weight of the body that pressed down on him. The brown rat rolled over and twitched once. There was a mess of blood already congealing at its throat.

'Poor rat,' Rattus Rattus said quietly. 'Forgive me! But it was you or . . .' then he stopped speaking and looked up, listening.

All around him the fighting continued, both in the air and on the ground. But what had caught his attention was not the sounds of the battle but that of a hunting horn and a moment later Cinnabar, the fox, leaped a gate and landed on the soft earth of the Four Fields.

'They're coming!' he shouted. 'The hounds are . . .' Then even Cinnabar was silenced and his sharp, staccato barking turned into a squeal of surprise.

For suddenly and totally unexpectedly out of the forest appeared a red deer, running fast, with its noble head held high and the sunlight shining on its glossy coat. A strange, expectant hush settled over the field. The barking and the baying and the innumerable gruntings and squeakings of all the creatures gradually faded away as every one of them turned and stared with wonder and disbelief at this new arrival in their midst. Even the humans seemed to sense some extraordinary presence.

Then the youngest and most innocent of the company, the baby, Stephanie, reached out towards the deer with both her hands and gave a high-pitched, strange and cheerful burble of welcome.

At once, as if to some signal, the fighting started again, fierce and dreadful.

The deer ran towards Phoebe and Stephanie, her instinct to protect them and, at the same moment, the hounds poured in through the narrow opening from the bridlepath, leaping the gate, followed closely by the first huntsman, galloping fast on a sweating horse.

The deer swung round, facing the hunt, blocking the way to Phoebe and Stephanie. For a moment the hounds seemed afraid to make a move. They stood in a tight pack, heads raised, baying and snarling. Then Cinnabar appeared, with William chasing after him.

'No, Cinnabar!' William shouted.

But the fox was deaf to his cries. He ran straight at the hounds, ploughing his way through them, making them turn, snapping and biting at him as he led them away from the deer and the humans.

Not all the hounds attacked the fox. Others smelling the wild scents all around them, set upon rabbits, stoats, rats, and all the other creatures of the battle.

The Four Fields became a scene of even greater pandemonium and carnage as the hounds rampaged through the grass and undergrowth snapping and tearing at any living creature they came upon.

The Huntsman blew his horn to no avail.

Some of the hounds turned savagely on the deer, gnashing and tearing with their teeth and claws. But the deer was a match for them. Backing away, she led them further and further from where Phoebe was standing holding Stephanie tightly. Then, when enough distance had been made between the hounds and the humans, the deer swerved, leaped a fence and drew the dogs away from the battlefield.

William meanwhile was in the thick of the pack, fighting off hounds with his bare hands. Ahead of him he could see the fox with a dog on his back and another tearing at his neck.

'Run, Cinnabar! Run!' William screamed. Then, as he turned once more to defend his friend, beating off a fresh wave of attack, a single gunshot shattered the tumult, making birds rise out of the trees and rabbits run for cover.

A surprised yelp of pain made William spin round.

Cinnabar was lying stretched out on the rough grass. As William watched he saw his breathing stop and an ugly stain of red blood seep from the back of his neck. Mr Jenkins, the farmer, was standing over him, his rifle still smoking in his hands as he faced the Master of the Hounds.

'Get off this land!' he bellowed. 'Your so-called sport is finished. The fox is dead. So go – and take your hounds with you. Go!'

'Cinnabar!' William sobbed. 'Cinnabar! They've killed you.'

'There's that wounded deer up ahead,' the Master of the Hounds shouted. 'We can't just leave it.'

'Get off this land *now*!' Mr Jenkins repeated savagely.

'William!' Mary cried, running to him and throwing her arms round him.

'Cinnabar,' William sobbed, kneeling beside his dead friend.

'It's all over,' his sister whispered, holding him in her arms. 'The hounds have scattered the animals. The battle's over, Will.'

'Cinnabar!' he cried, gasping and choking with grief.

'Come on, dearie,' Meg said gently, putting an arm round him. 'All over now. A quick death! A quick death!'

'He came this way,' William gasped, 'to make the hounds follow him. He knew they'd scatter the other animals. He could have got away easily. He could . . . We could . . . We could have got away.'

Meg and Mary held him between them. Alice stood a little apart, with her hands in her pockets, not bearing to look at his distress.

Jack came over to them and stood beside Mr Jenkins.

Mark Crawden ran forward and then hung back beside Phoebe, as if he were shy.

'Odd thing the whole of it,' Mr Jenkins said to Jack. 'I don't know when I last saw a deer in these woods. Nearest herd is the other side of the forest, over towards Wales. Though, come to think, she must have been someone's pet animal. Did you notice? She had a collar round her throat. A golden collar! Now there's a funny thing.'

The children turned slowly, listening to him.

'Are you sure?' Mary asked.

'Positive,' Mr Jenkins replied. 'Saw it with my own eyes. I'd best go and look for her. Most of the hounds that were after her seem to have have returned – but God knows what sort of a mess she'll be in. I'll have to put a bullet in her if she's in a bad way . . .'

'Come on, William!' Mary exclaimed.

'Where are you going?' Jack called as all three children now turned and started to run fast towards the gate in the hedge.

'To save the deer,' Alice called and looking back she saw Spot limping after her. 'You come with us, Spot,' she called.

'I will,' the dog thought, 'but I hope it isn't far!'

'City kids!' Mr Jenkins remarked. 'They're too soft-hearted. If a creature's wounded, the kindest thing is a quick death.'

The adults turned slowly towards the cars on the forest track.

'What's the baby's name?' Mark Crawden asked Phoebe, shyly.

'She's called Stephanie,' Phoebe replied.

'Stephanie,' the small boy said, savouring the sound. 'That's a funny name!'

'Some to-do it's been here today!' Mr Jenkins grumbled. 'Never seen the like! 'Course the hunt, we're used to – but, all this other . . .'

'It's over now,' Meg said quietly.

Phoebe glanced at her.

'Yes,' she said. 'I feel it as well! As though we're suddenly free!' and she held Stephanie higher on her shoulder and felt Jack's hand on the back of her neck.

'You all right?' he whispered.

She nodded, but didn't speak, because the sense of relief made her want to cry.

'It's all over,' Meg repeated, in a whisper. And looking up she saw Henry Crawden's eyes on her.

250

She smiled at him and, after a moment, he smiled back.

'Let's all go home,' Jack said.

'The children . . .' Phoebe said, looking back.

'They'll come when they're ready,' Jack told her. 'They'll be all right.'

The huntsmen had left, the hounds had gone. Dead bodies littered the field.

'Look at that big brown rat!' Mr Jenkins exclaimed. 'Did you ever see the size? I'd best be off myself. Whatever your kids say, that deer will thank me for putting her out of her misery. Goodbye now!' and, with a wave of the hand, he stalked off across the field in the direction the children had taken.

24
The Circle of Energy

Spot ran ahead, his nose down, sniffing and searching. Although his body hurt in so many places, it was good to be moving freely again, good not being attacked any more. It helped him to stop thinking about the friends who had gone, and he sobbed and gasped as he briefly remembered Cinnabar, lying on the earth. So quickly cold, so soon gone.

'This way!' he called, blotting the image out of his mind.

The trail led in the direction of Goldenwater. But in his heart Spot knew it was also the way to the silver path, that dark and dreadful path where his friends and relatives went for their final resting. The scent on the earth in front of him was filled with death and he dreaded what he would find at the end of it.

'Cervus can't have gone far,' Mary said. 'She was badly mauled by the dogs . . .'

William looked back over his shoulder and Alice, who was just behind him, moved forward and slipped her arm round his waist.

'You all right?' she whispered.

William shook his head.

'Why did it have to happen?' he asked. 'Why? Why to Cinnabar?'

252

'I don't know,' Alice said. 'And not only to Cinnabar . . . How many more of our side have been killed? At least you were out there trying to help, Will. Mary and I just sat in that Land-Rover . . . watching. Look at Spot – the state he's in! But I didn't do anything to help him. I was too scared. I just sat there . . .'

'Stop it, both of you!' Mary said sternly. 'That's all in the past. We've got more important things to worry about now.'

Ahead of them Spot stopped suddenly and raised his head, looking into the distance.

'What is it, Spot?' Mary asked, running forward.

'More blood,' the dog said thoughtfully. 'There's more than one creature up ahead. Come on!' and, turning to his left, he led the way along the shore of the lake, in the direction of the standing stone.

The bright day sparkled all around them. The light flashed on the surface of the lake and the sky above was blue and cloudless. The air was scented with wood smoke and damp earth. Autumn leaves glowed russet, brown and orange on the skeleton branches and in great drifts beneath the trees. A warm sun shone down. Thin bands of mist floated above the water and tiny wavelets lapped and splashed against the shining boulders.

'It's such a beautiful day,' Mary said sadly.

'It's such a beautiful place,' Alice added.

But William just stared out across the lake and shook his head. His heart was so full of tears he couldn't speak. But if he had, he'd have cursed the sun for shining and the morning for being so bright.

Somehow Alice understood his silence. She put the hand that had been round his waist up onto his shoulder and hugged him.

253

Ahead of them Spot barked once; a sharp, excited sound.

Mary hurried to join him. The dog was standing with his head lowered and his tail between his legs.

'What is it?' she called. As she drew level, she saw a squirrel lying on the ground. For a moment she felt panic surge through her and she remembered the creature that had waylaid her on the way to the Land-Rover. Looking closer, however, she realized that this one was different. Its fur was the colour amber; red and glowing. 'It's Rus!' she shouted to the others as she ran to him.

The Magician's squirrel was in a bad way. He had been battered in an encounter with a big buck rabbit and half his tail had been taken off by the beak of a crow. A wound gaped in his left thigh and he was weak from loss of blood.

When Mary picked him up, she felt his body stiffen, as if he were preparing for yet another fight. But once he had recognized her he sighed and lay back motionless in her arms.

'We must hurry!' Spot said, forcing his weary body to move more quickly.

They reached the end of the lake and started to climb the gentle slope towards the standing stone and the yew tree beyond.

Cervus had almost reached the stone before she had collapsed. The hounds had ripped at her so voraciously with their claws and teeth that there were open wounds all over her body. She lay, panting desperately, her head cradled between her two outstretched front legs.

Stephen Tyler, the Magician, leaned on the ground beside her, one arm thrown over her shoulder and the other supporting his own weight.

He could feel every one of her wounds on his own body and her weakness was his weakness.

'My deer,' he whispered. 'Is this the end for us? Is this where it must all finish? Let us go home, Cervus. Come, my deer . . . Be up! Be up!' But the Magician hadn't the strength to raise himself off the ground and the deer was beyond moving. 'We must go home,' he whispered. 'If we die here in a foreign time, we will be ghosts. Come, my Cervus! For I will not leave you. Come now . . .'

At first Mary thought it was a trick of the light, a shadow cast across the ground. An insubstantial shade, a dream almost . . .

'Mr Tyler?' she whispered.

'Where?' Alice asked and then also she saw him. 'Look, Will!' she cried, pointing towards the stone.

The children and Spot ran forward. At first Stephen Tyler didn't seem able to see them. His face was lined and his eyes were staring.

'Mr Tyler!' Mary called out when they were almost upon him.

'Come, Cervus! Come!' they heard the old man mutter and, as he spoke, he tried again to climb up off the ground but then he fell back once more, groaning. The children saw tiny drops of perspiration on his brow and his eyelids flickered as though he were falling asleep.

'Spot,' Alice whispered, 'please help him!' and her voice broke as tears unexpectedly started up into her eyes.

But Spot had collapsed on to the grass, utterly exhausted himself and unable to move another step. So it was Mary, still carrying Rus in her outstretched arms, who crossed towards the old man.

'We must hurry!' she said firmly. 'If Mr Jenkins

finds us, he'll shoot Cervus.' As she spoke she placed Rus on the ground near to Stephen Tyler. The movement seemed to wake him. He opened his eyes, frowned, reached out with his hand and felt the stiff little body beside him.

'Rus?' he whispered. 'Is it you?'

The squirrel pulled himself forward until he was nestling against the old man's side.

'So many casualties!' Stephen Tyler sighed.

'What must we do?' Mary asked him, kneeling down in front of him.

He opened his eyes again and squinted at her as if the bright light were dazzling him.

'Who's there?' he demanded, his voice shaking.

'It's all right,' Mary said gently. 'It's us; William, Alice and me. We're here to help you.'

'Ah!' the old man sighed and he nodded. 'Good! Good!' he whispered. 'You'll know what to do, you Constant children.' Then he opened his eyes wide and stared fiercely at her. 'Don't let us die in your time, whatever happens! We don't want to have to haunt the Golden Vale for the rest of eternity. You hear me? Get us home now! That's your task! You'll know what to do!'

'We must get him back,' Mary said thoughtfully, speaking to herself.

'All of them,' William agreed and, as he spoke, he took the pendulum out of his pocket.

As the sun caught the surface of the lump of gold, a hooting call made them all look up.

'Wait!' a voice trilled in an agitated tone. 'Don't go!'

Mary looked up in surprise.

'Jasper?' she called.

The great owl dropped out of the blue sky, flapping his wings and pushing downwards with his legs. Clearly visible, clenched between his two claws, was a black rat, his colour easily recognizable, despite the clotted wounds that covered his body.

'He's got Rattus with him!' Alice shouted.

'Found this poor creature limping along, going no faster than a snail,' Jasper announced, depositing the rat on the ground near to Stephen Tyler. 'If I hadn't chanced by, goodness knows what would have happened . . .'

'Varlet!' squeaked the rat. 'Bounder! Unspeakable coward! Where were you, owl, when your friends needed you? Where were you when Pica led the attack and Falco rallied the forces?'

'Doing my bit,' Jasper replied, hooding his eyes and hunching his shoulders disdainfully.

'Doing what?' Rattus demanded, staggering on to his four feet and facing the bird.

'Spent the entire day sorting the dead and dying from the living and wounded, if you must know!' Jasper replied testily. 'Ambulance service! Red Cross duties!'

'What are you blathering about?' the rat thundered. 'You are a coward, sir! You were too scared to join in. That's the truth . . .'

'Rattus,' Stephen Tyler said quietly. 'Enough now! We cannot all be born to fight, as it would seem you were.'

'I was not born to fight,' Rattus Rattus replied. 'If you must know, if I could have my life over again, I'd have been a performer. The roar of the audience; the groundlings and the gentry; the flickering lights . . . Though, no doubt, I'd have always

257

pined for the smell of the ocean . . . But be that as it may, it did not stop me doing my bit today . . .'

'You have all done your bit,' the old man protested.

'And if it hadn't been for me, rat,' Jasper cut in hastily, 'you'd still be wandering about in a daze looking for the way to the Dark and Dreadful Path.'

'I was not wandering about!' Rattus Rattus exclaimed. 'I was exhausted, I'll grant you. I was battered and bleeding, I'll admit. But I knew precisely where I was . . .'

'Well you wouldn't be here now, if it hadn't been for me spotting you and picking you up – instead of eating you, which I would have been quite at liberty to do!'

'Oh, exactly!' squeaked the black rat. 'Then you would have been behaving true to form, wouldn't you? This entire day has been a picnic for you, hasn't it . . . ?'

'You say that again,' the owl hooted furiously, 'and I'll . . .'

'Oh, stop it!' Mary shouted. 'Both of you! We've had enough fighting and squabbling! So stop it, both of you, please!'

'Well, I certainly didn't start it,' Jasper hissed.

'Mary, my child,' the Magician murmured, 'are you going to take us home, or are you going to leave us here to slowly expire?'

'We're going to take you home,' Mary answered. 'Only we do need a bit of help.'

'You know I will help you,' the old man whispered.

'Then tell us,' Mary pleaded, 'what we are supposed to do?'

'What you must always do,' he replied. 'Harness

the maximum energy for the task in hand and attend to nothing else.'

William stood up, looking at the standing stone and still holding the Magician's pendulum in his hand.

'If I touch the stone,' he said thoughtfully, 'and you, Alice, if you hold my hand and stretch as far as you can . . . Can you reach Cervus?'

'Just!' Alice said, doing as he instructed.

'Then, if Mr Tyler is touching Cervus with one hand, as he is, and the other hand is touching Rus . . . If you, Rattus, let Rus take hold of your tail . . .'

'Anything to oblige!' the rat said, turning his back on the squirrel and stretching out his tail.

'And . . . Mary,' William continued, reaching as far as he could with both his arms between the stone and Alice, 'if you hold Rattus's front claw . . . Can you stretch with your other hand back to the standing stone here, beside me?'

Mary tried to do as he suggested, but it was impossible. However hard she tried the standing stone remained out of her range.

'Why are we doing this, anyway?' Alice asked spreading her arms wide between William and Cervus.

'I thought if we formed a circle with the standing stone we could . . . somehow . . . channel the energy and use it to help us to time travel . . .' her brother replied.

'Very good, William!' the Magician murmured. 'An excellent conceit. It won't work, but it's a fine attempt!'

'Why won't it work?' William asked.

'You are trying to travel too many beings at one

259

time,' the old man replied. 'The earth energy through the stone is strong, I'll grant you. But my power is waning and you will need a far greater magnetic pull than the pendulum can supply . . .'

'If I lie on the ground, full-length,' Mary announced, 'and if you, Rattus, touch my foot . . .'

'No sooner asked for than done,' the rat squeaked.

'. . . Then I can . . . just reach it!' Mary exclaimed triumphantly and, as she completed the movement, the tips of her fingers grazed the rough surface of the stone.

'So!' the Magician said, sounding almost amused. 'The circle is complete! It still won't work, I'm afraid. It would be perfect for one or two of us. But there are too many creatures . . .'

Then Mary remembered Phoebe's necklace, still safely deposited in the pocket of her jeans.

'But if we had two pendulums,' she said, feeling in her jeans and producing the pendant.

'Ah!' said the Magician. 'That would be altogether different!'

'What about us?' hooted Jasper, indicating with a nod where Spot was watching them all from a distance, with his head tilted to one side. But Jasper might just as well have been speaking to himself, for the circle of friends had all vanished and he and Spot were alone on the bright grass beside the lapping lake.

25
A Walk Through the Woods

The day was colder. The frost had lifted but the ground was still hard and the grass crunched under their feet as they moved.

The old man could manage to walk, albeit only slowly, but they'd had to leave Cervus beside the lake. Rus had chosen to stay as well. His strength was returning, little by little, and he wanted somehow to reach his own home.

'I'd feel better up in a tree,' he explained.

'I'll send someone later to look to you,' Stephen Tyler whispered to his beloved deer, and he stroked Cervus' head, not wanting the children to urge him away.

'We must hurry,' Mary told him. 'You haven't much strength yourself.'

'Strength enough,' the old man said, straightening up and taking a deep breath of the cold air as he leaned heavily on her shoulder.

Rattus limped beside them until Alice was unable to ignore his condition any longer. She bent down and asked him, in her politest voice, if he would like her to carry him.

'That would be most civil,' the rat replied. 'Most surprisingly generous of you!'

So Alice lifted him up more than a little nervously and held him at arm's length.

'Why don't you put me on your shoulder?' the rat said and, when she had done as he suggested, he snuggled up to her and she could feel his whiskers tickling her cheek. 'It's a funny thing, life,' he squeaked in her ear. 'You used to misunderstand my people. You used not to even like rats. And now . . . we're the best of pals!'

Alice walked on doggedly, not looking at him. It was true that she had grown fond of Rattus Rattus, but she couldn't altogether forget what sort of a creature he was and, as such, he was still rather frightening to her.

William and Mary supported Stephen Tyler between them. As they walked slowly through the autumn trees towards the yew and on towards the edge of the forest he kept stopping and looking at all that they passed.

Later Mary would remember that it was as though he was wanting to see everything for one last time; to drink in the beauty that surrounded him; to feel the warm sun and the cold air on his skin; to smell the tang of the damp earth and the rotting leaves; to hear the birds, choiring the day with full-throated joy. At the top of the hill by the yew he paused for a longer rest.

'Which of all the magic places in our magic vale do you each love the best?' he asked them.

Alice answered him without hesitation.

'The tree house,' she replied. 'I like the fact that it's waiting there to be discovered and yet it's so well-hidden. I like being up in it and feeling it sway slightly in the wind. I like the windows being open and the glimpses of sky through the branches. I like the view from it and the safety of it. I love the tree house,' she finished breathlessly.

The old man nodded and reached out a hand towards her, touching her cheek.

'Minima!' he said gently. 'When first I knew you I called you Minimus! I insulted you. I gave you the masculine form – because I didn't think a girl would be any use to me! Two girls indeed! Well, I am a silly, stubborn old man and you have all shown me a great deal! You are a part of me, my Minima. You are also very dear to me.'

Alice swallowed and stood back. She felt a little foolish. She always did when she was singled out, with everyone looking at her.

'I think I love the area round the lake best,' William said quietly. 'And the cave behind Golden-spring most all. It's so secret and when you showed us the paintings on the wall . . . it seemed special, somehow.'

'It is special,' the Magician agreed. 'And only those who are very special ever find it. I also think the lake a particularly good place. Water is one of the primordial wonders. Water is the life-bringer. Water is the life-energy made manifest. Try to hold water in your hand and it will slip away; try to hold life and the same will happen. You cannot hold water. You cannot hold life. Without water there could be no creation – and the creation is always . . . now. Look around you! All your memories of the past are only present dreams. All your hopes and aspirations for the future are only present fantasies. This moment . . . has gone already . . .' as he spoke he waved it away. 'The moment to come . . . does not yet exist. So then what are we left with, William?'

William shrugged and frowned.

'Come on, boy! You know the answer. If the past is no longer with us and the future is constantly still to come. . . . Then with what are we left?'

'The present,' William said quietly. 'Now.'

'*Now*!' Stephen Tyler cried. 'That is all the time that ever exists. Now! How long is a moment? How long is now? A fraction of a second? Shorter even than that? Now's . . . gone. Now's now! Now's . . . gone again! How long is now, William?'

William shrugged again.

'When you put it like that,' he said, 'you make it sound as though there only ever is now. As though it's as long as for ever . . .'

'As long as eternity!' Stephen Tyler cried. 'As short as time! That's right. There is only now. Don't let your minds worry about the future. Don't let your minds regret the past. Remember with gladness and expect with interest. See, feel and be here. . . . *Now*!' He made the word suddenly urgent. The sound was loud and clear. It caused each of them to look towards him with surprise. The old man smiled at them and nodded. 'You see? Now! And you will be. . . immortal! Now! And you will be. . . invincible! Now! And you will be . . . in tune with the day, with the world of nature, with the whole of humanity. That's the only secret you need. That's how to time travel. That's how to move stones and mountains. That's how to make gold. . . . To be . . . gold. Squeeze your attention tighter and tighter to the very centre of now and you will find vast space and limitless horizons. Only be here – now – and you will each be gold! Then the alchemy is complete. The dross separates away and the truth, the purity at the very heart of each of us, may be revealed. That is all. That is the work on which we are engaged. Just keep touching the true centre . . . the gold..' and, lowering his voice to a whisper so light that it was no more than an exhalation of breath, he said again that one word: 'now!'

The birds sang loudly and the sunlight dazzled through the sparse leaves and the restless branches. But now it seemed as though the living, breathing world was not outside but was a part of each of them and that they were a part of everything they could see and feel; the view was inside each of them as much as it was out there; there was no beginning nor end to the mind of William nor to the mind of Mary nor to the mind of Alice.

'All joined!' the old man said, hearing their thoughts. 'No separation! All one!' Then he laughed gently. 'What a wonderful thing it is when the little mind becomes still and we may hear, see, smell, touch, taste. . . . Now!'

Again there was silence between them for a moment.

'So Mary,' the old man said, turning to her, 'which is your favourite place?'

Mary had dreaded him asking her the question because she didn't have an answer ready. She could feel her cheeks scalding as she started to blush and she looked away from him to hide her embarrassment.

'We haven't been everywhere yet,' she said.

Across the valley, on the other side of Golden House, she could see the curious V-shape cut between the trees that marked the place where the central, mysterious energy line left the valley. 'For instance, we haven't been over there yet,' and she pointed as she spoke.

'There always has to be somewhere left to go,' the old man said quietly. 'If you have been everywhere and done everything the danger is you will be dead before your time!'

'What is over there, I wonder?' Mary said to herself.

'Greater wonders than you ever dreamed of!' Stephen Tyler told her, but when she looked at him, she found he was smiling at her. 'Where is your favourite place?' he repeated gently.

He was looking at her so kindly. His face was lined and loving; his eyes less bright than she expected, his red hair flecked with silver. She realized suddenly that he was an old, old man. The discovery made her gasp. It was as though she was looking at him for the first time; as though she had never really seen him before. He wasn't a dream or a vision. He was flesh and blood. She gasped at the realization. It was as if the very act of seeing were new to her; as if her eyes were open for the first time ever. She saw the texture of his skin and where each hair grew out of his forehead. She saw the lashes round his eyes, his fine arching brows, his thin lips. A vein was throbbing on his temple and she could hear his breath escaping from his partially-opened lips.

'I like it best wherever you are,' she said quietly.

'And I like it best with you,' he told her gently. 'My Mary, who reminded me that love is part of eternity; that it cannot die, that it cannot go away. While there is breath in the lungs, there is love in the heart! And when the breath itself passes away, the love is released and it is . . . everywhere.'

Then this old man, so newly seen by her, turned away and looked himself out over the view.

'It has been a good life,' he said quietly. 'So quickly gone! Dear children! You have each . . . affected me . . .' And they realized that he was silently crying.

'Don't,' Alice whispered. 'Please don't.'

'Have no fear, Minima! Tears are but the heart's way of letting go. And that is what, in the end, we all must learn. . . . To let go! Come! Let us walk again. If we stay here much longer we will take root beside this ancient yew!' He reached out a hand and stroked the lowest branches of the tree, where they leaned to the ground beside him. 'This tree was ancient when it was created, I think! It was born old!'

Slowly they wound their way down the steep hillside, passing the badger sett and going in amongst the forest's shade. Stephen Tyler's hand shook sometimes as he leaned heavily on William's shoulder and upon Mary's arm. Behind them Alice moved carefully, not wanting to dislodge Rattus Rattus from his perch on her shoulder. He had grown strangely silent and when she glanced at him she saw that he was gazing ahead with twinkling eyes and a twitching nose.

'What are you thinking about?' she asked him.

'I'm thinking how very pleasant it is to be carried by you,' he replied and he grinned, revealing sharp white teeth. 'I'm thinking that I feel decidedly better and that any minute now, I might hop off for a bite to eat. I'm thinking that we must soon say goodbye.'

'All of us,' Stephen Tyler added, walking ahead of the rat and not looking round, though he was obviously joining in this conversation. 'We must all be very brave and say goodbye.'

'Not yet!' Mary gasped.

'Not quite yet. But soon, dear children. Soon! When the now that is to come is now and this now becomes then!'

They walked on in silence, stumbling sometimes on the rough ground. Sometimes William went ahead and held Stephen Tyler's hand, to help him down particularly steep portions of the path. Once the old man almost fell and Mary had to reach out with her other hand to hold on firmly to his arm.

'Oh, my children!' he laughed. 'What a trial it is to be old! The mind remains young but the body slows down.' Then he shook his head. 'Not true, old fool! The mind slows down as well. I am quite likely, these days, to call a book a flagon or a nightingale a pea pod! Old people should learn to hold their tongues . . . !'

'Please don't! Not you!' William exclaimed. 'There is still so much you have to teach us.'

'Not one little item, my dear boy. You know as much as I do; as much as anyone can. Listen to your hearts. Be true to yourselves. Act bravely – now. That is all the knowledge you need.'

'But why did there have to be a war in our time?' Alice exclaimed. 'Why did Morden want to destroy everything?'

'He didn't . . . doesn't. He only wants the power and the glory and the riches and . . . the gold – for himself. That is all. Listen to me, one last time!' He paused again and turned so that he was including Alice. 'The straight and narrow way leads to understanding. Move off it by as much as the breadth of one hair and chaos will ensue. Morden is a good scholar. He could become a wise master. Be he still has to find his true worth. He makes gold that perishes – as Jonas Lewis made gold. But with your help, your influence, over the years to come he could eventually make the great leap. You are his light. He is your dark. You all need each other. The work never ends until . . . until . . .' The old man shook his head. 'All Morden must do is curb his greed.'

'All!' Mary cried out. 'All? It seems pretty hard to me. How can we be sure that we're not, each of us, just like Morden? I want things for myself. I want people to love me. I want to be admired. I want . . . not power, exactly . . . but . . . well, I want to be superior, I want to be rich and famous . . . I'm no different from Morden myself!'

'Good!' Stephen Tyler exclaimed. 'Want as much and more than you can possibly hope for. Seek the darkness. How would a person know if they were awake – if they had never been to sleep? How would a person recognize the day – if they had never seen the night? There is no right – without there be a wrong; no positive – without the negative; no hope – without despair. But each time you notice you have strayed from the centre path – come back to it! Come back! That is all that is required. Each time you see the darkness – search for the light!'

'But – creatures died during the battle of the Four Fields,' William cried. 'You weren't there. You don't know.' Tears started to well up into his throat, a terrible rage was shaking his body. 'This is all talk. But then. . . . Then . . . there was fear and beastliness. There was pain and suffering. Cinnabar died. Rus is almost dead. Cervus is lying back there, fighting for her life . . . You weren't there.'

'William,' the Magician said sternly. 'Where

were you when the hounds ripped at my body? Had you your eyes closed? Did you not see?'

'Your body?' William gasped.

'You think I would let my Cervus go alone into the field? You think I would leave all of you to face the battle alone? Shame on you, William! I thought you knew me better.'

'You were in Cervus?' Mary asked.

'Of course,' the old man replied.

'But, all the same,' William cried, his voice broken, his body shaking, 'why did Cinnabar have to die? Why?'

'Ah!' the old man sighed, gently stroking William's head. 'The great cry of humanity, "*Why*?" It is a question without an answer, my dear! Unless the answer be only "*Because. . .!*" '

They walked on in silence until they reached the valley floor. Then slowly they moved along the forest track towards the door in the brick wall of the garden behind Golden House.

'Here's where I set out from this morning. Here is where we must part. Old Kate will be angry with me for being gone so long. She will scold and I shouldn't like you to see that! You think I am a master! You should see me with Mistress Kate. Then I am no more than a small child, late home from the schoolmaster having dawdled in the woods! As for you, you must hurry as well! The only way you can possibly return to your own time will be with the aid of my glass. Go to my study. Use both the pendulum and the necklace. Travel carefully!'

As he spoke, he was pushing them ahead of him through the gate. Rattus Rattus jumped off Alice's shoulder and stood on the ground beside the old man, watching silently.

'Won't we see you again?' William called as they started down the neat path through the garden towards the yard gate.

'No,' the old man called. 'We shall not meet again. Goodbye, my Constant children . . . !'

Alice who was the last through the gate was half-way to the dovecote when she stopped in her tracks.

'No!' she gasped. 'No!' And she started to cry. 'We can't just leave you!' And, turning, she ran back to the Magician and flung her arms round him, clinging to him and sobbing.

William and Mary also turned and, hanging their heads, they waited for their sister.

'Alice!' the old man said gently, cradling her head in his hands. 'My Minima! What's this? Tears from my brave girl? Stop now! Stop! Or you will have me blubbing as well!'

'You're going to die, aren't you?' Alice wailed. 'We'll never see you again.'

'Alice, listen! All three of you. Come here!' He beckoned to the other two and when they had walked back to him he laid a hand on Mary's shoulder and the other on William's. Alice, meanwhile clung to him, with her arms clasped round his waist.

"Listen!' he said again, gently. 'If I gave you a gift – something rare and special, something so priceless and beyond compare that it was unique, something that you could never lose, something that was to be yours for ever – and if, when I gave you this gift, I had placed it in a casket to make it look more important . . . Which would you value the most? The gift or the casket?'

271

'The gift,' Mary mumbled, swallowing back her tears.

'The gift!' the old man said gently. 'This body is only a casket. Let it go! Keep the gift! I will always be with you. We've grown to love each other. We cannot lose each other. Whenever you walk in the woods of the Golden Vale – I will be there. Whenever the rain falls or the sun shines; when the swallows first come, and the owl hoots – I will be there. When darkness fills your minds and the days seem long and wearisome, remember me! When clouds gather, blotting out the sun and there seems no purpose, no hope . . . look for the bridge – the bridge in the clouds! I will be there at the other side, waiting for you. My dear, dear children! When Stephanie marries – as marry she will – I will be there! Remember then, on that day, that I am with you. . . . Remember me! Now go, my children! Be brave for us all! Be brave for Jasper and for my Sirius, your Spot! Be brave for Lutra and Falco and Pica and Merula, the blackbird! Be strong for Jack Green and for Phoebe – they have their part to play as well! Let the sun shine on the moon and the moon will shine! Hide the one from the other and there is darkness. Go! Go! Go, my children! You are taking me with you . . .'

'Master Tyler!' a voice called, and the old woman appeared at the yard gate.

'Quickly now,' Stephen Tyler hissed, pushing the children down a side path.

'Master Tyler, I have been calling you! Your nephew is here from Avonside. He would speak with you . . .'

'I'm coming, Kate. I'm coming!'

26
Departures and Arrivals

The children stayed hidden on the side path while Mr Tyler and the woman walked slowly back down the length of the garden, grumbling and chattering together. As soon as they had disappeared from view, William led the way and, moving cautiously in case the old couple were still in the yard, they went out through the gate themselves.

The house that faced them was completely different from the one to which they were accustomed. The kitchen door had vanished and the Georgian wing was replaced by a tumble of low eaves and dark beams.

'I'm not sure of the way in from here,' William said, surprised and perplexed. 'We'd better go round to the front.'

But as they turned the corner from the yard, they saw a number of horses tethered near the front step and they could hear the sound of peoples' voices coming from the hall.

'Now what should we do?' William asked, drawing back.

'D'you suppose we can be seen or not?' Mary asked.

'I don't know,' William admitted.

'Phoebe couldn't see Mr Tyler that time he was talking to us on the front lawn and she called to us from the house,' Mary said thoughtfully.

'Which time?' Alice asked.

'Don't you remember,' Mary began. 'It was after the baby had been born and . . .'

'Never mind about that now!' William said irritably. 'We've got to find a way of getting to the steps up the chimney.'

'In that case,' a voice said, 'you'd better all come with me!' and Rattus Rattus stepped out of a clump of nettles and beckoned them into him.

The way the rat took them was dark and rough. They went along innumerable twisting tunnels and scaled sheer, wooden beams. They leaped gaping chasms that took all their concerted energy and they squeezed through openings that seemed impossible for their body size. At one moment, having crossed a particularly wide crevice between two beams and being in pitch darkness at the time, Rattus lost his footing and they started to slip over into the gaping void below. But the rat summoned up every last ounce of their strength and energy to the rescue and they managed somehow to regain a footing and pull themselves to safety.

'Whew!' he exclaimed, brushing their whiskers with their front claws. 'That was a bit nasty!'

Eventually they arrived on a flat wedge-shaped stone and, as the children became detached from the rat, they recognized the steps up the chimney.

They had arrived at a point somewhat higher up than the smoke door.

'Just a stride and you'll be in the Master's study,' Rattus told them, standing on a higher step than

274

Mary, who was in the lead, with Alice and William crowding behind her. 'I shall leave you here,' he continued, with a flourish. 'The worst should be over for you – unless, of course, you find the travelling itself tricky and I won't be able to help you there – so I'll say goodbye. I want to get back to the Master. It's going to be a sad house, no matter what he says. When his time comes, I'll let you know through the owl. Though I doubt there'll be a creature in the Golden Vale who won't be aware, the moment it happens. I have enjoyed your company! Give my best regards to the troops. We had a good fight, didn't we! If you're ever down in Bristol town, look up my family. If there are any left in your time, of course. Just ask at the inn down near the docks. The Rattus family are pretty well known along the quays. We have a reputation for bravery and, though I say it who shouldn't, quite a following among the sea-faring crowd! Goodbye then!' and, with a deep bow and a flick of his tail, he disappeared through a gap between two stones.

As soon as they were alone, Mary led the way up to the top of the staircase and swung open the door into the Magician's study.

Matthew Morden was seated on a high chair, poring over an ancient document that was spread out on the cluttered table in front of him. As Mary entered the room he looked up with surprised eyes and seemed, for a moment, to be unable to focus on what it was that he thought he had seen. William and Alice pushed in behind her and the three children stood by the door, uncertain what they should do next.

'Who's there?' Morden asked, searching in the half-light cast by the glowing candles.

'Matthew! It's us,' Mary said, taking a step towards him.

Morden's reaction took her completely by surprise. He lifted his hands and spread them out in front of his face, as if he were trying to ward off a series of blows.

You?' he gasped. 'What are you doing here?'

'We brought Mr Tyler back from our time,' William explained, stepping into the room behind Mary.

'Get away from me!' Matthew Morden cried. 'What are you? How are you here? Ghosts of my dreams – be gone!' And he started up from his chair, knocking it backwards.

'Matthew, it's all right!' Mary said gently, moving slowly towards him.

But Morden started back, feeling with his hand and picking up a thorn walking-stick that had been leaning against the side of the table at which he had been working.

'Back, I say!' he snarled, lifting the stick and brandishing it in front of him, as though he intended to hit them with it.

'Watch out!' Alice hissed. 'He's obviously totally loony!'

'Matthew,' Mary pleaded with him. 'There's no need for this. We are your friends. You remember? We brought your mind back from our time. We helped you . . .'

'Aaagh!' howled the poor man, dropping the stick and covering his ears with his hands as though he was in terrible distress; as though some dreadful pain within his head was tormenting him to distraction and was in danger of breaking out of his skull. 'Get away from me, creatures of my madness,

276

demons of my mind!' he wailed, shaking his head from side to side and backing still further away from them with desperate, staring eyes.

'We must get to the glass,' William whispered to his sisters and, as he did so, he began to edge slowly round the room, keeping as far away from Morden as was possible, and making for where the circular bowl of mirror in its plain wooden frame hung on the wall behind Morden.

'Stay away from me!' they heard the man sob and then, with a sudden movement, he dodged forward and picked up the stick again, holding it out in front of him, like a weapon.

'William!' Alice wailed as she pushed past the table. 'What now?'

'Give me your hand,' her brother whispered. 'And, Mary, you hold her other one.'

Mary reached forward and took Alice's hand without for an instant taking her eyes off Morden.

The three of them were now standing, hand in hand, in a row in front of the circular glass. Dully, at its centre, a pinpoint of light shone; the reflection of one of the candles in the room.

'We must all concentrate on the very centre,' William whispered. 'And, Mary, when I say the word take out Phoebe's necklace and I'll produce the Magician's pendulum at the same time . . .'

'Will it work?' Alice gasped.

'I don't know, do I?' William said.

'Then what?' she whispered.

'We just hope,' William replied and he swallowed nervously.

Behind them, Morden was pacing the room, muttering to himself. He obviously could not believe that they were there. In some mysterious way he believed them to be a figment of his imagination.

'Get away from me!' he kept whispering. 'This is my doing! This is my creation! This is what the dangerous art can bring one to. I am gone *mad*!' and he screamed and wailed the last word so that it echoed and reverberated round the room.

'Now, Mary! *Now*!' William cried and at the same moment both he and Mary produced from the pockets of their jeans the pendulum and the pendant necklace.

'The Master's gold!' Morden screamed and he lunged forward as if he would wrest the pendulum out of William's hand. Just in time William swung his arm away, making Morden stumble and fall against the wall and, at the same moment, he forced his attention to rest on the pinpoint of light in the deep centre of the mirror.

The whole bowl seemed full of swirling clouds. Dark and threatening, they billowed and moved, sucking the children in amongst them. Then, with a sensation not unlike that of being on a big dipper at a funfair, they felt themselves being drawn into the bowl until they were surrounded by the clouds and a terrible rushing sound of wind enclosed them on all sides.

Distantly from another time they heard Matthew Morden shouting:

'I will be satisfied. I will have the gold . . .'

Then the noise was replaced by a sudden, deathly silence.

In front of them the clouds cleared for a moment and to their astonishment they saw two faces staring at them from the other side of the mirror, with expressions of terror and surprise.

'What's happening, Mark?' a girl's voice gasped.

'I don't know,' a boy's voice replied. 'Steph, are you all right?'

'I'm frightened,' the girl sobbed.

She was tall and obviously very young, perhaps no more than ten years old. She had long tresses of red-gold hair that hung in a sheet down her back. Her companion was a teenager, probably older than he looked, with short cropped hair and a pale skin.

'We must stop this,' he whispered.

Mary knew at once what had happened.

'We've gone too far!' she shouted. 'We're ahead of our time. We must go back!'

'How?' she heard Alice cry.

'Think – backwards!' William exclaimed and, a moment later, they felt themselves hurtling back as though they were falling from a great height.

'I will stop you now!' a voice behind them yelled and turning in spite of themselves, they saw Matthew Morden raise his walking-stick and run at them.

'*Now!*' William screamed.

"Now!' Alice echoed. 'Oh, Mr Tyler, help us now! Please help us now . . .' she gasped and sobbed, as she forced her attention back to the centre of the glass.

'Yes,' Mary echoed her sister's words as though they were a prayer, 'please, Mr Tyler, help us!'

The clouds that filled the glass parted. Thin afternoon light filled the view. They walked away from the wall into the dusty, twilight room. Behind them a shattering, splintering crash made them spin round. They saw the convex mirror on the wall behind them split into millions of glistening fragments of glass.

'I will be free of you!' Matthew Morden wailed across the centuries.

And then there was only silence.

'Are we in the right time?' Mary whispered.

'I don't know,' William admitted. 'Too late now anyway. We can't ever use the mirror again . . .' Then he stopped speaking for, distantly outside the window, he heard Jack's voice, calling:

'Kids? Where are you? Children?'

William crossed and looked out of the front circular window. Down on the lawn he could see his uncle, with his back to the house, standing searching the hillside beyond him. The late afternoon light was pale and golden. Everything looked very ordinary.

'We're home,' William said, quietly. For some reason he felt almost depressed.

Mary walked slowly back across the room to the broken mirror and stared at it.

'I wonder what they were looking into,' she said, thoughtfully.

'Who?' Alice asked.

'Steph and that boy,' Mary replied. 'It couldn't have been this mirror – because . . . well, just look at it! It's completely broken.'

'Was it really our Steph?' Alice asked.

'I think so. I'm sure of it. She looked exactly like Phoebe, didn't you think?'

'I hardly dared to look,' Alice replied. 'What was the boy called?'

'Mark, I think,' Mary said.

'Who's Mark?' Alice wondered.

Mary shrugged.

'I don't know. A friend of hers, I suppose. Some-

280

one she hasn't met yet, maybe. Actually, she looked very like Stephen Tyler, as well!'

'So Steph will get involved in all this one day,' William said thoughtfully. 'In that case we'll have to find somewhere safe to keep this for her,' and as he spoke he held out the pendulum.

'She'll have one of her own, one day,' Mary said, holding out the necklace. 'I expect Phoebe will give her this eventually.'

'Well at least we know that Jack and Phoebe will stay on here,' Alice said. 'Steph looked almost a teenager.' Then she added, almost as an after-thought. 'Isn't that revolting little grandson of Henry Crawden called Mark?'

They were all silent for a moment. Then Mary smiled.

'That'd really put an end to everything, wouldn't it?' she said.

'What would?' Alice asked.

'If Steph eventually married Mark Crawden,' Mary replied. 'The Tylers and the Mordens . . . joined together. Any children they had would have both the families' blood in their veins!'

'We'll just have to wait and see what happens,' William said, leading the way to the top of the staircase. 'Come on! We'd better go down.'

Phoebe was standing in the middle of the hall when they stepped out of the fireplace.

'There you all are!' she exclaimed. 'We've been searching for you everywhere. There's such exciting news!' and she held out in front of her a piece of paper. 'Look what's come! A letter from your parents. Obviously posted ages ago. They're on their way back! They should be here by the weekend!'

27
The Bridge in the Clouds

Sometime, just before the first light of dawn, Mary woke from a troubled sleep. The room was in darkness, but dimly silhouetted against the night sky outside the window she could see Alice kneeling on the foot of her bed.

'What's happened?' she asked.

'Listen!' Alice whispered. As she spoke, the door opened and William came, in stepping silently on his bare feet.

'You've heard it?' he said.

'What?' Mary asked.

Alice slipped off her bed and crossed to open the small window, pushing it wide. A thin rain was falling and the breeze blew the dampness into the room. But none of them noticed the cold or the wet.

The dark woods outside were filled with sounds. Long anguished howls and mournful, fluting whistles. Sad sounds, filled with despair; mournful sounds, full of pain and tragedy. Somewhere a dog whined and a fox barked, an endless yelp of unhappiness.

'It been happening for a few minutes,' William whispered. 'It just suddenly started.'

'It's him, isn't it?' Alice said, in a small voice. 'It's Mr Tyler. They all know . . .' and then she stopped speaking and the tragic overture of sound continued to echo and resound through the night, filling the room and each of their hearts with its message of bereavement and desolation.

As dawn glimmered in the eastern sky, the children let themselves out by the kitchen door. Spot wasn't there, so they had to go without him. They walked up the centre path of the walled garden through that curious half-light, neither night nor day, that comes in those moments before the sun first breaks over the horizon. Then, reaching the forest gate, they went out on to the track beyond.

The sounds were louder here. A requiem of pain and suffering, encapsulated into the long, swooping cadences of sadness and loss, echoing and re-echoing among the dark trees, on and on, seemingly without any end.

The children didn't choose which path to take. It was an automatic and unanimous decision. Indeed it seemed as if there were no choice to be made, as if they were guided by some unseen force. With heavy steps they climbed slowly up through the gloaming light towards the top of the valley and the yew tree.

Reaching the badger sett, they disturbed one of the sows still out and about. She looked at them with surprised eyes but didn't wait to greet them before she dodged down into the ground and out of their sight.

Thin drizzling rain began to fall as they reached the flat ground beside the yew and a dreary dawn inched a new day over the distant, easterly hills. Darker clouds were blowing in from the west, spreading across the sky above Goldenwater and the waterfall beyond.

William turned his back on the lake, and crouched down on the ground, with his hands in his pockets. The lake had too many memories for him. Mr Tyler was in every single view; in every single memory. Mr Tyler in the boat. Mr Tyler at the standing stone. Mr Tyler . . . everywhere. He had said it would be like this. But why did it hurt so much?

Nearby, Alice covered her mouth with a hand and scratched her cheek. She feared that if her mouth were allowed, it would open and a cry of such anguish would come out of her that she might never be able to stop it, never be able to speak or act normally again. So instead she held her lips together in her cupped palm and she stared into the endless distance on the other side of the Golden Valley. She was trying not to see his face smiling down at her, the time when she had told him how the moonlight had filled the Dark and Dreadful Path when she had set off alone to face the badger baiters at Blackscar Quarry, all those months ago, and he had cheered and said she had given them back the silver path.

'Mr Tyler,' she whispered, and a tear trickled out of the corner of her eye and ran down her cheek.

Mary walked away from them both. She felt suddenly angry. She wanted to cry out. She wanted to shout and scream.

'Why?' she sobbed. And she could hear him whispering the only possible answer; '*Because* . . . !'

The rain was heavier now. It slanted out of the west at an angle, wetting them and dripping off the branches of the yew.

284

A sudden barking lower down the hill made Alice run forward, hopefully.

'Spot,' she called and when the dog appeared, she ran towards him with open arms and flung herself down on the wet ground in front of him. 'Oh, Spot,' she sobbed. 'I'm glad you're here. He's dead, isn't he? Mr Tyler is really dead?'

'In the night,' Spot growled. 'He went in the night.'

'The rat sent word,' a voice hooted from the yew tree branches, and looking up, Mary saw Jasper. 'But he needn't have bothered. We all knew at once,' the owl continued mournfully. 'It will be a strange world – without the Master!' and his voice broke into a dying fall.

'Oh, Jasper!' Mary sobbed, great big tears mixing with the rain that was falling on her face. 'I'm so glad you're here. I was so lonely . . .' Then, at once, she wished she hadn't said the words, for there in front of her, crouching on the ground, was William, staring at the earth. She ran quickly to him and put an arm round his shoulder. 'Will,' she whispered, 'I'm sorry.'

'It's all right,' William said, turning his face away from her, so that she shouldn't see his own tears.

As he did so, a flash of red, lower down the hill beyond the badger sett, caught his attention. He moved forward, rising, a sudden, ridiculous hope in his heart.

'Cinnabar?' he called.

A young fox broke cover, stepping out into the clearing and then stopping with one paw raised and his mouth half-open.

'It's one of Cinnabar's cubs,' Spot said.

The cub looked up at William with deep, questioning eyes.

'Has he a name?' William asked.

'Shouldn't think so,' Spot replied. 'The Master used to do the naming. Now it'll be up to you three.'

'Let's call him Bushy!' Alice said suddenly.

'No!' William exclaimed. 'Certainly not!'

'Because of his bushy tail,' Alice explained.

'He is not going to be called Bushy,' William said firmly.

'What then?' Alice asked in a sulky voice.

'He shall be called Cinnabar,' William declared, after a moment, 'in honour and memory of his father!'

'Cinnabar!' Spot barked.

'Cinnabar!' the owl hooted.

And the young cub took a shy step towards William and looked up at him with amber eyes.

'Oh, William! Alice! Look!' Mary gasped and as she did so she pointed towards the Golden Valley.

The rain was falling fast but a brilliant shaft of sunlight had broken through the clouds and there, dazzling and sparkling in a great arc from one side of the valley to the other was a perfect rainbow.

'A bridge in the clouds!' Mary cried and, as she spoke the words, so Stephen Tyler's presence flooded in around them, until they felt him everywhere.

He was in the trees and in the grasses; in the breeze and in the rain.

Everywhere.

The sunlight grew in strength, brilliant against the black clouds. The rain was shattered into a thousand prisms of colour.

The bridge in the clouds spanned the space in

front of them and they each knew without any doubt that somewhere at the other side he would always be waiting for them. And that he would never leave them. And that he was as much a part of the valley as the valley was a part of him.

Then the young Cinnabar, the first of the new generation, trotted up the slope and looked up at the three children.

'Now,' he seemed to say, 'where shall we begin?'

Share the magic of the Magician's House by William Corlett

There is magic in the air from the first moment the three Constant children, William, Mary and Alice arrive at their uncle's house in the Golden Valley. But it's when they meet the Magician, William Tyler, and hear of the Great Task he has for them that the adventures really begin.

THE STEPS UP THE CHIMNEY

Evil threatens Golden House in its hour of need – and the Magician's animals come to the children's aid – but travelling with a fox brings its own dangers.
ISBN 0 09 935370 1   £3.99

THE DOOR IN THE TREE

William, Mary and Alice find a cruel and vicious sport threatening the peace of Golden Valley on their return to this magical place.
ISBN 0 09 997390 1   £3.99

THE TUNNEL BEHIND THE WATERFALL

Evil creatures mass against the children as they attempt to master time travel.
ISBN 0 09 997910 1   £3.99

THE BRIDGE IN THE CLOUDS

With the Magician seriously ill, it's up to the three children to complete the Great Task alone.
ISBN 0 09 918301 9   £3.99

THE SNOW-WALKER SEQUENCE

Book 1

CATHERINE FISHER

THE **SNOW-WALKER'S SON**

Short-listed for the WH Smith Mind Boggling Books Award

*S*ome say he's a monster, others hope he is
dead, and no one has seen him for many,
many years. Until now...

'I'm sending you to live with my son,' the Jarl said.

For a moment they couldn't realize what he meant.
Then Jessa felt sick; cold sweat prickled on her back.

Thorkil was white. 'You can't send us there,' he
breathed.

'Hold your tongue and let me finish.' Ragnar was
looking at them now, with a hard, amused stare.

'Call it exile, and think yourselves lucky. At least you'll
have a sort of life. You leave tomorrow for Thrasirshall, at
first light.'

Jessa saw Thorkil was trembling. She knew he couldn't
believe this; he was terrified. It burst out of him in a wild
despairing cry.

'I won't go! You can't send us out there, not to that
creature!'

Out now in paperback from Red Fox at £3.50
1 THE SNOW-WALKER'S SON, ISBN 0 09 925192 2
2 THE EMPTY HAND, ISBN 0 09 925182 5
3 THE SOUL THIEVES, ISBN 0 09 953971 3

THE
SNOW-WALKER
SEQUENCE

Book 2

THE EMPTY HAND

Catherine Fisher's riveting fantasy adventure continues...

*R*emember the wicked ice-witch Gudrun?
*If you thought she couldn't get any more
evil... Think again. She just has...*

Hakon turned, clutching the sword that felt hot and heavy in his hand. And then, among the undergrowth, among storm-stirred leaves and snow, something shifted, and he knew he was looking at a face, a narrow, inhuman face among splintered branches and shadow. It watched him, its small eyes pale as ice, a big, indistinct shape, and he swore for a moment that the snow drifted through its body.

Like a man, but bigger. Like a bear, but... not. Hakon felt a sudden pulse of terror that he squashed at once, deep down.

Barely opening his lips he said, 'It's here. Don't move. Don't speak. Whatever happens don't make a sound.'

Out now in paperback from Red Fox at £3.50
1 THE SNOW-WALKER'S SON, ISBN 0 09 925192 2
2 THE EMPTY HAND, ISBN 0 09 925182 5
3 THE SOUL THIEVES, ISBN 0 09 953971 3

THE SNOW-WALKER SEQUENCE

Book 3

CATHERINE FISHER

THE SOUL THIEVES

'A thrilling, chilling world of magic and menace' MAIL ON SUNDAY

*W*hen a powerful spell-storm settles over the Jarlshold, Kari knows it's a Sign. A Sign to take up his mother's final, most dreadful challenge...

Kari raised the cup to drink and stopped; so still that Jessa looked at him. He was staring into the wine as if something had poisoned it, and when he looked up his face was white with terror.

'She's here,' he breathed.

Alarmed, Wulfgar leaned forward. 'Who is?'

But Kari had spun round, quick as a sword-slash. 'Close the doors!' he yelled, his voice raw and desperate over the hubbub. 'Close them! NOW!'

Jessa caught Kari's arm and the red wine splashed her dress.

'What is it?' she gasped. 'What's happening?'

'She's here.' He stared over her shoulder. 'Gods, Jessa. Look!'

Out now in paperback from Red Fox at £3.50

1 THE SNOW-WALKER'S SON, ISBN 0 09 925192 2
2 THE EMPTY HAND, ISBN 0 09 925182 5
3 THE SOUL THIEVES, ISBN 0 09 953971 3

❖ Tales of Redwall ❖
BRIAN JACQUES

'Not since Roald Dahl have children filled their shelves so compulsively' *The Times*

An award-winning, best-selling series from master storyteller, Brian Jacques. Discover the epic Tales of Redwall *adventures about Redwall Abbey - and beyond!*

- **Martin the Warrior**   0 09 928171 6
- **Mossflower**   0 09 955400 3
- **Outcast of Redwall**   0 09 960091 9
- **Mariel of Redwall**   0 09 992960 0
- **The Bellmaker**   0 09 943331 1
- **Salamandastron**   0 09 914361 5
- **Redwall**   0 09 951200 9
- **Mattimeo**   0 09 967540 4
- **The Pearls of Lutra**   0 09 963871 1

❖

Tales of Redwall by Brian Jacques
Out now in paperback from Red Fox priced £4.99

Book **1** in the FELIX TRILOGY

GO SADDLE THE SEA

*A*ction-packed adventure, high-tension
drama and heroic swashbuckling!
*Join dashing hero Felix Brooke as he boldly
embarks upon the journey of a lifetime...
Here's a taster to tempt you!*

'Ye've run yourself into a real nest of adders, here, lad,'
Sammy whispered.

'I know they are smugglers,' I began protesting. 'That
was why the fee was low. But I could take care of my — '

'They are worse than smugglers, lad – they are
Comprachicos,' he breathed into my ear.

'Compra — c-comprachicos?'

At first I thought I could not have heard him aright.
Then I could not believe him. Then I *did* believe him –
Sam would not make up such a tale – and, despite myself,
my teeth began to chatter.

THE FELIX TRILOGY by Joan Aiken from Red Fox

Go Saddle the Sea	£3.99	ISBN 0 09 953771 0
Bridle the Wind	£3.99	ISBN 0 09 953781 8
The Teeth of the Gale	£3.99	ISBN 0 09 953791 5

Book **2** in the **FELIX TRILOGY**

BRIDLE THE WIND

*I*f you're an adventure addict then you'll love BRIDLE THE WIND – it's un-put-downable!

Here's a taste of what's in store...

Shipwrecked, imprisoned and then haunted by a ghoulish premonition – brave Felix may be down on his luck but he'll never, ever give up...

'*Oh*, but I don't want to die!'

And then, a second time, putting the fear of death, such as I had not felt, even through the shipwreck, into my own heart, '*Oh – but – I don't – want – to – die!*'

Petrified, I stared all around me. From where could the voice possibly come?

Trembling uncontrollably, I looked upward, and now, just for a moment, it seemed to my dazed senses that I could see something - some *body* - suspended from one of the arching boughs overhead, that I could see a thin form swinging, dangling at the end of a rope not three feet above me... It faded, melted, and was gone.

THE FELIX TRILOGY by Joan Aiken from Red Fox

Go Saddle the Sea	£3.99	ISBN 0 09 953771 0
Bridle the Wind	£3.99	ISBN 0 09 953781 8
The Teeth of the Gale	£3.99	ISBN 0 09 953791 5

Book 3 *in the* FELIX TRILOGY

THE TEETH OF THE GALE

*G*rab a copy of the thrilling finale of
*THE FELIX TRILOGY. It's an action-
packed read – so hold on tight!*

*Pulses race when brave Felix leads a rescue mission with
his sweetheart, Juana. It's a deadly dangerous task – will
Felix keep his head and return a hero?
Here's a tingling taster...*

'Juana! Keep very still!' I called hoarsely.

My heart seemed to fall clean out of my body into the
gorge below. There she was, defenceless, in deadly danger, and here I was, strung on two ropes over the gulf,
with my gun strapped out of reach, useless on my back;
however fast I moved, I would never be able to get back
in time to save her if the bear flew at her.

The massive bear turned, at the sound of my voice, and
eyed me intently. I joggled frantically on the rope, to
hold its attention.

'Bear! Bear!' I yelled. 'Look at me! Look at me on the
bridge. Come and get me, bear! Here I am!'

THE FELIX TRILOGY by Joan Aiken from Red Fox

Go Saddle the Sea	£3.99	ISBN 0 09 953771 0
Bridle the Wind	£3.99	ISBN 0 09 953781 8
The Teeth of the Gale	£3.99	ISBN 0 09 953791 5